# PRAISE FOR *KLARA*

"In *Klara's Truth*, themes of identity—personal, cultural, religious, and familial—are interwoven with echoes of intergenerational trauma. Klara finds her past . . . and herself. Thoroughly enjoyable from beginning to end!"
—STEPHANIE NEWMAN, PhD, clinical psychologist, author of *Barbarians at the PTA* and *Madmen on the Couch*, and coeditor of *Money Talks*

"In this page-turning novel, Susan Weissbach Friedman integrates her experience as a trauma therapist with her gifts as a storyteller to share a beautiful story of healing and transformation. Klara's personal journey is embedded seamlessly into a background that captures the traumatic impact of the Holocaust on Polish Jewish families. Friedman guides the reader back and forth from the depths of Klara's wounded heart to the history of Poland beyond World War II, instilling hope in the reader that both the individual and the nation are capable of moving beyond a past of devastation toward a more optimistic future."
—SHARI A. BECKER, PhD, licensed clinical psychologist, yoga and meditation teacher, and Somatic Experiencing Practitioner

"Susan Weissbach Friedman has written a compelling story of family and heritage and self-discovery, of family ties and friendship and second chances, and has added a side of possible romance. She also gives us another perspective on how the sharp fingernails of war reach through generations and prick the skin decades after the guns stop firing. A great read!"
—ELLEN BARKER, author of *East of Troost* and *Still Needs Work*

"In Susan Weissbach Friedman's empathetic and appealingly written debut novel, protagonist Klara's unresolved trauma and fragmented memories from her past drive her to cautiously revisit them in hopes of finding the resolution and authentic connection that have eluded her into adulthood. Friedman writes with both clarity about and insight into how trauma impacts a life, and the importance of connection with the self and others in the healing process, as she captures this complex journey amidst a compelling historical and cultural setting."
— MARY CULLEY, LCSW, EMDR certified therapist and somatic experiencing practitioner

"As someone whose mother was a Holocaust survivor, I was eager to read *Klara's Truth* to see if it was also my truth. It took only a few pages to see it does ring true. I think only a psychotherapist like Friedman could write a novel that so richly captures the intra- and interpersonal dynamics of families still seeking to heal from the Holocaust. Yet this is not a heavy read by any means—I gobbled it up in a few sittings, quickly drawn in by the beautiful love story."
— JUDE BERMAN, author of *The Die*

"*Klara's Truth* is a beautiful story of discovery about a grown woman who is finally told the real circumstances of her father's death. This revelation sends her on a journey to meet the family she never knew and discover even more previously unknown truths about her family's history."
— T. M. DUNN, author of *Last Stop on the 6* and *Her Father's Daughter*

# KLARA'S TRUTH

# KLARA'S TRUTH

## A NOVEL

SUSAN WEISSBACH
FRIEDMAN

SHE WRITES PRESS

Published 2024
Printed in the United States of America
Print ISBN: 978-1-64742-610-1
E-ISBN: 978-1-64742-611-8
Library of Congress Control Number: 2023911721

For information, address:
She Writes Press
1569 Solano Ave #546
Berkeley, CA 94707

Interior Design by Tabitha Lahr

She Writes Press is a division of SparkPoint Studio, LLC.

This is a work of fiction. Names, characters, places, and incidents either are the product of the author's imagination or are used fictitiously. Any resemblance to actual persons, living or dead, is entirely coincidental.

In 2013, I had the pleasure of traveling to Warsaw and Krakow, Poland, where there are many wonderful sites, great food, and culture to experience. While there is accuracy regarding buildings and locations in this story, such as the Jewish museums and synagogues referred to here, the story of *Klara's Truth* has been created by this author. For example, Poland has never given reparations to Holocaust survivors and their families — or to non Jewish property owners from Poland — whose land was taken by the Nazi Germans and their collaborators during the Holocaust and World War II, and subsequently nationalized during the Communist regime. I also made up clandestine operations I refer to funded by an American during the Holocaust and WWII.

To Alan, Olivia, and Bella
With all my love

*"The ultimate key to freedom is to keep becoming who you truly are."*
—DR. EDITH EGER, *THE GIFT*

# CHAPTER 1

<hr>

## *May 6, 2014, Bangor, Maine*

It was the first springlike day Klara could remember in what felt like forever, a whopping sixty-two degrees. Feeling the warm sun on her arms and noticing that several purple-and-yellow crocuses had just sprouted by her front porch in the last twenty-four hours momentarily brightened her mood. She was walking home for some lunch after teaching two classes that morning when she grabbed her mail from the postbox next to the street curb. In quickly leafing through her letters, mostly junk mail, Klara spied a large red, white, and blue FedEx envelope with her mother's name and return address.

She picked up her pace, quickly unlocking the antique oak front door to her small white Colonial and throwing down her jean jacket along with the rest of the mail. Tearing open the cardboard envelope, she found a letter from her mother and a more official one from the Polish government. She read her mother's letter first.

> *Dear Klara,*
> *I have surprising news to tell you, and what good news it is! We are inheriting money in your father's name. The Polish government has finally gotten*

*around to reimbursing Polish Holocaust survivors and their families—as well as non-Jewish property owners from Poland and their families—for property the German Nazis and their collaborators stole during the Holocaust and WWII that was subsequently nationalized by the Communist regime all those years ago.*

*I know it will be a shock, but I must tell you that your father is dead. When I first found out many years ago, you were so young, and I didn't want to upset you. After that, it just seemed easier not to talk about it.*

*The truth is, we were fighting all the time, and he decided to leave after he lost his job due to his drinking. He refused to understand that your grandfather was as important to me as he was, and I couldn't just move out, just the three of us, leaving your grandfather alone to fend for himself. What kind of daughter would that make me? He took a train to Philadelphia from New York City to look for work. There was a job a friend had told him about, and, well, the train was in an accident. He was among five passengers who were immediately killed. You were so young, only six years old.*

*His sister, Rachel, still lived in Warsaw at the time. When I told her about the accident, she somehow had your father's body flown to Warsaw, where he was buried. I know I should have told you sooner. I'm forced to bring it up now as there's a lot of money at hand, $250,000. We could handle it by mail, but I'm worried that your father's sister, if she's still alive, or her family might try to finagle all the money for themselves, so I think it's best if you travel to Poland.*

*Call me right away!*

*—Mom*

The letter from Poland's government outlined the details of the restitution—and her mother must show proof that she and Klara's father were married at the time of his death. Otherwise, the money would go to any living children her father might have.

After reading and rereading the letters, Klara paced around her living room, shaking her head.

Unbelievable. All these years, she's denied she knew what had ultimately happened to him, only allowing that he walked out and left us, never turning back. Now that there's money involved, she reveals the truth. That's just so like her. And why didn't she call me first to discuss this before sending the letters? Again, it's just so like her.

After running around her home like someone who had lost her way, ignoring her mother's multiple phone messages, Klara finally called Sheila, her closest friend at Holbrook College. In the seven years since Klara had first come to teach there, Sheila was the one person who knew her story, or at least much of it.

By then it was dinnertime, and although she knew Sheila was likely in the middle of her evening family routine, Klara had to speak to her.

"Hi, Klara," Sheila said cheerfully from the other end of the phone line, but with an underlying frenzied tone. "The kids are finishing their homework, Jack has the study door closed, and it's my night to make dinner." She paused for a moment, and then yelled, "Tommy, don't take your brother's pencil away from him! He's using it." Klara heard muffled conversation, and then Sheila was back. "Sorry about that. What's up?"

"I don't mean to bother you." Klara's voice dropped. "It's about my mother. I mean, it's about my father. He's dead," she said, bursting into tears.

Following a moment's silence, Sheila exclaimed, "Oh, my god, your father's dead . . . but I thought you never found out what happened to him?" she said, trying to follow what Klara had just told her. "How did you find out? Are you okay? You don't sound okay . . . I'm so sorry."

"My mother told me in a letter, and now she wants me to call her. Can I come over to your house? *Please?*"

Sheila immediately replied, "Yes," and a half hour later at dusk, Klara arrived at her friend's picket-fenced home. Once inside, she followed Sheila around several piles of student papers and waved from the other room to Jack as he served their four- and six-year-old kids dinner, mouthing, "Thank you" to him. The women made their way into the over-furnished study for privacy, Sheila first grabbing a bottle of pinot grigio from the fridge. Klara told her more about the letters—her mother's letter, and the one from the Polish government—as Sheila poured two glasses of wine.

"Here, see for yourself," Klara said, passing them to her friend.

Sheila scanned the letters, looking up at her. "What are you going to do?"

"I have to go," Klara insisted. "I have to go, not because she wants me to, which she does, but because I have to try to find any family my father may still have. Maybe his sister's still alive and living there. From her letter, my mother seems to believe she might still be, or might have children who are," Klara said, her words bursting out of her mouth, like fireworks. "Also, I need to visit my father's grave. I want to pay my final respects and have closure. I *have to* go."

Sheila's husband knocked on the door, popping his head in. "Should I start their baths?" he asked. Seeing the two women were in deep conversation, he knew the answer was yes before Sheila had a chance to respond. He nodded his head and smiled, closing the door behind him, before Sheila could finish saying, "I'll pay you back."

"You know," Sheila said, crossing her legs and leaning

forward, "if you're really serious about going, the timing couldn't be better. The semester's ending in two weeks, and from what you've told me, you don't have any big summer plans that can't wait."

"You don't think I'm crazy for wanting to jump on a plane? Just tell me I'm not crazy," Klara said, sighing and shaking her head.

"You're *not* crazy," Sheila replied. "You should go. You have one more week of classes, and then you just have to finish marking your papers and grading your exams. You can do this. I'll drive you to Portland to catch the airline transport van to Boston." She grabbed Klara by the shoulders. "I'm really happy for you. As hard as this is, you're finally getting answers." Klara smiled, exhaling deeply.

❈ ❈ ❈

Two weeks passed at tornado speed. The last thing Klara took from her dresser drawer was a small, white cardboard box previously hidden under some winter sweaters. Inside the box sat a gold oval locket with an engraved floral design, tucked underneath a cotton pad. The last time she'd laid eyes on the locket was when she first arrived at Holbrook College and was unpacking. She held it up to the sunlight while gingerly opening it. Two old, miniature black-and-white photos stared back at her, one of her father's parents, the other of her father and his sister as young teenagers. Klara could feel them beckoning to her from the dim past.

Sheila kept her word, kindly driving Klara the two hours from Bangor to Portland in her family's Ford SUV two weeks later. It was cluttered with reusable grocery bags, children's school projects, and half-eaten granola bars, but Klara took in none of it, given her laser focus on her upcoming trip ahead.

"Keep me posted," Sheila said. "I want to hear all about it, and not just when you get back. Email me as soon as you get there. Good luck!" she added as she reached out to hug her friend goodbye. Klara smiled and hugged her back.

"Thank you for everything," Klara said before waving farewell.

And then she was in the Logan Airport–bound van with six other passengers for the next two-plus hours. Using her faded jean jacket as a makeshift pillow, Klara fell into a half-sleep state, in and out of consciousness, recollecting how she had ended up at Holbrook seven years earlier. A few years before arriving there, she had been working at Harvard University, where she first began as a college student, then moved on to graduate school for seven long years. She'd finally landed her dream job as an anthropology professor with a specialty in archaeology. However, after happily living in Cambridge's busy college town for twenty-five years, something within her was starting to give out. She was forty-two years old, juggling a full schedule of classes and research, and barely able to get out of bed in the morning. Her engine was running on fumes. Although she had two close grad school friends, Barbara and Diane, who were now her colleagues, they had their own relationships and families. Klara still had no significant other to speak of, so her ties to the area didn't feel very deep-rooted.

Then, one particularly gray morning, her mother called with sad news. She got right down to business, announcing that Klara's grandfather had died and ordering Klara to return home immediately. "We're burying him tomorrow," she declared.

Of course, Klara knew she'd need to go right away, as Jewish tradition required the dead to be buried as soon as possible. And then her mother added, "And don't forget to bring a black dress," as though she were a child. Klara drove five hours in her vintage VW Beetle to Queens, New York, for the funeral the next day, sitting shiva with her mother for the remainder of the week. Seeing her mother, shut down and emotionally detached as usual, in that dark, staid, pre-war apartment she'd grown up in, drained every last bit of energy Klara had left. Klara's mother and grandfather, Sigmund—or "Siggy," as he was better known—had shared a claustrophobic, symbiotic relationship that her mother expected Klara to duplicate with her.

Luckily, a colleague had just mentioned an anthropology PhD position at a small northeastern liberal arts college in Southern Maine. The school was over seven hours from Queens, another two and a half hours farther from where her mother lived. Between Klara's mental exhaustion and her need to slow down the pace of her life, she jumped at the opportunity—a chance to have more time to herself, with the added benefit of putting more distance between her and her mother. Holbrook College was interested in her archaeology background, and she was not deterred by the fact that the department was small, offering only a minor in anthropology, with a smattering of archaeology classes. And she wouldn't have to regularly publish!

"How could you go from an urban, high-caliber research university to a small liberal arts college three hours away, even a strong one?" her good friend and colleague Barbara asked. "You've always been so ambitious in the past."

"It's going to be so lonely for you," their other friend and coworker Diane chimed in. "We're going to miss you. You'd better keep in touch. I know you, Klara; you have to promise to come down to Boston for the weekend once a month or so."

"I'm going to call and check on you. I'll come up there myself to get you if I need to," Barbara said in her typical maternal manner.

It was true. Klara had always been so ambitious—first spending hours studying the archaeology and history of Mesoamerica, then participating in Central American digs, even leading some expeditions, and of course, there was the constant pressure to publish her research. She was ready to slow down and have less pressure, having already done the publishing thing. And yes, although she had a great academic position, she had barely anything else to show for herself and was far too tired and worn out for someone in her early forties.

When she first arrived at Holbrook, she did make regular monthly trips to Boston for long weekends to see her friends, but then they became less frequent. These days, her friends had gotten busy with kids and other family members. Although Barbara and Diane would periodically call and email, Klara wasn't very good about being in touch. She was lucky enough to have met her Holbrook colleague Sheila in her department. Sheila's life was quite hectic between work and family, but the two had lunch a few days a week. They mostly talked shop, discussing their course syllabi and areas of expertise. Sheila occasionally invited her over for family dinners.

"Come on, Klara, you can't spend another Friday and Saturday night by yourself," Sheila would say.

"How do you know I'm spending it by myself?" Klara would tease.

"Really?" Sheila would reply. "Really?"

Klara wouldn't say anything at first. Usually she *was* by herself, but she did have some company here and there, although it was more often than not quite short-lived. Despite knowing Sheila would love to hear any juicy details, she kept those to herself.

"No," Klara would typically say, "it's just me." And sometimes she'd take Sheila up on the invitation and enjoy a lovely, albeit noisy, family dinner with her good friend and her friend's family. Other weekends when she didn't have something of her own going on, which was usually the case, she'd self-isolate for the weekend with her archaeological and historical Mayan texts.

As Klara pondered her mother's letter, she thought about how this wasn't the first time in recent history her mother had contacted her with consequential news that had resulted in Klara heading off to another country. This had happened just a year earlier when her mother announced she was getting remarried to a relative of an old family "friend," at which time Klara responded by barreling off to co-lead a dig with a former colleague/boyfriend in the Yucatán Peninsula. So, truth be told, she wasn't completely unprepared for more shocking news. But learning that her father was dead and buried in Warsaw, Poland, was beyond anything she could have anticipated.

When Klara finally opened her heavy eyelids, the airport van was somewhere along I-93 south. Knowing it wouldn't be too much longer before they arrived at Logan, she was trying to reorient herself. She was now paying the price of exhaustion from sleep deprivation, as she had packed too much into too little time. Klara felt jolted when she suddenly remembered where she was going and why, and a wave of anger flashed over her as her fists tightened. She was ready to finally get some honest answers.

# CHAPTER 2

Klara's early life was a blur. She was sure she would have remembered it better had her mother and grandfather allowed her to ask questions about her missing father and regaled her with stories about him when she was little. Instead, there seemed to be an unspoken rule forbidding such discussion. "Why are you always asking about when you were little and before your father left?" her mother would whine. "You're a big girl now, and you, me, and Grandpa are a family." Even at the still-tender age of eight, Klara knew it was a non-answer, but after many such pressing questions eliciting limited and dead-end responses, she finally learned to no longer ask.

As Klara stopped questioning where her father was and why they never heard from him, she also began to forget the wonderful times the two had spent together, such as how her father played with her every day after he first came home from work, taking her to the playground at the park down the street. After he walked in the door, he'd greet her and her mother, taking off his hat, tie, and work jacket. When he rolled up his shirtsleeves, she knew it was time for them to go out. They'd walk together to the corner park, hand in hand, met by green grass, trees, birds, bees, and butterflies, each talking about their day. She'd run around while he sat on the grass, supported by a big old oak tree. When she was ready to go on the swing, he pushed her as she yelled, "Higher, higher!" As she got a little older, around five or so, she learned to raise her legs at the top of each swing, increasing her overall height, and then folding them under her thighs. She loved how it felt to pump her legs as she tried to reach the sun with the tips of her toes, pointing them up to the sky. Her father would cheer her on, yelling, "That's my girl!" while they giggled together.

After her father had gone, she'd ask her mother to take her to the playground. At first, she did when Klara pushed hard enough, but there was never any joy in it. Instead, her mother seemed to do it out of obligation.

"Please, I haven't been to the park in over a week," she'd beg.

With pursed lips, after finishing a host of chores, her mother would finally acquiesce, but her face always looked bitter, as if she had just bitten into a lemon. After another year or two passed, once Klara was no longer "little," her mother would reply, "You're too grown-up for that now, Klara. Anyway, I need your help in the kitchen." Then she returned to chopping the vegetables or cleaning the kitchen counters.

"What about Grandpa? Can he take me?" she'd ask.

"Your grandfather has much more important things to do than to take you to the park, Klara," her mother would reply.

Klara knew her mother was responsible for keeping the house clean and the family fed, but wasn't Klara important too? Important enough for either her mother or grandfather to spend time with? Instead, she turned to her books, art supplies, and Steiff stuffed animals imported from Germany. She'd gotten one as a birthday present and one as a Hanukkah present every year until she was ten. Although her mother and grandfather were German Jewish, and Hitler had tried to exterminate all the Jews only twenty years earlier, they still felt great German pride. Klara's few gifts consisted of a Steiff stuffed animal, usually a small teddy bear or dog, or occasionally an untouchable Madame Alexander doll to view as it collected dust on her shelf, but not to play with. Klara preferred her Steiffs to the dolls.

Although she had some school friends, her mother insisted she come home every day immediately after school, so there were no playdates, and weekends were for "family time."

By age ten, Klara was a small adult. Her fourth-grade teacher commented to her more than once, "Klara, you look so serious. There must be a smile in there somewhere."

Klara hated having attention called to her—being noticed was the worst. She and her best friend, Charlotte, played hopscotch together at recess every day, but by the time middle school rolled around, Charlotte had moved away, and the other girls regularly had sleepovers with one another on the weekends.

"Sleepovers?" her mother would repeat, when she'd bring up the subject. "No, that's not something I approve of. You can't sleep over at someone else's house, and they can't sleep here. I don't know who these girls or their families are. I'm not going to let you have a sleepover with them."

Klara would try to explain, "Well if you let me invite them over after school, then you could get to know them," but that fell on deaf ears. It was strange because her mother was second-generation American—born and raised here. One would think she'd be more acculturated and understand things like sleepovers, but she was standoffish and possessive of her daughter.

Their one regular visitor was Jacob Herschler, Klara's grandfather's boss and longtime good friend, whom Klara rather disliked. He came over for dinner most Sunday evenings, and as she got bigger and older, he'd ask to stay over.

"I'm just so tired," he'd announce while stretching his

arms. "I'm not sure I can make it back to Manhattan tonight." Klara's mother practically tripped over herself making up the extra bed in the guest room for him. "Anything for you, Jacob." She'd smile so hard it seemed her face might crack.

Saturdays were reserved for mother and daughter to visit the Metropolitan Art Museum, where her mother focused on the European painters and sculptors from Classical to Renaissance to Neoclassical to Impressionist—her mother's interest stopped there. While Klara appreciated the artwork, she was more drawn to archaeological finds from earlier cultures, loving when she got to walk through the Egyptian, Greek, and Roman exhibits. Later, as an older teenager, when she took the bus there by herself, she'd spend hours exploring Ancient Near Eastern art, along with the art of Africa, the Americas, and Oceania.

She was so interested in drawing and knowledgeable about art history that her eighth-grade art teacher encouraged her to apply to Music and Art High School, offering to help her put together her portfolio. She recalled telling her mother, "Mr. Rand thinks I should apply to Music and Art. He thinks I have enough talent to get in."

Her mother had replied, "Art is a hobby, Klara. It's important to be well-versed in, but it's not something that will prepare you for a real career, like math, science, or English." And that was the end of that.

Although it was no longer the fashion to skip a grade or two if you excelled in school, Klara knew she needed to separate her life from her mother and grandfather as soon as possible. From the time she started high school, she planned to finish in three years, and she did. While her mother only wanted—no, only *allowed*—her to apply to New York City–based schools, Klara knew she needed to go elsewhere if she were ever to be free and independent.

"Why look elsewhere when there are so many good colleges and universities right here in the city?" her mother asked.

In private conversations with her guidance counselor, Mrs. Carter, Klara expressed her desire to go to another city, maybe Boston. Mrs. Carter encouraged Klara to look at Boston University, Tufts, and Harvard.

"You have the grades to get in, and the SAT scores too," she said.

Klara asked, "What about financial aid? I'm going to need it."

"I'll help you fill out the form, and you'll just have to see." Mrs. Carter crossed her fingers and held them up in the air. Klara repeated the gesture.

That April, she got a thick envelope from Harvard University.

"What is this?" her mother asked, waving a white-and-maroon envelope as Klara walked in from school one afternoon. "When did you apply to Harvard? We said you'd go to school here in New York and live at home."

Klara took the envelope from her mother's hand and ran into her bedroom, shutting the door behind her. Her heart raced as she locked it with the hook lock she'd recently installed.

Ripping open the envelope, she read:

*Dear Miss Lieberman—*
*Congratulations! I am delighted that the Committee*
*on Admissions has admitted you to the Class of 1987.*
*I hope you decide to join us at Harvard.*

As she scanned the letter to the final paragraph, she read:

*As we were extremely impressed by your quali-*
*fications and understand your financial need, we are*
*able to offer you a partial scholarship and additional*
*financial aid, including a part-time job on campus.*

Klara screamed into her pillow. This was her golden ticket. No one could stop her now, not even her relentless mother.

*Knock. Knock. Knock. Bang. Bang. Bang.* "Open this door right now, young lady! I insist!" Eventually she did, but her mother no longer wielded the same power over her that she'd had just a few moments ago. A few months later, against her mother's and grandfather's wishes, Klara waited at Penn Station with two large khaki-green duffel bags, ready to board an Amtrak train bound for Boston's South Station, followed by a quick MBTA Red Line subway ride to Cambridge.

Klara's new life was beginning. Making her way to Harvard Yard, where all the freshman dorms were, she could feel her breath become lighter. Despite the heavy duffel bags, her shoulders softened. Twirling around in the campus quad, she pinched herself to make sure it was real, not just a dream. She'd certainly had dreams like this before, only to awaken to the four walls of her childhood bedroom.

"You must be our other roommate," a red-haired girl said. "I'm Lisa."

"Hi, I'm Klara."

Looking at the Klara's two duffel bags, Lisa asked, "Is that all you have?"

"Yes," Klara said, looking down.

"Well, that's good, because I have enough stuff for the both of us." Both girls smiled.

The next four years flew by. Klara was busy with classes, schoolwork, professors, and research. The need to maintain a 3.5 average to keep her scholarship, on top of her part-time job, left little time for socializing, but she was used to solitude.

After taking an Introduction to Anthropology class her freshman year, Klara was hooked, particularly when it came to archaeology. By the end of that course, she was ready to declare her major. She loved learning about ancient cultures and the fact that the study of archaeology provided the opportunity to see physical proof of those cultures. In her more advanced classes, when she had the opportunity to touch and feel artifacts, something inside her awoke that she never realized was there: a desire to know more.

The summer between her junior and senior years, Klara volunteered with a handful of other students—undergrad and graduate, along with two professors—to help excavate a site in Central America. Her friends Barbara and Diane were with her, and the three of them bonded over shaking screened trays of dirt and gravel in the hot Guatemalan sun, searching for shards of vases, bowls, and plates. Holding a ceramic shard from seven hundred years earlier, Klara felt connected to generations upon generations that had come before her. Every being mattered, because everything was connected, she thought. This meant she was no longer alone in the world, at least intellectually. Emotional connection would take much longer for her.

Klara returned home to her mother and grandfather's apartment as infrequently as possible.

Her mother would constantly ask, "When are you coming home, Klara? We never get to see you anymore."

"I'm busy with school and my job," she would answer.

"What about your grandfather and me? Did you forget about us?"

But her mother never came to visit her in Cambridge. Klara thought, *If she really cared, she'd come see me here.* But her mother never did. *The truth is, it's all about her and her needs*, Klara realized. This was one more piece of evidence.

After graduation she stayed in Cambridge, getting an apartment with Barbara and Diane. All three had started a PhD program at Harvard's Department of Anthropology, which offered doctorates in archaeology and social anthropology. She dated here and there, but nothing lasted very long, whereas her friends had long-term relationships—one had a serious boyfriend, the other a serious girlfriend. It bothered her that she didn't, but not enough to really question why she'd never had a relationship.

Time went on, and after seven years and a few major digs in Mexico, Klara graduated with a doctorate in archaeology. In addition to earning a master's degree and taking further courses toward her PhD, she had to complete a dissertation that included thirty months of field research. Neither her mother nor her grandfather came to Klara's college or graduate school graduations.

"It's just too long a trip for your grandfather," her mother explained each time, "and I can't leave him home alone."

*Of course not*, Klara thought. To say she was disappointed was an understatement. She was more than a little disheartened but not at all surprised. Her good friend Barbara invited her along to dinner with her family both times, and while they were all quite gracious, Klara's heart sank deeper each graduation. Nevertheless, she graduated with honors. Her friends expressed their pride and happiness, but it wasn't the same as having her family do so. Their kudos came in the form of a Hallmark graduation card, with the printed words *Happy Graduation* and her mother's and grandfather's signatures.

Dr. Klara Lieberman began her career as a junior faculty member of Harvard University's Department of Anthropology's graduate program in archaeology in August of 1994 at the age of twenty-nine and a half. She was sure the next chapter of her professional and personal life was just around the corner, but she didn't realize just how emotionally unequipped she was.

The next thirteen years passed quickly, with Klara teaching, assisting, co-leading, and eventually heading up multiple major archaeological digs related to ancient Mayan civilization. Traveling to various parts of Central America and Mexico for digs was the exciting part, followed by months of meticulously researching unearthed shards in a prominent high-tech lab. Although she had certainly learned how to crank out the research papers, all of this took time. After assisting at the university's graduate program for a year after graduation, Klara rose through the academic ranks, first becoming an assistant professor, then an associate professor, and finally, after many research publications and academic accolades, attaining the coveted position of full professor.

The truth was, she judged Barbara and Diane for not pushing themselves harder. By their mid-thirties, they'd decided they wanted to settle down and have children. Klara was like a machine. She didn't believe she needed any of that, which was why she was more shocked than anyone when she began sleeping in and missing classes.

"Barbara," she said on more than one occasion, "can you please fill in for me? I don't know what's wrong. I must be coming down with a virus or something." The next time, she asked Diane.

Finally, her friends confronted her. "What's going on with you? You haven't been feeling well for a few months now. We're worried about you. We'll go with you to see the doctor; just make an appointment."

Klara always yessed them but ignored their concerns.

However, upon returning to Cambridge after her grandfather's funeral and shiva, she was so run-down that she could no longer keep up with her job's busy pace. All she wanted was to rest. The doctors she finally saw said she was fine other than needing to exercise, relax more, and take Vitamin D. They did mention something about depression, offered to start her on an SSRI antidepressant, and suggested she consider talking to a therapist.

It was around this time that Klara heard about the professorship at a small liberal arts college a few hours away in the Maine countryside, with fewer responsibilities. Klara was convinced the solution was to leave her high-pressure job, and all would be fine. The fact that it was two and a half hours farther from Queens, where her mother lived, only made the position more desirable.

Now, after seven years of coasting as a professor with some teaching responsibilities but few expectations of leading digs or publishing, Klara was forty-nine years old. *How did that happen?* she wondered. The most adventurous thing she had done since coming to Holbrook College was co-lead a dig in the Yucatán with a former colleague, Arthur, the year before. She was right to be suspicious of his motives. She knew from a brief romantic relationship with him in the past that he was untrustworthy, but she felt compelled to go.

While in Mexico, she formed a close relationship with a female Mayan shaman, Rosario, whose husband she worked with. Through that unexpected friendship, Klara became close to a group of other Mayan village women as well.

It was Rosario who made her question her obsession with other peoples' cultures and history, particularly when she seemed so uninterested in her own. Klara considered staying and perhaps teaching at a local university nearby. In the end, she realized that staying might be just another escape, and she returned to her life teaching college in Maine, giving her more time to reflect on her next move. Or maybe it was just easier.

While often regretting her decision to return to Holbrook College and the United States in general, she knew her mother's letter, along with the one from the Polish government, was just the inspiration and direction she needed.

*My father is buried in Warsaw. After all these years, I'll finally get the answers I've been waiting for,* Klara thought. She couldn't pack quickly enough.

# CHAPTER 3

It was two o'clock in the afternoon when Klara arrived at Warsaw's Chopin Airport. As she looked around at the people milling about, rushing to their gates, and checking their cell phones, Klara felt like she could have been in any Western city in 2014, particularly given their modern dress and the newness of the airport. She had to admit the fast-paced feel here surprised her, at least in this wide-open anonymous airport. However, as she heard Polish spoken all around her, she remembered where she was. She chastised herself for being ethnocentric and out of touch, half expecting it to be a cold, gray Eastern European winter day, although it was June with hot summer weather, just like in New England.

Once she got her bearings and retrieved her luggage, she hopped on a city bus to her hotel, after inquiring of an airline worker. Once situated, Klara showed the hotel address to a young woman seated next to her, asking in English while pointing to the address, if she might tell her when she reached her stop, Nowy Street, to which the other woman nodded. Peering out the window, she noticed low-rise gray block buildings interspersed with more updated, colorful ones and some high-rises in the distance. The outmoded gray buildings looked drab and industrial, straight out of the Communist era, while the brighter ones had clearly been built sometime during the past twenty years or so. While peering out the window, she played with the gold locket her father had given her so many years before—the one she only just began wearing after receiving the recent letters. She was rubbing it for strength and good luck when the other woman tapped her shoulder, saying, "Nowy Swiat."

"Thank you," Klara said. Klara had read that it was along the Royal Way, part of the ancient processional route near Old Town and Lazienki Park. She disembarked at a tree-lined corner, her backpack over one shoulder and a small suitcase in tow. After walking a few blocks with the aid of a map, the help of a few kind people, and lots of hand gestures, Klara finally arrived at Novotel Warszawa Hotel, a small efficiency she had found in her guidebook.

*At least it's within my budget.*

Walking in, Klara spotted a tall, lanky young man at the front desk who wore a name tag that read *Szymon*. He chatted with her in reasonably good English while checking her in. "Are you here on business or pleasure?" he asked, smiling.

Confused by the question, as she wasn't sure whether finding her long-lost family qualified as "pleasure," Klara said, "Business, I think." She noticed him staring back at her as he tilted his head. Jet-lagged and more than a bit disoriented, Klara was chattier than usual, surprising herself. She was shocked to find that she had told a total stranger, "I actually came to Warsaw to seek out family roots"— something she would normally keep to herself, or share only with her closest confidants.

"I have a friend who's a local tour guide," he replied. "From time to time, she helps foreigners searching for their Polish ties. I can call her if you'd like."

Before Klara knew what she was saying, she blurted out, "That would be terrific, thank you." Smiling, she asked him, "Do you know where I could find something to eat?"

"Old Town, it's just a few blocks away," he said, circling the area on her city map. "It's a much prettier area there, with pastel-colored homes, rebuilt to look as they did before the war, so it's got a true traditional Polish feel. There are plenty of cafés and restaurants to choose from."

"I have one more question," she said, "if you don't mind."

He nodded.

"Your English is so good. Is it just you, or is it common for people here to speak English?"

"Thank you, madam. Over the past twenty-five years, English and other European languages like German, French, and Spanish, rather than primarily Russian, have been taught as a second language in our schools. Two-thirds of students learn English, so many young people speak it."

Klara nodded and smiled. She was so famished that she thanked Szymon, left her bag at the front desk without even going to her room, and headed to Old Town in search of sustenance.

It was a bright, clear day with blue skies and a seasonable summer temperature of seventy-five degrees. The afternoon sun shone brightly, although it looked as though the workday was over, as women in heels and men in loafers, both wearing suits, hurried by. Some carried their jackets and had rolled up their shirtsleeves. The air was warm, and an occasional breeze blew through her hair. Klara walked past gray postwar buildings until the colors began to brighten and the landscape transformed into a sea of pastels, while the streets changed from paved asphalt to cobblestone. She had arrived at the Old Town Square with its many indoor and outdoor cafés and colorful canopies with the names of the establishments, like Café Epoka, overhanging small tables.

The large square was filled with people strolling, sitting, talking, smoking, eating, and drinking, just like back home, but Klara was here in Warsaw. She inhaled the atmosphere—a relaxed early dinner crowd at the beginning of a warm summer's evening. Sitting at an open-air café, she imagined what it might be like to be one of them, a Polish resident, while she waited to order. Contemplating this, she momentarily felt a sense of belonging, rather than like the tourist she was. Recalling that she was a visitor, Klara remembered to email Sheila that she had arrived safely.

Taking out her laptop, she wrote: *Thank you again for the ride. I can't believe I'm here, sitting in a beautiful European square, having a glass of white wine and a cigarette at this moment. Talk soon!*

The restaurants, vendors, and dwellings surrounding the square were noticeably pristine and charming. Klara stopped under a dark blue canopy with several silver jewelry vendors when her eye caught the glint of burnt-orange, cherry-red, and chartreuse-amber items set in silver.

"Do you speak English?" she asked one vendor.

The woman nodded.

"Is that all really amber—even the red and green colors?" Klara asked.

"Yes," the vendor answered. "Lots of people are surprised to learn this, but amber comes in many colors," she said, smiling.

"Thank you," Klara said, returning the smile.

She looked around, taking in the atmosphere. *I'm really here*, she thought. She tugged on her locket and shed a few tears. She knew there was no turning back, and she didn't want to. She wanted to forge ahead, meet her father's family, and finally say a proper farewell to him at the cemetery where he was buried.

❖ ❖ ❖

Upon returning to Novotel Warszawa Hotel, Klara approached Szymon, who was still behind the hotel desk. She intended to touch base about his friend and pick up her bags.

"I have good news, madam," he said with a smile. "Although my friend Anna is not available this week, she knows someone who can help. You can call her tomorrow; her name is Alicja. Here's her number," he added, handing her a slip of paper.

Retiring to her room, Klara felt more optimistic about the next day but couldn't stop pacing back and forth across the drab, shoebox-sized bedroom, its pale walls dimly lit by a small desk lamp. She picked up her new Frommer's travel guide to Poland, focusing on Warsaw, mindlessly leafing through it.

What if she doesn't want to see me? What if she doesn't like me?

Perhaps she should have tried to track down her aunt before making the trip there, but she had to talk to her in person—a letter wouldn't have been sufficient. She had to look her in the eye and explain why so many years had passed with no contact from her. And who knew if her aunt had tried to find her? Her mother had certainly never said, but then again, Klara knew she couldn't count on her mother. Feeling for the locket once again and staring into the photos it held of her father, aunt, and grandparents, she breathed a little more deeply.

Although she was exhausted from the long journey from Maine to Warsaw, Klara tossed and turned all night. By the time she awoke, her covers were strewn about the bed. She had dreamed of meeting Aunt Rachel, but Rachel didn't know who she was and perhaps didn't even know she existed. Her body felt sluggish and achy, and she didn't recognize where she was at first. Looking out the window, she recalled she had arrived in Warsaw just the day before.

Szymon's acquaintance Alicja wouldn't be able to see her right away, so Klara had a few days to kill. After using the hotel's computer, she tried to Google "Rachel Lieberman," her aunt's name. When nothing came up, Klara switched gears, grabbed her Lonely Planet guide, and headed out to tour the city. She spent the next two days visiting museums, Warsaw University, and the stately Royal Castle by the banks of the Vistula River, which divided the large city of Warsaw into two parts. Couples were seated on the freshly cut green grass in the park near Vistula River, holding hands and taking pictures, as families walked by. She felt a deep ache in her chest, wishing she could be among them.

As Klara sat there on that overcast, warm afternoon, she thought about the last conversation she'd had with her mother before her bombshell of a letter arrived. She had been nagging Klara about something or other, as usual—probably not calling often enough. She imagined her mother sitting with her new second husband, Morris, at the round kitchen dinette table that was still covered in the same yellow-and-brown polyester tablecloth. In Klara's mind's eye, she could see her mother holding the pickle-green 1980s-style telephone receiver that hung from the mustard-colored wall, connected by a twisted nine-foot cord.

Everything except the food in her mother's apartment had been bought in or before 1990, around the time Klara stopped coming home on any kind of regular basis. She sincerely doubted her mother had replenished her wardrobe since then, wearing the same dark, below-the-knee skirts with plain, long-sleeved blouses, and always with a pair of nylons and her white faux-leather house slippers. Her short, dyed brown hair was always in a stiff coiffure that she had styled every Friday at Miriam's beauty parlor down the street.

Klara had one particularly vivid memory of her father, as she was only six years old when he left. He wore his black fedora with a well-fitted gray suit and had magically willed a lollipop to appear from his suit jacket pocket. "Just for you," he said with a smile that lit up her world as she ran to hug him. But the memory was fleeting, evaporating in seconds. It must have been right before he left, as it was what she could best remember.

Her memories of the two adults who subsequently raised her, her mother and grandfather, were not nearly so pleasant. Klara was always a good student, bringing home A's from the time she was in first grade. But rather than commending her, her mother and grandfather would criticize her instead when she got a ninety-eight on a test rather than a hundred.

"Where did the other two points go, smarty pants?" her grandfather, Siggy, asked mockingly. His nose was always in a serious, thick hardcover book by a well-respected man like Sigmund Freud, Franklin Delano Roosevelt, or Douglas MacArthur.

"You think you're so smart. Next time you should get them all right," Klara's mother, Bessie, would add, dish towel in hand and a gingham apron tied around her waist. She was forever cleaning—dusting, vacuuming, and washing dishes. When she wasn't cleaning, she was in the kitchen cooking flavorless meals that were either overly boiled or overly baked. Bessie was in constant motion, with an air of busy efficiency like a factory conveyor belt. Klara often felt like her mother didn't really take her in as a separate being; it was as if she were just another object in the apartment, expected to look neat and tidy, perform her duties as a good student and daughter, and do as she was told.

Klara's grandfather had lived with them for as long as she could remember. Her emotional recollections informed her that her mother constantly sided with him, never standing up for her father. How she wished her father could have taken her with him. She couldn't understand why he never returned or tried to reach out to her. As time passed, this loss created a deep hole in her heart that she could feel even now—like a constant pain she had learned to live with. Making matters worse, her mother expected her to treat her grandfather, whom Klara secretly called "Siggy" rather than "Grandpa," with the same deferential manner that she did, assuming she would forever wait on him. Bessie would often lament, "I'm sorry, Papa. I just don't know what I'm going to do with that girl. She must learn some manners." He would nod his head in agreement as he sucked on his dark brown pipe, slowly exhaling smoke rings that hung in the air around him as he relaxed in his brown corduroy La-Z-Boy recliner.

Although Klara's mother anticipated her daughter would follow her example as a dutiful homemaker, instead Klara mostly did what she pleased, preferring her own company with a good book in her bedroom or the local public library down the street. She read for hours, occasionally catching the attention of a librarian, while escaping her emotionally disconnected reality of chores and expectations. Her mother did not appreciate Klara's independent streak, viewing it as insubordination and repeatedly punishing her for it. "No dessert for you," she would decree. "My mother would never have tolerated this insolence. I was running the entire household and doing all the cooking and cleaning when I was only sixteen. That was when your grandmother came down with pneumonia and died shortly afterward." This was meant to make Klara feel bad, which she did, but the feeling passed when she thought of how her own mother treated her.

And then there were Jacob Herschler's recurring visits. They were too frequent and lasted too long, always leaving Klara shaken. Jacob was her grandfather and mother's very dear family friend, and they treated him like he walked on water—but to Klara, he was a pest who kept coming back. Jacob was around sixty years old at the time, just a few years older than Siggy. He was balding, with strands of gray-and-white hair combed across his clammy freckled forehead, and he had dark, beady brown eyes. As Klara became pubescent, he'd openly leer at her and find reasons to touch her arm, shoulder, or back. His mere presence sent waves of the willies up her spine. She had no power over whether or not Jacob was in their lives. Her family's admiration of him and their shared history were too strong. When she tried to complain to her mother about how often he came around, she'd call Klara a "willful, ungrateful child."

Her grandfather frequently reminded her that he and Jacob had arrived on the docks of Ellis Island from Germany in 1924, when they were teenagers. They had met as neighborhood friends, both having their own reasons for wanting to escape their families. Jacob had been nineteen, Siggy only seventeen. Jacob was the one with the charm and drive, eventually founding his own men's shirt factory from what was once a small men's outfitting operation, and Siggy worked there his whole life. It was there that Klara's father, along with a number of other Eastern European Jewish immigrants, also worked. In fact, it was rumored that Klara's father, David, had been part of a group of twenty young men rescued from Nazi-occupied Poland during World War II through a clandestine operation funded by Jacob, who also funded other such clandestine operations in Germany. While they were not all successful, his storied efforts allowed him to appear as a hero in his community, despite then using these young men to work in his factory for long periods of time at low wages to pay off their debt to him.

Siggy and Jacob ultimately introduced Klara's father and mother, and soon they wed. Even though David was considered of lower socioeconomic status, given his Eastern

European roots and recent immigrant status, as opposed to their more upscale and long-standing German Jewish background, Jacob convinced Siggy that it would be a good match because his daughter, Klara's mother, would never abandon Siggy for her new husband. With David as a son-in-law, Siggy would never lose his daughter, as she would always put her father first.

How long does one have to be grateful or beholden to someone who essentially saved your family? Ten years? Twenty? Fifty? One's whole life?

While her mother and grandfather treated Jacob as if he were God himself, it wasn't long before they started treating her father like dirt, ignoring and dismissing him. And then, just like that, he was gone. Klara was barely out of kindergarten when he disappeared. Whenever she asked her mother about her father, she would yell, "I've told you over and over again, he walked out on us—you, me, and your grandfather!" Finally, at around the age of eight, Klara stopped asking for her father when it became clear that he was never coming home, and that there would be no answers forthcoming. From that time forward, Klara understood it was an unspoken rule not to bring him up, so she didn't. Instead, she buried almost all her memories of him, except for the gold locket he had given her the last time they were together. The one she now wore. Her father had told her it was a family heirloom that first belonged to his mother and then to his sister, who had given it to him when they exchanged farewells in Poland. At the time, Klara put it away in the back of her bureau drawer for safekeeping from her mother. She now gently pulled on it, stroking the pendant with her fingers.

As a breeze blew across her bare shoulders, Klara returned to the present and decided to head back to her hotel room and retrieve her jean jacket. As she looked around and saw people congregating together, she was reminded that Wednesday couldn't come soon enough. She sorely wanted to find her father's family. What she wanted more than anything was to belong.

# CHAPTER 4

K lara awoke early Wednesday morning, anticipating her meeting with Alicja. Secretly harbored hopes of connecting with her father's family had piled up and now weighed heavily on her chest. During the twenty-minute bus ride to Alicja's office, she stared out the window, trying to concentrate on the sights around her, but worries buzzed through her mind. By the time she reached the office, her heart was racing, and her legs felt like jelly. She stood in front of a small travel agency with the number "127" printed on the glass door. After a few moments, Klara tucked her long, unruly hair behind her ears, played with her locket, and willed herself to step one sandaled foot in front of the other. A stylish sixtyish woman with gray-streaked hair, wearing a crepe blouse and pleated slacks, greeted her at the front desk.

"Hello, I'm Alicja," she said, extending her hand. "You must be Klara."

Klara nodded.

"I work as a travel agent here, but I also do genealogy research for tourists on the side. I understand you're looking for your father's family. Please come sit down." She gestured to a cushioned office chair across from her, taking a seat at her desk.

Klara settled herself, crossing her legs and smoothing her gauze skirt. Even its long length couldn't hide her trembling foot. Klara knew she was that much closer to finding her aunt Rachel.

"I've come to find my father's sister, who may or may not still live here. It's a long, complicated story. You see, we've never met, and I'm worried I might shock her popping up like this. While I certainly don't want to upset her, I do want to meet her in person." Klara's words quickly tumbled out of her mouth.

"I see," Alicja said, with another nod.

"Oh, and I should mention, I'm not certain if she stayed in Warsaw after the war, particularly as the family was Jewish," Klara said, almost out of breath.

"They may not have," Alicja said. "Many of the Jews who survived the war ultimately left. May I ask what makes you think she's still here?" She spoke in a low voice, speaking to Klara as she might to a young, frightened child, which was exactly how she felt at the moment.

"My mother received a letter from the Polish government mentioning that they were sending a copy of the same letter to my aunt, so it seems the government knows she's still alive. I'm hoping that she still lives here, although I don't know," Klara said, wondering if she had just traveled over four thousand miles for nothing more than a hope.

Alicja looked at her, tilting her head as if asking a question. "Why don't you tell me your aunt's name," she said, again smiling.

"Her maiden name is Rachel Lieberman, and she was born in Warsaw in 1925."

"Okay. Well, it's quite helpful that you know her maiden name. Is there anything else you can tell me about your family?"

"My father, David Lieberman, was born here in 1927 and was buried in a cemetery here in Warsaw in 1971. He died in an accident in the United States, but his body was flown here and buried by my aunt," Klara said, biting her lip.

"I'm so sorry to hear about the sad circumstances of his death. How unusual for him to be flown here!" Alicja remarked, as she jotted down this information with pen on paper. Looking up, she asked Klara, "Are there any other family names you can give me?"

"My grandparents were Meyer and Sarah Lieberman. Sadly, I know very little about them, except for the horrible fact that they perished in Treblinka sometime around 1940." Klara gazed at the floor, concentrating on its black-and-white tiles as though something fantastic might burst from it.

Alicja listened attentively, patting Klara's hand as she continued to stare at the floor, exhaling loudly.

"When I was young, my father told me that they sent him and his sister away, soon after the Nazis invaded Poland in 1939, in order to protect them. They were supposedly sent to the countryside near the Polish–Ukrainian border, and raised there as Catholic children."

Alicja looked at Klara with glassy eyes. "I'm so sorry to hear your story. Unfortunately, it is not an uncommon one for Jewish families under Nazi rule back then. Most of the children who survived the war did so by being converted, hidden, or sent away." She swallowed and added, "If your father and aunt were able to get away, it would have been early in the war, as you said. Let me look up their surname and your aunt's married name," she continued, turning toward her computer screen. "Oh, and if your father was buried here, perhaps he was buried in a Jewish cemetery. There's only one left in Warsaw."

"Really," Klara said, trying to wrap her head around the enormity of what this meant—that the rest had been bombed or razed, or that there weren't enough Jews still living here to create a need for further cemeteries. Whatever the case, she wanted to cry, but instead she simply sat there, shook her head, and said, "I don't know my aunt's married name."

For the next half hour, Klara waited as Alicja researched her family. She almost fell out of her seat when the other woman invited her back to her desk. "Okay, I found the name Lieberman with details that appear to match the information you've given me. A couple with this last name sent their two young teenage children, a boy and a girl, away to the eastern countryside before they were sent to Treblinka in 1940, as you mentioned." Alicja looked down, avoiding eye contact when she added the last part.

"How'd you find their name so quickly? I was hoping to get some answers, but I thought it would be more arduous."

"Two things—the Nazis were fastidious about their record-keeping and simply could not destroy all the evidence of their crimes fast enough. Also, we have a new website; it's like Warsaw meets Ancestry.com. Only professional members of a particular genealogical society can access it, and only here in Poland."

Klara couldn't help herself from asking, "You're certain?"

"There are details that match your story, as well as the same surname. It has to be the same family. While there were easily well over one hundred Lieberman families living in Warsaw in 1939, at the outbreak of the war, your grandparents, Majer [Meyer] and Sara [Sarah], were thirty-six and thirty-four at that time, and their two children, Rachel and Dawid [David], were fourteen and twelve. It makes sense that Rachel and Dawid were sent away, because only Majer and Sara were sent to Treblinka in 1940, where, as you mentioned, they sadly perished," Alicja explained.

"And what about Rachel?" Klara almost shouted.

Alicja looked again at her screen for a few more moments, scrolling down. "I can't be sure, but yes, it looks like she returned to Warsaw after the war ended and stayed here," she replied. "It's unusual she did, since most of the Polish Jews who returned to Warsaw, Krakow, Lodz, and other major cities and towns weren't exactly welcomed. Later many of them went to Israel in the 1960s, when they were forced to emigrate by the Polish government. They say that there are only about three to ten thousand Jews still living in Poland, while there were approximately three million Jews residing here before the war. Give me a moment. I'll see what else I can find," she said with a frown.

After typing on her keyboard and navigating other websites as well, Alicja smiled and looked up at Klara. "It looks like she may still live here after all. As you said, I see she married, and now her last name is Sheinberg. Her husband appears to have died a few years ago, but it seems she still lives here in Warsaw with her adult daughter, Hanna [Hannah], age fifty-nine, and her family. She's now eighty-nine years old. Let's see if we can find a current address." She continued typing and looking at her screen while Klara tapped her foot incessantly. After about another ten minutes, which felt like an eternity, Alicja announced, "I have it. I've written the address for you along with the telephone number. It's only about a twenty-minute bus ride from here," she added, handing her a piece of paper.

Klara took the paper and stared at it. It read:

*Rachel Lieberman Sheinberg, Potocka Street 35*
*apt. 4F, Warsaw, telephone number 022 750 32 34.*

She read the name aloud, "Rachel Lieberman Sheinberg," enunciating each syllable with emphasis, as though it were the final clue to a long-unsolved puzzle. "Oh, my god! I don't know what to say. Are you sure it's right?" she asked, her mouth agape. Now that Klara had her aunt's information, the likelihood of finding her became that much more real.

"There's only one way to be sure. Would you like me to call her for you?" Klara immediately nodded. Alicja picked up the receiver and dialed. It was clear that someone answered the phone at the other end. Although she could only hear Alicja's end of the conversation and understood little of the rapid Polish dialogue, Klara soon heard a change in Alicja's tone. While it was originally upbeat, it had become quieter, and then the call ended.

"What did they say?" Klara blurted out.

"That was Rachel's daughter, Hanna. She said she needed to go. She couldn't talk," Alicja said slowly.

"I don't understand. What exactly did she say?" Klara demanded, wringing her hands.

"I don't understand either." Alicja shook her head. "That's what she said, and then she hung up. As you heard, I told her who I was, and that I was calling because you were searching for her mother and family. I'm sorry. I think she was in shock," Alicja continued, gently putting her hand on Klara's shoulder. Klara felt the blood rush from her face and felt like she might easily faint. Alicja noticed, quickly getting a glass of water for her. As she drank it, the phone rang. After she answered it, Alicja's countenance transformed from flat to quite animated. Her mouth hung open, and she raised one finger in the air toward Klara.

"That was Hanna, believe it or not," Alicja said, grinning. "She apologized for hanging up so quickly and explained that she'd been overwhelmed by the unexpected news that you're here in Warsaw. She said she knew of you but was blindsided by your sudden arrival without any warning. She'll meet you later this afternoon."

"Just her?" Klara asked, thinking perhaps she'd misheard.

"Yes, just her. She said she speaks fluent English, so you'll be able to communicate with each other. She wants to meet at a nearby restaurant, Café Bocian in Old Town, at two o'clock."

Klara thanked Alicja for all her help and paid her for her services. "Wish me luck," she said, waving goodbye as she left.

# CHAPTER 5

Klara walked into Café Bocian at two o'clock that afternoon, tugging on her gold locket for some much-needed
support. The café was narrow, with white-and-royal-blue
ceramic plates charmingly hanging from long white ribbons on
the wall. She immediately spotted a medium-built middle-aged
woman sitting at a table in the corner, smoking a cigarette and
drinking a cup of coffee.

Walking up to her, she asked, "Excuse me, are you Hanna?"

The woman quickly extinguished her cigarette and
stood, as Klara awaited her response. "Yes, I am," she replied
flatly and without expression.

"Hanna, it's so good to finally meet you," Klara said,
forcing a smile despite Hanna's cold reception.

Hanna nodded curtly.

Following Hanna's lead, Klara avoided attempting to
embrace her cousin, instead sitting down in silence. No
sooner had they sat than Hanna began shooting questions at
her: "Why have you come to Poland now? Where have you
been all these years? Why didn't you ever contact us before?"

Klara felt like she was in front of a firing squad. "I'm
sorry," she said quietly, trying to keep an even tone, "but my
mother never spoke of your mother or her family. She was very
secretive about my father's background, and he disappeared
from my life when I was a young child, so I never got to learn

much about him. My mother only recently told me that he died many years ago, and that his sister—your mother—had flown his body back to Warsaw." She took a breath. "Please believe me; I just found out about your family."

Hanna did not appear mollified by Klara's explanation, and the interrogation continued. "Why now? How long has it been? Let's see, it's been forty-three years since your father died. Why have you finally come to meet my mother after forty-three years?" she asked, glaring at her from across the table.

"Um," Klara said, fumbling over her words, completely taken aback by this unwelcome reception. "As I said, I really didn't know about your mother and your family until very recently. That said, for certain reasons, maybe I wasn't ready to delve into my family history until learning of your existence." Klara looked down at her hands, realizing she was pulling on her fingers. "When I received the letter from my mother two weeks ago finally revealing the truth about my father, I hopped on a plane here."

"My mother was ready to meet you a long time ago. She wrote letters and tried to telephone. She waited and waited. I still don't understand," Hanna persisted. "She made many attempts to get in touch with you over the years; how can you say you didn't know she existed?" Hanna hissed.

"I knew she existed, but only as an old photograph and a story my father told me when I was a child. It was like a fairy tale about a once-happy family, a brother and sister, with their mother and father, but then they all got separated, and no one lived happily ever after." Klara opened her locket to show the black-and-white photos of her father's sister and parents.

"Where did you get that?" Hanna snapped, now staring intently at the old photographs.

"From my father, the last time I saw him. He said it was given to him as a parting gift by his sister, your mother,"

Klara replied. None of this was going the way she had imagined. Hanna sat there gritting her teeth, and Klara was at a loss for words. She was unprepared for her cousin's anger and the revelation that her aunt had indeed tried to connect with her. She knew she sounded defensive when she replied, "My mother must have blocked the calls and letters. That's the only explanation I can think of. I really had no idea!"

"That might have made sense until the time you were in your twenties, maybe, but it's been another twenty-five years since then."

Klara sat there staring at Hanna, considering how to proceed. "You don't believe me? Why else would I be here?" she asked, looking into her cousin's eyes, trying to make some connection. "I finally got enough information about my father's family and have the emotional wherewithal and means to search you out at nearly fifty, and you turn your back on me? My mother and grandfather kept me from knowing anything about you and your mother for all this time. But now that I know the truth about my father, you're going to shut me out?"

Klara again opened the locket, pointing to the small photos inside, and said, "I remember my father giving this locket to me and telling me about his sister, your mother, and his parents, and how one day I would get to meet his sister. I've only recently learned that she is the only person left out of the four people in these photos. Now that day has finally come, and I very much want to meet my aunt. I'm sorry if that seems strange to you, but I want nothing more than to meet the family I've been kept from." Klara spoke in a rush of words, a tear rolling down her cheek.

But Hanna remained unimpressed. "I'll tell you what seems strange to me," she said, sipping her cup of coffee. "My mother recently received a letter from the Polish government, only a month ago, saying that land our grandparents purchased here many years ago is now worth something. As with other property wrongfully seized by the Nazis and then nationalized by the Polish government, Jewish families in particular are only now finally being compensated. And now that land is worth much more than anyone would have imagined, as its location has suddenly become desirable, and a private company wants to develop it. My mother may soon be a more comfortable woman. Might that have anything to do with why you're here now?" Hanna stared at Klara with her steely blue eyes. "Are you trying to make sure you and your mother get a piece of the action? Is that why you're really here now, Klara?"

Klara could feel her eyebrows furrowing as her mouth was frozen half-open. She paused, feeling like a criminal caught in a web of lies, but she knew she was neither a criminal nor a liar. She had just omitted a part of the truth—one that didn't seem as important as the rest of it. "Yes," she finally said, looking down, "I did know that. That's why my mother came clean and told me about my father and your mother, but that's not the reason I came here. I could have dealt with that by mail. I came because I just found out from my mother what really happened to my father, after decades of not knowing— that he died in a train accident and was buried here in Warsaw by your mother, whom she thought might still be living here. I always wanted to know about my father's true whereabouts and to meet his family," she said, leaning toward Hanna. "I live a quiet academic life. The money is secondary. I'm most interested in family," Klara insisted.

"I don't believe you." Hanna abruptly pushed back her chair from the table. "And you're twenty-five years too late. Your mother clearly put you up to this. From what I've heard of her from *my* mother, this feels like just the sort of thing she would do: manipulative, ruthless, and con-niving. Of course, it's about the money, isn't it? How is it possible you didn't know your father was dead and buried here? What did you think happened to him?" she asked, her nostrils flaring.

Klara could understand Hanna's perspective—why *hadn't* she questioned her mother about her father's whereabouts sooner? She didn't know the answer. She had lived her whole life doing what was necessary to survive emotionally and burying her head in the sand when it came to anything else. While she could see Hanna's point, her feelings took over. At that moment, an uncharacteristically high-pitched voice came out of her mouth. "I barely talk to my mother. Yes, she did write to me about the Polish government compensating our family with money for the seized land, but that's not the reason I came! I came to find and visit my father's gravesite, and to meet your mother. You have to understand, my mother always told me that my father left us and never wanted to see me again. She turned him into a villain. I was so young that I never questioned it," Klara cried, resting her face in her hands. Taking them away suddenly, she demanded, "Just tell me, does your mother even know I'm here?"

Hanna took her time in replying. Tight-lipped, she said, "No, and she won't, because I'm not going to tell her, and you're going to go quietly back to wherever it is you came from." She got up from her chair and wrapped her white cardigan around her shoulders.

Klara's eyes welled up with tears. She had finally learned about her father's family, had committed to seeking them out, and was being turned away at the outset. Before Klara could stop her, Hanna turned and walked away.

"That's it?" Klara asked loudly, now standing.

"Yes," Hanna said as she kept walking.

❖ ❖ ❖

Klara remained seated at the café table for barely a moment after Hanna left, before getting up and discreetly following her. Although she had Rachel's address from Alicja, she thought it better not to simply barge in on her. Instead, she would follow Hanna, as according to Alicja's information, they lived together. Trailing Hanna felt like a game of cat and mouse; while unfamiliar with this strategy, Klara was determined to catch up with her and continue to try to convince her to introduce her to Rachel. Working under the assumption that Hanna was heading home, Klara didn't think about what she'd do once she finally got there. She was on a mission with adrenaline pulsing through her veins, propelling her forward, so much so that she could feel her heart pumping. Hanna jumped into a taxi, and Klara followed suit.

"Please follow that taxi," she said in English to the thirty-something taxi driver. She gestured wildly at the cab in front of them. Thank goodness, he seemed to understand her, though he likely thought she was half-mad.

Of course, it made sense that Hanna would think she was just there for the money. The next time she looked up, Hanna's taxi had stopped, and she was getting out on her street—Potocka Street. "Stop here!" Klara called to her driver. She tried as politely as possible to excuse herself while pushing through a crowded street of people walking side by side. However, once Hanna was in sight, Klara was shocked, not knowing what she should do next. In order to get her bearings, she popped into a bakery for a moment, peeking out the door as she visually followed Hanna, who walked toward a red brick pre-war apartment building. Klara assumed it was Potocka 35, the address Alicja had given her. Quickly leaving the bakery, she hid around the corner, trying to remain out of sight. A couple of older gentlemen stared at her, tipped their hats, and kept going. She tried to smile kindly at them and waited, knowing she'd need to come up with another plan. A few minutes must have passed, and when she looked up the block, she spied Hanna walking slowly with another woman, a much older one. Her heart jumped when she saw the other woman, white-haired and with a slight limp, leaning on a wooden cane. *It must be Rachel!* she thought.

Although Klara so badly wanted to walk right up to Rachel and introduce herself, she swiftly turned her back on them as her legs froze and her throat tightened. Rachel looked her full eighty-nine years, just a few years older than her own mother. She stepped back into a doorway as the two women neared and passed by slowly. As she snuck a look at the older woman, she noticed a faraway sadness in her eyes that made her want to reach out and take her arm. Instead, she waited another ten minutes until they were gone, exhaling a long breath as she felt her body relax. At least she had finally laid eyes on Rachel, which was one more step forward.

❖ ❖ ❖

The next morning, Klara returned to Potocka Street promptly at nine, stopping at Sosnowa Bakery, approximately where she had hidden herself the day before. This time, she followed the sweet smells wafting from the bakery and went inside, where she bought a loaf of *chalka*, what the Poles called challah bread. Spotting an open bench by the sidewalk, she sat down and began eating the bread and sipping her cup of strong Polish coffee. As it neared eleven o'clock, she finally saw the front door to her aunt's apartment building open and the older woman from yesterday emerge. Aunt Rachel walked slowly, and this time, she was by herself, again leaning on a cane. Klara took a deep breath, realizing that she was essentially stalking her aunt, but she was convinced it was for a good reason.

After Rachel walked in her direction and then passed by, Klara stood up from the bench and followed her aunt for a short distance. The older woman was probably less than five feet tall. Her white hair was tied back in a neat bun. Her body swayed from side to side as she moved, leaning more heavily on her right side, the one with the cane. Despite her slow pace and slight limp, she moved adeptly.

As they waited together at the street corner for traffic to pass, Klara approached her aunt, holding out her hand.

"Can I help you cross the street?" Klara asked in English, illustrating her speech through body language, extending her hand.

"*Dziekuje ci* [Thank you]," Rachel replied, and they walked side by side, crossing the street as Klara held Rachel's arm.

"You're welcome," Klara answered in English, with a smile.

"American? Canadian?" Rachel asked in English, pointing to Klara.

Klara's mouth dropped. "Yes. American" — she pointed to her chest and nodded — "New York."

They were now standing in front of a bus stop. Rachel sat on a bench, gesturing for Klara to sit next to her.

Klara faced Rachel. "Yiddish? German?" she asked, hoping Rachel spoke some Yiddish from her childhood, as Klara spoke German from hers, growing up in a German Jewish household. Between the two of them, perhaps they could find some common language. For once, Klara was thankful for the amount of German her mother and grandfather had spoken when she was growing up.

"*Yiddish i German*," Rachel replied, wide-eyed.

"I speak German, not so much Yiddish," Klara replied in German, imagining Rachel was wondering whether she was Jewish, given the mention of Yiddish, but was simply too reserved to ask.

As the two women sat together, Klara reached into her

bread bag and pulled out a chunk of challah. "Would you like a piece?" she asked her in German, their newfound common language.

"Challah? I haven't heard it pronounced that way in a very long time. We call it *chalka* here," Rachel said, almost laughing.

Again replying in German, Klara said with a smile, "Yes, they told me that at the bakery. I'm just so used to pronouncing it 'challah.' It's amazing, though, that halfway around the world, challah looks the same and tastes pretty similar too, regardless of how it's pronounced."

"Thank you, dear." Rachel beamed, accepting the piece of bread. "Where'd you buy it?"

"Sosnowa Bakery," Klara replied, mirroring her grin.

"Sosnowa is good, but you haven't tried real *chalka* until you've tasted mine," Rachel said with a twinkle in her eye.

"Is that so? You make your own challah? I bet it's delicious. I've never eaten homemade."

Rachel was gazing into Klara's face with what appeared to be a glimpse of recognition. "There's something about you . . . I can't quite put my finger on it, but you look so much like someone I once knew," she said. "It's something about the shape of your face, and the color of your eyes. But even more than that, it's your smile. How is it that you speak such good German?" Rachel asked.

"It was spoken in my home when I was growing up. How about you?" Klara asked.

Rachel's eyes looked faraway at that moment.

Klara thought Rachel must have clearly figured out she was Jewish, and thus was someone safe to share her story with.

"I had to learn it when the Nazis took over Poland, in order to survive by working as a housekeeper in a Polish German household. My German had to be perfect," Rachel said, placing her thumb, middle, and index fingers together, "so they'd never guess I might be Jewish."

Klara so wished she could tell Rachel who she was at that moment, but she didn't want to scare her away. Instead, she panicked and stood up from the bench abruptly.

"I forgot. I need to go to the pharmacy to pick up some toiletries. It was so nice meeting you. Have a good day." Klara got up, leaving a puzzled Rachel staring after her.

# CHAPTER 6

The next day, after it stopped pouring, Klara took a bus to Potocka Street, planting herself on the same park bench near Rachel's apartment as she had the day before, hyperaware so as not to be spotted by Hanna. It was an overcast day with just a slight sprinkle of rain, but Klara didn't mind. She graciously nodded at people, generally trying to fit into the neighborhood, when she spotted her aunt walking toward her. Rachel wore her hair pulled back again, but this time with a floral kerchief covering it, a dark raincoat, and sensible shoes.

"Hello," Rachel said with some surprise upon seeing Klara. "What brings you back here today, dear?" she asked in German, and then recalled, "You left rather quickly the other day."

Klara replied in German. "It's Shabbat, and I wanted to buy a challah. I mean a *chalka*," she said, pointing to Sosnowa Bakery, a few shops away. "I'm sorry for leaving so abruptly the other day." She said no more about their last encounter, as she could think of no good excuse for her erratic behavior.

"You celebrate Shabbat?" Rachel asked wide-eyed, sitting down on the bench next to Klara. "Me too. I'm Jewish," she whispered, half-conspiratorially, forgetting she had mentioned this fact just yesterday. "There aren't too many of us left here in Poland, but maybe a few more than you might think." She looked at Klara's uncovered head. "You must be getting wet out here."

"I'm fine. It's not too bad," Klara replied, although her hair was damp and frizzing even more than usual.

"Come, dear, let's go inside the bakery," Rachel said, putting her free arm through Klara's. She led her into the busy bakery, where they sat down at a small round metal table in front of rows of glass-encased, just-baked pastries wafting sweet aromas and making Klara's mouth water.

"Are you traveling alone, dear?" Rachel asked.

Brought back to the present moment by Rachel's question, Klara replied, "I am," consciously speaking from her belly in order to make her voice sound more self-assured than she actually felt.

"You're all by yourself, and it's Shabbat. Perhaps you'd like to come over to my home tonight and have Shabbat dinner with me and my family?" Rachel asked.

Klara wanted nothing more than to say yes, but she knew Hanna would be furious with her. "Thank you so much, but I do have other plans this evening. I really wish I could," she said as she pushed her chair back from the table. "It was so nice meeting you again, but I should probably go now. Thank you," she said, touching Rachel's elbow.

Rachel sat there staring at her. "You have such a lovely face. You look so much like someone who was very dear to me," she said, appearing to arrive at a sudden realization. "It's your blue eyes. My brother David's eyes were the same shade of ocean blue with yellow flecks like yours. It's been so many years since I last saw him, but I'd recognize his eyes anywhere," she said, more to herself than to Klara. "He lived in New York City too, but he died many years ago." Her voice trailed off before she continued. "Where do you need to be, dear? Are you visiting family?"

"I hope to visit family, but it hasn't really worked out," Klara said, biting her upper lip.

"Why not?"

"It's a long story." Klara's heart was pounding so wildly she wondered if her aunt could hear it.

"I have time," Rachel said gently.

Klara shifted around until she got more comfortable in her seat, and then began speaking rapidly. In one long breath, she explained, "It's taken me a really long time to come to Poland to visit my family. I wish I had come years ago, but until recently, I didn't even know I had family here in Warsaw. I was so busy with my career and trying to run away from my past."

"Well, you're here now."

"Yes, I am, but my newfound cousin mistakenly thinks I'm here for other reasons. She doesn't trust my motives," Klara said, the words spewing out before she could stop them. At that moment, it occurred to her that she didn't know what her aunt knew of her existence, so perhaps she should be more careful about what she said. Hanna had said that her aunt did know about her, but what exactly *did* she know? Automatically placing a hand on her locket, she wondered: *Did Papa tell her about me? He must have. If he did, how much did he share? Has she ever seen a photo of me? That's silly; it would have only been up to when he died, when I was six years old.*

Suddenly, her aunt's eyes were drawn to the distinctive gold locket hanging around Klara's neck, the one she was palming. Rachel seemed to notice its intricate design, allowing her eyes to linger on it. Her hands were drawn to it as if it were magnetic; they moved toward it in slow motion. Once reaching the oval-shaped pendant, her fingers nimbly opened it. While her eyes grew bigger, Rachel's body lurched back and she dropped the locket as if it were hot coal.

With wide eyes and a face drained of color, she asked, "Klara, is that you?"

Klara slowly nodded her head.

"Oh, my god!" Rachel exclaimed, placing her hand over her chest. "After all these years, it's really you!" She grabbed Klara's hands across the table, and wouldn't let go. "Why didn't you tell me?" she asked, still astonished.

"I was going to, but Hanna asked me to wait. She was trying to protect you," Klara said, fibbing a bit to soften the truth that Hanna preferred Klara go away entirely. "She thought I was after money you recently acquired from the Polish government for land that had belonged to your parents." The words rushed out like water from a collapsed dam.

"Is that why you're here?" Rachel asked, peering directly into Klara's eyes, studying them as though they were windows into her soul.

"I swear to you, no!" she nearly shouted. Other customers looked at her. Lowering her voice, Klara explained, "My mother did recently tell me about the land and the money, but that's not why I came. I wanted to meet you and your family. You must believe me: I only just learned about you. My mother finally told me the truth—that my father had died and been buried here in Poland many years ago, and that perhaps you might still live here," Klara insisted, practically sobbing. "That's why I came now, and then I found someone to help me locate your family. She called your home number and reached Hanna. We met a few days ago, but she didn't trust me. I hate that I've been so secretive, but I've been waiting for the right time and the right way to introduce myself to you."

"You really didn't know your father was dead? You didn't know he was buried here, or about my family?" Rachel asked, clearly shocked, trying to process this astonishing information. After a brief pause, as though deciding to believe Klara, she waved her hand dismissively and said,

"Oy, Hanna is too protective. She worries about me so much and doesn't trust other people that easily. Certainly not ones who show up out of the blue after so many years." Again, she stared at Klara, shaking her head, still in shock. "But here you are—Dawid's daughter. I've waited a very long time for this moment." She grabbed both of Klara's hands again, giving her a warm embrace.

"I'm so glad you feel that way." Realizing her hands were shaking, Klara sighed in relief. "I thought you'd be angry with me too."

"Not angry, dear, just curious about the timing. I still don't understand why you would come now, if not just because of the money. The timing just seems like too much of a coincidence. You have a right to your half of the money, of course, but I don't comprehend why, after all these years, you're seeking me out. I know you said you just learned your father was dead and buried here, but it's hard to believe, if I must say." Rachel studied her face.

"All I can tell you, Rachel, is the truth. My mother and I rarely speak. I've kept her out of my life because she's always been very demanding, calculating, and secretive. It would be just like her not to share what happened to my father until it was to her advantage. In this case, she thinks there may be more money to gain. As for not trying to find out more, I've lived my life up until now trying to put my past behind me. Some months ago, I was on a dig in Mexico when a friend asked me why I was so interested in other peoples' artifacts and culture, and what about my own? It made me start to think more about my family roots, and then I recently learned about my father. I guess the answer to your question is that I'm finally ready to get to know my family. I'm sorry if it seems odd to you."

As Klara spoke, Rachel continued to stare at the gold locket. "That locket you're wearing was a gift from my mother to me, and then from me to your father the last time I saw him alive, over seventy years ago. It's traveled so far and through so many years," she said with tears in her eyes. Her shoulders dropped, and it appeared as though she might collapse as she again reached out and stroked the locket. "It brings back so many memories."

Klara placed her hand on Rachel's shoulder without thinking, gently rubbing it. "My father gave it to me the last time I saw him," Klara said. "He was planning to go away for a while, apparently to look for a job. He told me this was a very precious locket, that it belonged to his mother, then to you, then to him, and now it was mine, and I needed to take extra special care of it. He said you gave it to him just before he left Poland to come to the United States at sixteen, and that your mother had given it to you. I've treasured it, keeping it safe all these years, as it has been my only connection to him. I just recently started to wear it again. I'm sorry. Do you want it back?" Klara asked, suddenly removing her hand from Rachel's shoulder, ready to unclasp her necklace chain.

"No, of course not, child. It's yours," Rachel said, making a shooing motion with her hand. "It has just been forever since I last saw it."

Klara opened the locket, displaying the old black-and-white photos—one of Rachel and David as young teenagers, and one of their parents just before they were taken to the concentration camp in Treblinka.

"Those were taken shortly before the war began," Rachel said solemnly, pointing to the photos as tears ran down her pained face. She took out a well-washed cotton handkerchief and wiped her eyes.

"I'm so sorry to upset you," Klara said, certain she had made a mess of things.

"No. It's not you. Seeing those old photos just brings back so many memories from such a long time ago, when my parents and your father were still alive. It seems like another lifetime," she said, staring past her niece with a faraway gaze.

All Klara could think to say was, "I'm so sorry."

Rachel perked up. "No. It's wonderful to see you wearing my mother's locket, your grandmother's locket," she said, squeezing Klara's arm and smiling.

Klara could tell that her mind was still somewhere else. She waited a few moments before asking, "What are you thinking about?"

"It's Shabbat, and every Shabbat I visit your father and my late Benjamin's gravesite at Cmentarz Zydowski, the Jewish Cemetery."

Before she could think, Klara heard herself asking, "May I come with you?" She certainly didn't want to intrude on her aunt's private ritual, but she so wanted to go with Rachel to visit her father's gravesite.

Rachel's face momentarily froze like a still frame, not moving for a few moments. Klara was sure she had gone too far with her request and ruined everything. Instead of responding, Rachel completely changed the subject. "Why don't you tell me what you've been doing with yourself all these years, dear? I haven't heard a peep about you for over forty years, since your father was alive."

Klara proceeded to fill in the details and activities of her adult life—that she was a professor of anthropology with a specialty in archaeology at a small northeastern college, and had taught, led digs, and published a number of research papers at one point. Her aunt was kind enough not to ask about her personal life. As Rachel listened, Klara could feel her body relax; her chest felt lighter and her stomach calmer.

After about an hour of chatting, Rachel buttoned her jacket, announcing, "Why don't we head to the cemetery, dear?"

Now Klara was the one who was surprised. She followed along as Rachel stood up from the table where they had been sitting for the past two hours. The two women walked arm in arm to the bus stop on the corner, chatting and laughing as they waited for the bus, as though they had known each other forever.

# CHAPTER 7

The bus wasn't too crowded, so aunt and niece were able to sit next to one another, continuing their conversation.

"So, my father's buried in Warsaw's Jewish Cemetery?" Klara asked, feeling slightly lightheaded, as if in a dream.

"Didn't your mother tell you he was buried there, in Cmentarz Zydowski?" Rachel asked.

Klara shook her head, feeling the need to explain once again that, until recently, she hadn't known what happened to him. "She never even told me he was dead, only that he had left us. I just recently learned the truth, after she received a letter from the Polish government, explaining there was money to collect in his name. Only then did she tell me he was dead and buried here in Warsaw, but not exactly where. I don't think she knew."

"Oh, my," Rachel replied, shaking her head. "It's true. I flew him here when I was first notified that he had passed. I had to. Once I heard from the coroner's office and Bessie that Dawid had died, and that your mother was washing her hands of him, wanting nothing to do with his burial, what choice did I have? He was the last of my family of origin, and I needed to make sure he was well cared for, even if I could only assure this in death rather than in life."

Klara stared at her octogenarian aunt, trying to imagine her accomplishing such a feat. "But how did you manage to bring him back here? It was during the Cold War. There were such poor relations between Poland and the United States, right? In fact, between the whole Eastern Bloc and the US?"

"Yes, that's right, but I spent the last of my savings bribing the Polish officials to fly your father's body back here and then buried him in Cmentarz Zydowski, Warsaw's last active Jewish cemetery," she recalled. "I told my late husband, Benjamin, may he rest in peace, that I had to do it. Thank goodness, he loved me enough to understand."

Klara was speechless. She couldn't believe the lengths her aunt had gone to in order to bring her brother, Klara's father, back to Warsaw and properly bury him. Her admiration for this woman who had lived through so much tragedy multiplied even more. Not wanting to embarrass her, Klara kept these thoughts to herself. Instead, she said, "There's so much I don't know about my father—so much my mother never told me—and I was quite young when he left. And I'm sorry I never met Benjamin; he sounds like such a compassionate man who clearly loved you dearly."

Her aunt smiled, more to herself than to Klara, showing off her deep laugh lines. "He was a true *mensch* [a person of integrity], as they say in Yiddish. The best. I was very lucky to have him in my life. We understood each other."

"It sounds like it was *bashert* [destiny], as they also say in Yiddish," Klara replied, and they both laughed.

"You know some Yiddish too," Rachel said, patting Klara's hand as she smiled some more. "You know, dear, we have plenty of time to fill in the details of our lives. There's no need to rush." She looked up and, seeing the gates to the cemetery in front of them, declared, "The next stop is ours."

Klara knew that something special had just transpired between them, and a part of her felt a little more whole. As she inhaled, she could feel her breath fill her lungs more deeply. She was sure she made the right decision in making the trip to Poland.

The bus stopped in front of Okopowa 49/51 at Cmentarz Zydowski, the Jewish Cemetery. An old, large black set of wrought-iron gates stood, surrounded by two red brick pillars. Descending from the bus with Rachel and walking closer to the gates, Klara saw two stone signs set into the brick. Rachel explained that the gates were original to the cemetery but had been resurrected in 1998, as they had been torn down during the war. She then read, "In eternal memory of the six million Jews that were murdered by the Nazi regime." As Rachel read these words, a chill ran through Klara's body.

"You come here every Friday afternoon?" she asked, trying to calm herself with small talk before actually seeing her father's grave.

"Yes," Rachel replied solemnly, bowing her head. "I do. In a strange way, it gives me a sense of peace, visiting your father and Benjamin, and reminding me that once there were many Jewish people living here in Warsaw, and that my mind doesn't deceive me. I didn't make it up. There are two hundred and fifty thousand marked gravestones here, as well as mass graves of victims of the Warsaw Ghetto. Before World War II, there were approximately three million Jews living in Poland. Today, people say there are only three, maybe up to ten thousand. This graveyard is a living memory to so many, and your father is buried here among them."

As they walked through the gates and passed a small brick office building, Rachel waved to a middle-aged man who was working nearby.

"Who's that?" Klara asked, looking over her shoulder at the man, as they continued walking.

"That's the groundskeeper, Filip Jablonski," she said. "He's a nice man. I see him every week when I come and visit. He's always here overseeing this place. It's an enormous job. You'll see there isn't nearly enough upkeep, especially of the older stones."

They walked slowly along a stone path, viewing tombstones in various states of disrepair. Klara noticed it was still busy, even late in the day, as they passed others—tourists mostly. "Summer is a busy time for visitors to Warsaw in general," Rachel explained, "and as this is Warsaw's only active Jewish cemetery, it is a special spot for Jewish tourists in particular."

The gravestones were lined up haphazardly and in rows, some standing tall, others tumbling down. Some were simple, some elaborate. Many of the stones had inscriptions in Hebrew; others were in Yiddish, Polish, and Ladino, the language of Sephardic Jews. All had weeds and trees growing around them. Downed tree trunks lay on their sides among the graves, and in some areas, it was difficult to distinguish between the two.

Finally, they reached a small, newer section.

"Dawid's grave is here," Rachel said, pointing.

The narrow green plot of land she indicated held the graves of people who had passed away in the last seventy years, postwar. The grass appeared to have been mowed, and the trees were cut back. There were small stones set on top of many of the graves, as is customary in the Jewish tradition. Klara was helping Rachel walk over the still-uneven ground when she suddenly saw a simple stone with the name *Dawid Lieberman, 1927–1971* in front of them. It read, *Beloved Son of Majer and Sara, Beloved Brother of Rachel, Beloved Father of Klara*, in Polish and Hebrew.

Klara gasped as the hair on her arms stood up. She was finally seeing tangible evidence of her father's death after all these years. But there was something even stronger—she was reacting to being acknowledged as his daughter. At that moment, it made him all the more real to her. In an instant, she was six years old again, and he was holding her tightly in his arms. In her mind's eye, she thought she could see tears in his eyes.

"Daddy, why are you crying?" she recalled asking him in her most grown-up, six-year-old voice.

Although remembering he had denied it, she knew, even at that young age, that he was trying to hide his tears. Now, forty-three years later, she felt a large lump in her throat as she imagined the scene from so many years before. She was begging him to tell her why he was so sad as he wiped tears from his cheeks. She would never forget his answer: "I have to go away for a while, sweetie, but I promise to come back." At that, he became so choked up he couldn't say another word. He took something out of his pocket, silently putting it into her hand. It felt cool and smooth.

Klara opened her small hand to discover a shiny, engraved gold locket hanging from a gold chain. Her father helped her open the locket; inside were two small black-and-white photos, one of a boy and a girl, the other of a man and a woman. He explained that the children were him and his sister, and the adults were their parents. He told her to keep the locket hidden in her drawer for safekeeping. She jumped into his arms, but he tried to put her down as he struggled to regain his composure.

She was sure her heart was breaking and that she'd never be the same. "No, Daddy, please don't go," she cried, trying to cling to him. "Why do you have to go?" And then her father hugged her tightly for what would be their final time. She hugged him back while her mother tried to pry her out of his arms, scolding, "You must let go of him, Klara."

In the final scene, she imagined running into her room, slamming the door, and throwing the locket her father had just given her on the floor as she collapsed onto her bed with her head on her pillow, crying. Nothing would ever restore her broken heart.

"What is it, my child? What's wrong?" It was Rachel's voice, bringing her back to the present moment.

She hadn't realized it, but there she was, in Warsaw's Jewish Cemetery, sobbing about her lost relationship with her father, about the forgotten part of her child-self, and for all the hurt she had felt over the forty-three years since the final time she had seen him. After all the years that had passed, she was finally mourning the loss of her father. Rachel, who had stopped at Benjamin's grave, found her there.

❀ ❀ ❀

The trip back to Klara's hotel felt much longer than the outing to Potocka Street and the Jewish Cemetery combined. Although Rachel had insisted that she join her and her family for a Friday night Shabbat dinner, Klara was much too exhausted, both physically and emotionally. The last thing she felt like doing was facing her suspicious and unwelcoming cousin, especially after going behind Hanna's back to meet Rachel. Her aunt had stopped insisting, but only after Klara agreed to come over the next morning for a visit.

"But what will Hanna say?" Klara had asked, still worried about her cousin's reaction.

"Don't worry about Hanna, I'll take care of her," Rachel reassured her, putting a sturdy hand on her shoulder. In the end, Klara acquiesced, but she still had misgivings about another confrontation.

When she arrived back at her poorly lit, narrow hotel room, Klara collapsed onto her twin bed. She quickly dropped off to sleep, even though it was only seven in the evening. Her internal clock was still off from her recent international travels, but more overpowering was how emotionally drained she felt. It was all so much to take in—the warm reception from her aunt, the visit to her father's gravestone in the cemetery where he had been buried so many years ago, and the recollections of her time with her father as a small child. Just before she fell asleep, Klara drafted an email to Sheila, back in the States.

> *I met my father's sister today, and visited the cemetery where he is buried. It's a lot! I actually have family other than my mother and my late grandfather. Who knew? So happy to be here!*
> *Fondly, Klara*

Closing her eyes, she thought briefly of her mother. Fighting against her more selfish instincts, she pushed herself to draft a postcard to her. She could not help her biting tone:

> *I arrived in Warsaw earlier this week. I've met Aunt Rachel and she's wonderful. I visited Dad's grave today. Yes, he really is dead. I will be in touch when I can. Klara*

# CHAPTER 8

It was dark outside the next morning when she awoke, feeling sweaty and disoriented. Rubbing her eyes, she slowly sat up and pulled off the covers. The moon shone brightly and was almost full. Klara loved full moons. They made her think of her time digging in the Yucatán last year when she had met her dear friend and mentor, Rosario, who encouraged her to learn about her own culture, not just everyone else's. *How right she was.*

She got up and paced around the room before showering and getting dressed. Feeling refreshed, she was now ready to face whatever the day might bring. Around nine o'clock that morning, she began her trek back to Potocka Street, taking the bus that dropped her right near Sosnowa Bakery, where she picked up some warm sweet rolls to bring to Rachel's. The smell of freshly baked breads and pastries comforted her, but only momentarily. The bakery was more crowded with people than during her previous visits earlier in the week, but of course, now it was the weekend. Her stomach flipped for the hundredth time that morning, since Hanna would be at the apartment, likely with her husband and her adult daughter too.

Potocka 35 was a handsome four-story, pre-war sand-stone building set back from the street, sandwiched between two more contemporary apartment buildings. Several well-maintained flowering shrubs surrounded the front steps.

As Klara walked toward the building, a young woman in her mid-twenties and her small child were leaving. They exchanged smiles with Klara, which boosted her courage. Walking up the steps to the entrance, she wondered how Rachel navigated these stone steps with her cane at least twice a day. As she entered the spacious vestibule, she scanned the buzzers for apartment 4F, staring at it for a moment before she pressed it.

"*Dzien dobry* [Good morning]," she heard Rachel's friendly voice call out, just before she was buzzed in.

The elevator was small. As the dark paneled doors closed, Klara knew there was no turning back. When the elevator opened to the fourth floor, Rachel was waiting for her with the apartment door ajar. "I'm so glad you're here," she said with wide-open arms, switching from Polish to German, a language they both knew. On seeing Klara's downturned mouth, Rachel pulled her inside, adding, "Don't worry. I spoke to Hanna. It's fine."

Despite Rachel's assurances, Klara was still on guard when she walked into the apartment. It was newer than she had imagined, with exposed brick walls and finished oak floors. Folk art hung on the walls, and the rooms were naturally bright from the sunlight, although the furniture was ornate and imposing. Rachel invited Klara into a sitting room with heavy drapes and thick, textured floral upholstery. While the room, like the apartment, definitely had an old-world feel, there were also some contemporary accents.

*A mixture of both mother and daughter's tastes*, she thought.

"So, you found my mother on your own, I see," Hanna said as she entered the room, standing in front of Klara with her arms crossed, frowning. "Still after the money?"

"Hanna, stop it. We discussed this," Rachel interrupted, trying to wave Hanna away. "Klara is our guest. Why don't you make some coffee for us all?"

"I brought these," Klara said as she held out her bag of sweet rolls. "They're still warm."

"They'll be perfect with the coffee. Thank you, dear." Rachel took the bag and handed it to Hanna, who begrudgingly accepted it and headed into the kitchen.

"Good morning, Grandma." A pretty young woman, around twenty years old, entered the room.

"Rebeka, this is my niece from America, Klara, your mother's cousin."

Rebeka stuck out her hand. "Nice to meet you," she said in clear English.

*How different she is from her mother in attitude and appearance*, Klara thought as she smiled. Rebeka was taller and slimmer than her mother, with long auburn hair and green eyes. Hanna was shorter and broader, with blue eyes and shoulder-length brown hair heavily peppered with streaks of gray.

Hanna returned, and the four women made awkward small talk about the weather for a few minutes before sitting down at the kitchen table to drink strong coffee and eat the sweet buns. They spoke a mixture of German and English for both Klara's and Rachel's benefit, although Rachel primarily understood German, and only some English.

"So how long are you going to be here?" Rebeka asked Klara with bright eyes and a soft smile.

"I'm not really sure," Klara said, looking down for a moment. "I only arrived a few days ago, and there's still so much I want to see. I just went to the Jewish Cemetery yesterday. I visited my father's grave."

"Of course. My grandma goes every week to visit her brother and my Grandpa Benjamin," Rebeka said, nodding.

"I know. We went together," Klara said, feeling Hanna's glare.

"Don't you need to get back to your job in America?" Hanna asked brusquely, her face a mask of stone. She clearly wouldn't be warming up to Klara anytime soon.

"I'm a professor, and its summer vacation," Klara said as she nervously watched her aunt leave the room. She didn't want to be left alone with Hanna, even if Rebeka was still there as well. "And I'm considering taking a sabbatical starting in September, so I'm not in any rush to get back." She said these words at the same time she came to this decision, surprising even herself. She went on to explain that she taught anthropology, with a specialty in archaeology, focusing on the Mesoamerican period about eleven hundred years ago.

"It sounds interesting," Rebeka said, making friendly eye contact with Klara. "I hope to take an archaeology class next semester."

"It certainly is," Klara agreed, relieved that Hanna's daughter seemed open to her. "There's so much to piece together about other peoples' lives and cultural history. What are you focusing your studies on, Rebeka?" Klara asked, but couldn't help noticing Hanna's glare.

"I'm studying to become a doctor. I'm taking all my pre-med classes now, like biology, chemistry, and physics, so I can begin my medical school education next year."

"That's wonderful you're planning to become a doctor," Klara commented. "Will you pursue your graduate studies in Warsaw?"

Before Rebeka could answer, Hanna chimed in, "We're very proud of her," but her smile was forced.

Just as Hanna opened her mouth again, Rachel reentered the room, carrying a worn light-blue box with some writing on the side. She carefully placed it on the table before them. "Klara, you'll never guess what I found last night."

"What is it?" Klara asked, picking up on Rachel's excitement, and happy to have a diversion.

"I remembered I have a box of some of your father's mementos and letters," she said as she delicately opened the box and held up a black velvet drawstring bag the size of a hand. "This was your father's. I know he'd want you to have it." She carefully reached into the bag and pulled out a glowing burnt-orange amber stone, about the size of a small apricot.

"Oh, my, it's beautiful!" Klara exclaimed, her breath taken away.

"Amber is the stone of Poland," Rachel explained. "Dawid had this from the time he was ten years old. I remember he used to carry it in his pocket. He called it his 'good luck charm.' Perhaps it will bring you good luck," said Rachel, smiling.

"It already has," said Klara.

"And this photo was found on him as well. The funeral parlor said it was tucked away in his shirt pocket." She held up a small black-and-white photo of a man in his early forties, holding a small girl in his arms. Both the man and the young girl were smiling. The edges of the picture were wrinkled.

"Oh, my god. Is that my father holding me?" Klara exclaimed, overcome with emotion, as she held her hand over her mouth.

"Yes, it is. It's a beautiful picture of the two of you," Rachel said as she held it up.

"This must have been right before he left. I look like I'm around six years old," Klara said, as her eyes welled up with tears. "I remember that dress."

Rachel reached out to hold her hand. "You should keep the picture along with the amber stone. They're yours." She handed both items to Klara.

"Thank you so much," Klara said.

"I'm not done yet. I have something else to share with you." Rachel took a torn white envelope from a pile of what looked like several similar ones. She gently pulled out a piece of yellowed stationery. "Let's see. He wrote these letters to me in Yiddish. I can translate them into Polish, and Hanna or Rebeka can then translate them into English." They both nodded, although Hanna did so more reluctantly.

She put on her reading glasses and began: "*Second of May, 1965. My . . . dearest . . . sister . . .*" Rachel paused, shaking her head, as she again addressed Klara. "I'm so sorry, dear, but these words are too faded for me to read, even with my glasses. They were written so many years ago. I'm going to need to spend some time studying them to decipher what they say, and I'm the only one here who reads Yiddish."

Klara was disappointed but didn't want to let on. After sitting and talking for over an hour, Rebeka excused herself to go to the library to study. Hanna also made some excuse to cut the visit short, and Rachel was tired, so Klara said her goodbyes. Offhandedly, she asked her aunt, "Do you mind if I hold onto the first letter, Rachel? I know a little Yiddish. I promise to bring it back soon."

"Sure, dear."

As she was leaving, Klara could have sworn she caught Hanna scowling.

# CHAPTER 9

Heading back to Okopowa Street and the historic Jewish Cemetery the next afternoon, Klara played with her father's amber stone in her pants pocket. It felt smooth and cool to the touch as her fingers moved over it. As she did so, Klara thought about the forty-something-year-old letter from Rachel she carried in her purse. Upon walking through the cemetery gates, she tried to recall where her father's tombstone was located but was quickly turned around. Although she'd just been there the day before yesterday, she hadn't been paying close attention with Rachel leading the way. With no idea which way to go, she circled around a few times.

"Can I help you?" A man who looked to be in his mid-forties addressed her in accented English. "Wait. I saw you the other day with Mrs. Sheinberg," he said.

"Yes, I was here with her a couple days ago. She's my aunt," Klara responded, recognizing the groundskeeper whom Rachel had pointed out. "We visited my father's grave, but I can't seem to find it today. His name was David Lieberman."

"Yes, Dawid Lieberman. He's buried in the newer section. I'll take you there. I'm the record keeper and part-time groundskeeper here. I'm Filip Jablonski," he said, nodding toward Klara.

"Thank you. I'd appreciate that," Klara said, smiling. "I'm Klara Lieberman."

Klara followed Filip as he led her down a wooded cemetery path.

"Your English is very good," Klara commented, making small talk.

"That's not too unusual for many people my age and younger. I studied it in school."

"Are you familiar with most of the headstones here? I understand there are over two hundred and fifty thousand." Klara was always curious about historical information, and this cemetery was a bastion of history. She had devoured many guidebooks on just this topic over the past few days.

"Not all, but many, and I know the location of the ones that families visit often. Your aunt visits your father's grave every week. Ah, here we are."

"Thank you for showing me the way," Klara replied, for the first time really looking into his face. It was his helpfulness and his warm tone that made her take further notice of him. His eyes were bright green, and pronounced dimples appeared when he smiled. His facial features were well-defined, and he was tall with broad shoulders and was somewhere around her age.

"Can you tell me a little of the history here?" she asked.

"Actually, most of the gravestones in this cemetery no longer have family to tend to them. In recent years, some Holocaust survivors from America and Israel have sent money for their loved ones' gravestones to be maintained, but many more have no one left to send money. This cemetery was founded in 1806, and as you can see, except for the newer area, many of the stones are in a state of disrepair—they have either fallen down or are covered by overgrown weeds. Only about one-third of the gravestones survived the war, but all the cemetery burial records were totally destroyed by the

Nazis during their occupation of Warsaw during World War II. I wish I could do more." Filip sighed, looking around at the unkempt gravestones.

"Tell me more about it," Klara said.

"The past manager before me made significant efforts to create an index of the gravestones, and I continue with this work, but there's not enough money or staffing to do all that needs to be done. In recent years, the Foundation for Documentation of Jewish Cemeteries in Poland has helped a lot, but there's always more work to do," he said, shaking his head.

"I'm curious, why is it so important that the gravestones be indexed?" Klara asked with genuine interest.

"Because, although the Nazis systematically documented everything, many of Warsaw's twentieth-century Jewish birth, marriage, and death records did not survive World War II. Information from these gravestones can be very helpful to genealogists researching people's families from greater Warsaw," Filip replied. "Actually, we're not the only ones interested in working on this project of collecting ancestral information. The new Jewish museum, POLIN, will house a genealogy department to this end, as well."

Klara had been looking around at the headstones while Filip was talking.

"Why do the tombstones have different languages in their inscriptions? Some are in English, some in German, others are in Polish and Hebrew," Klara remarked as she bent down and pointed to the writing on multiple tombstones.

"It's whatever the families of the loved ones chose. This one is in Yiddish," he said, pointing to a gravestone a few feet away from her father's.

"Yiddish?" she asked, surprised. "It looks just like Hebrew."

"Yes, it does, but the pronunciation is different," he said, pointing his index finger in the air.

"Do you know Yiddish?" Klara asked, with a touch of excitement in her voice.

"Yes, I do," he responded.

"It sounds like you know so much about Polish Jewish history and the Holocaust; have you studied history?" Klara heard herself asking.

"Oh, I've taken some classes here and there. Why do you want to know if I speak Yiddish?"

Klara paused for a moment, and then took out the old, faded envelope from her bag and extended it toward him. "Can you read the first few words of this letter for me? Would you mind?"

He took the envelope, squinting as he studied the writing. "It's quite faded . . . *Dear Rachel. I never thought I . . .*" An unexpected rain shower suddenly interrupted them. "Quick, follow me to my office," Filip said as he started running, Klara at his heels. They ran down a dirt path to the front of the cemetery, entering the small brick office building she had noticed by the entrance. By then, they were both soaking wet, but Klara's letter stayed dry in Filip's pocket.

"How about some coffee?" he offered, wiping the water from his face, as he gestured at the half-full coffee pot on a nearby desk, cluttered with papers and an old desktop computer.

"Thank you."

Filip sat down with two cups of hot coffee. As Klara shivered, he handed her a towel, with which she attempted to dry herself.

Klara realized that she was so excited that Filip read Yiddish, and could decipher her father's letter, that she hadn't considered he was a total stranger. *Who knows what might be in that letter? It could be personal and embarrassing to me. Maybe I should get to know him a little better before he continues reading it.* She decided to ask more about Poland and Jewish life here—*if* there was Jewish life here.

"Can you tell me a little about Jewish life—both before World War II and today?" she asked, sipping her coffee.

"Sure," he replied distractedly, looking up from the desktop, where he had been checking his emails. "I don't mean to be rude. I just had to check whether someone had gotten back to me." He continued, "As you might know, before the war, there were about three hundred and ninety thousand Jews living in Warsaw, thirty percent of Warsaw's total population before 1939, when the Nazis invaded. Warsaw had the second-largest Jewish population in the world, just after New York City. There were about three million Jews living in Poland at that time. Today, no one knows for sure, but they estimate there may be three to ten thousand Jews left in all of Poland. This is the only standing Jewish cemetery left in Warsaw, since the Nazis decimated all the others.

"What's really amazing is that ever since the Berlin Wall was torn down in 1989, there's been such a transformation of Poland to a pro-democracy state," Filip continued animatedly, warming to his subject. "It's become more tolerant, but as we all know, old habits die hard. After the war, some Jews tried to come back to their homes but generally found them either destroyed or occupied by Polish families who had begun living in them during the war. They were not made to feel particularly welcome, and in some cases, there were outright assaults against them. Then in the 1960s, the government tried sending the remainder of the Polish Jews to Israel. Most left, and the ones who stayed were very quiet about their Jewish identity. Slowly, though, since the Berlin Wall came down and Poland once again became a democracy, more people have been telling their children and their grandchildren of their Jewish backgrounds. My mother told me just before she died that she was Jewish. Many others have similar stories," he concluded, his intense eyes as expressive as his words.

"You're Jewish?" Klara asked, surprised given his last name and his strong Slavic features—pale skin, deep eyes, and a mildly roundish face. "Me too."

"Yes. I uh, figured that out. This is a Jewish cemetery, and you're visiting your late father," Filip replied with a gentle smile.

"Of course, you did," Klara replied, her face flushing with embarrassment.

"There aren't too many of us around these parts," Filip said, as his office phone rang. He answered and spoke for a moment, then turned to her, his hand covering the mouthpiece. "I'm sorry, Klara, but I have to take this call," he said.

"Can I take you out for dinner later, and then maybe you can finish translating my letter?" she blurted out.

Filip paused and looked at her for a moment before smiling. "Sure," he said. "Oh, and you should take this," he added, giving her back the letter.

"How about across the street, just after five o'clock?"

He nodded, returning to his phone call as she stood to leave.

❖ ❖ ❖

Klara walked out of Filip's office to a light rain. Opening her umbrella, she wondered, *Did I just ask him out on a date?* She walked back to her father's grave through what was now a light mist, this time remembering her way there. *What must he think of me? Is it a date? Maybe he's married. He couldn't be married, or he wouldn't have accepted. Or so I'd like to think.*

She arrived at her father's gravestone, shaking her head to clear it and then standing there for a few moments before silently addressing him as she never could before:

*Papa, it's been way too long since we were last together. Mother kept your death from me all these years. How could she? I love you so much. I never really stopped loving you, even when she made me believe you'd left us. I'm so very sorry for believing her lies. You'll be happy to know that I recently met your sister, Rachel. She's been so openhearted and generous to me. She's the one who brought me here to this cemetery for the first time, and now I'm back. We've missed so much as father and daughter.*

Here, tears rolled down Klara's cheeks, and she grabbed a tissue to wipe them away.

*I must sound silly to you, but I was hoping you could give me some fatherly advice. I just asked a man out. I can't believe it. I feel like I'm six years old, like the day you left, despite the fact that I'm now a forty-nine-year-old woman. I don't think that feeling will ever change. I feel like a scared little girl. I wish you'd never left. Now I'm all grown up, but I'm afraid. Look at what Rachel has given to me. She gave me your amber good-luck charm, and this photo of the two of us taken just before you left. Why did you have to go?*

Klara's eyes welled up.

*Oh, Papa. I only recently learned that you've been dead all these years. Although a part of me already knew that, another piece of me, my six-year-old self, wished you were still alive and just hadn't been able to find me. What did you say in those letters? I guess I will soon find out. I love you.*

# CHAPTER 10

B y the time she left her father's grave, it was already four o'clock in the afternoon. Although the sky was gray, the rain had finally stopped. Klara decided to look around the rest of Warsaw's Jewish Cemetery, which was rich with history. She had to smile when she saw a group of older British schoolgirls, perhaps young teens, in their navy-blue uniforms with white blouses, listening to their teacher discuss the cemetery. There were memorials to all those who had perished in the Holocaust, and mass graves symbolized by three aboveground stone coffins. As she walked on, she stopped in her tracks at the memorial to the one and a half million European Jewish children who were killed in the Holocaust, set against a tall red brick wall with poems cemented into it. In front of it lay an area of ashes and black-and-white photos of children. A large, six-armed menorah rising from the ground completed the memorial. One poem on the brick wall in particular captured her attention. It was named "The Little Smuggler," and Klara could not turn away. She read the second stanza:

> *And if fate will turn against me in that game*
> *of life and bread*
> *Do not weep for me, Mother,*
> *Do not cry,*
> *Are we not all marked to die?*

Tears burned her eyes as she absorbed the level of pain and annihilation this memorial and others represented. As she looked at the black-and-white photos of unknown children from seventy years ago, she realized that any one of them could have been her father or her aunt Rachel, but for the grace of God.

She pulled out the worn photo from Rachel of her father holding her young self just before he left. She stared at it, trying to decipher the look in his eyes. Was he scared? Uncertain? Sad?

Without realizing it, Klara began speaking her thoughts aloud. "What happened to you, Papa, should never have happened. I'm so sorry it did. I'm so very sorry for you and me both. We both lost so much."

With that, she began to sob. As she cried, a strange thing happened: the tightness in her chest that was there every morning when she awoke and every night when she went to sleep was suddenly a little lighter. It was as though the energy holding it in place had been released, and she could finally breathe a bit more easily for the first time she could remember. She imagined that her tears had washed away the rough, jagged edges of her hurt feelings, so they were a bit smoother and more bearable. She rubbed her chest clockwise as she tried to further release the chronic tension her body had amassed over the years. This visit had become a catharsis that she had not expected.

Realizing it was almost five o'clock, Klara stopped in the cemetery's restroom to splash cold water on her face and brush her hair before meeting Filip at the restaurant across the street. She arrived first, giving her plenty of time to fidget and generally overthink her dinner invitation. Mindlessly, she began playing with her locket. As the sun had reappeared, she asked to be seated outside at a table shaded by an umbrella. It seemed more spacious and brighter out there, and Klara felt less conspicuously alone. Perusing the menu, she saw that this restaurant served typical Polish fare, heavy on meat, especially pork, kasha, and winter vegetables like cabbage. It was hardy, and the dishes were made with lots of cream and eggs. Although she didn't normally eat pork, she was sure she'd make do.

Taking out her guidebook, Klara was marking several places she wanted to visit when she heard Filip's voice and looked up. "I'm sorry I'm late," he apologized as he sat down.

"I hope it's not awkward—my inviting you for dinner. I didn't mean to ask you out. I mean, I meant to ask you out . . . just not to ask you out like on a date," she stammered, biting her lip. *What about him makes me just blurt out these things?*

"That would have been fine too," he said, smiling in a way that made her relax.

"*Zupa ogorkowa* is very good. It's a soup made with pickled cucumbers," he added.

Klara said she'd try it. "Thank you for coming. Please don't think I'm rude, but I'm dying to know what that forty-plus-year-old letter from my father to my aunt says. Do you think you can take a look at it before we order? Please?" she asked, her eyes silently pleading.

"Of course," Filip answered, "although I have to admit, I'm a bit hungrier than usual. I typically have a big lunch around two o'clock in the afternoon, but I knew we'd be going out to dinner, and I've heard Americans eat their biggest meal at night."

She braced herself to listen to her father's letter. As she reached into her bag to retrieve it, her hands felt the smooth amber stone Rachel had given her from her father. It felt like a personal talisman that could soothe her.

"Let me see it," he said as he put on his reading glasses. He reviewed the letter and began reading aloud in English:

*The second of May, 1965. My dearest sister. I never thought I would live to see this day. I am so over-joyed. Bessie and I had a baby girl, Klara Anne.*

He looked up, and she looked at him. He continued:

*She's seven pounds, two ounces. She's so beautiful, Rachel. She was born with a full head of dark brown hair, blue eyes, and ten perfect little fingers and toes.*

He smiled again before continuing.

*I feel so blessed. After all we've been through with the war, coming here, and Bessie and I trying to have a child, miracles can still happen. Bessie is in the hospital with the baby for a few more days. She's tired and irritable, and she wishes we'd had a boy, but I'm sure she will change her mind once she and the baby are home.*

Filip paused, aware that what he had just translated was upsetting.

Klara's jaw clenched as her whole body tightened. *That would be my mother's first reaction*, she thought. She was not particularly surprised, though, as she had heard her mother say this a million times throughout her childhood—that boys were so much easier. But to say it on the day she was born was beyond belief. She looked at Filip, waiting to hear more. He looked down and continued reading.

*I wish more than anything that you could see Klara, but clearly that isn't possible any time soon, given the Cold War. In the meantime, I will send you pictures. Here's the first one.*
*Love, Dawid*

"Do you have the picture?" Filip asked, gazing at Klara.

She took a black-and-white snapshot of a newborn wrapped in a thin white hospital blanket from the yellowed envelope and handed it to him across the table. The baby in the photo looked like she had just been born with scrunched eyes and tightly swaddled in a tiny hospital blanket.

"Is that you?" Filip asked, pointing to the photo and smiling. "Are there more letters like this one?"

"Yes, Rachel has more, but I just asked if I could borrow this one. I thought I might be able to get a Yiddish dictionary and translate it myself, but of course, not nearly as well as you did. The writing was too faded for her to easily read, but I guess this is my lucky day. You were able to translate it for me," Klara said as she glanced away. "I thought this letter might tell me more about my father."

"What were you hoping to learn?" Filip asked, quietly staring into Klara's eyes.

"Everything. I was quite young when he left," she replied, fiddling with her fingers. "And everything I thought I knew turned out to be untrue."

"If it's not too forward of me to say, it's easy to tell from his letter that he was completely taken with you," Filip said with a grin.

"Really?" Klara asked. Much to her surprise, she was comforted by this suggestion.

"Can't you tell?"

"It's hard to take in."

"May I ask you what happened to him? I mean, he was born here in Poland but then went to America, right?"

Klara understood that her father's history was unusual. "He escaped during the war," she explained. "A wealthy Jewish American businessman committed to saving twenty young men by paying for their escape with bribes." Without realizing, she winced, but only for a moment. Someone less observant might have missed it. "My father was one of them. He lived in the United States for many years, until he died in a train accident, which I only learned about just before coming to Poland. My aunt had his body flown back here so she could bury him in Warsaw."

As she spoke, Klara found herself really looking at Filip, noticing his features. He had slightly long, light-brown hair worn to the side and tucked behind his ears, striking green eyes, a sideward smile, and a calming voice.

The waiter arrived at that moment, breaking the spell. They ordered full traditional Polish fare with three courses: *zupa ogorkowa* (pickled cucumber soup), *sledzie* (marinated herring), *zrazy wolowe* (stuffed beef rolls), *slata* (leafy salad), and *ziemniaki* (mashed potatoes). Klara couldn't imagine eating that much food.

"That's quite a story," Filip said, as they continued talking and sipping their cabernet. The waiter had just brought a second glass for each of them.

"Interestingly, because there are so few Jewish citizens still living here, it turns out that the Jewish cemeteries in Poland that still exist are looked after by Polish Catholics. Many have become interested in Jewish history, viewing it as an important part of Polish history. But in my case, I am Jewish. Although as I told you before, I only found out about it ten years ago, just before my mother died, when she revealed her true background to me. She and my father hid it from me until then. I'm sure they believed it was for my own good. This was, and probably still is, very common. I was brought up as a good Polish Catholic, going to church on Sundays. I know my parents thought I'd be safer that way, more accepted. I'm sure there are many others like me. My wife and I raised our son Catholic too."

"You're married?" Klara quickly glanced at Filip's ring finger, but there was no ring.

"I was. I'm divorced. I meant to say my ex-wife." He paused for a moment, perhaps to consider her surprise that he could have been married.

She blushed, looking down at her lap.

"When my mother was on her deathbed," he continued, deflecting from the awkward moment, "she told me she was Jewish, which technically made me Jewish, at least in Jewish tradition. I knew her family had perished in the war, but I didn't know until then it was because they were Jews. They died in the gas chambers of Treblinka, like so many other Jews from Warsaw." In saying this, his eyes watered, and his voice cracked.

"I'm so sorry," Klara said, setting her hand on the table and leaning in.

"Me too. I would have liked to know them. What a horrific way to die," he added, shaking his head.

"Yes, it most certainly is. My father's parents died in Treblinka too," she said.

Filip sat there continuing to shake his head. "I'm sorry for your loss too. So many of them died such tragic deaths. It's still hard to comprehend."

"Thank you," Klara said, pausing. "I barely knew my father, so thinking about his parents feels quite removed. But the knowledge of how they died is beyond awful and feels very personal, especially now that I'm here."

"*Personal* is a good word to describe the feeling," Filip agreed. "So, when my mother passed away, I wanted, of course, to honor her wishes to have a small Jewish funeral and to then be buried here in Warsaw's only active Jewish cemetery," he said, pointing across the street. "My father agreed. He understood."

"What did your wife say?" Klara asked, forgetting to add "ex" in front of the word *wife*.

"My ex-wife was surprised, but basically understanding about it at first. Then she became less okay with it as I spent more and more time searching out my own Jewish roots and ultimately took this lesser-paying job running the cemetery. She didn't know what to make of it at first. Eventually, she said she felt I was too different from the man she'd married twelve years earlier."

Klara detected a note of bitterness in his tone.

"That man was a good Polish Catholic who went to an office job each morning and brought home a dependable paycheck each week. That man did what was expected of him: he went to church, finished college, got married, and had a family. Now, I work as a part-time records keeper and part-time groundskeeper for a dilapidated and under-funded Jewish cemetery. I don't get paid very much, and I question assumptions that others might generally accept. Nina, my ex-wife, was very uncomfortable with my trans-formation. I, on the other hand, much prefer who I am now," he said with an air of certainty. "So that's my story." He lightly slapped his hand on the table, seemingly ready to move on.

"That's quite a story. So, you have a child?" Klara could hear her voice raise an octave higher. She was intrigued and wanted to know more about him, despite his apparent eager-ness to change the subject. He was nothing like what she had expected, although she wasn't quite sure what that was.

"I have a son, Jan. He's now seventeen and lives with his mother most of the time. He considers himself Catholic, but he actually thinks what I'm doing is pretty cool. Sometimes he comes and helps me at the cemetery when he's off from school." Filip's pride in his son was apparent.

"I understand your mother shared with you that she was Jewish just before she died, but what made you pursue your Jewish background so completely? It's like you did a full turnaround," Klara said. "I hope you don't mind my asking," she added, wiggling in her chair.

"No, that's fine. I'm happy to tell you. When I was growing up, we didn't learn about the Shoah, the Holocaust, in school under what was then Communist rule, as the schools were forced to follow Soviet ideology. It wasn't talked about, and anyone who was Jewish needed to practice their religion in secret, if at all. When I found out my mother was Jewish just before she died, and then learned that the rest of her family, and thus my family, had been killed in a concentration camp not far from Warsaw, I had to do something to honor their memory. So, here I am," he said. His lips pressed together in a thin line.

Klara nodded, aware that she had touched a raw nerve.

"Is there still much anti-Semitism here in Poland?" she asked, careful to keep her voice down.

"Of course, but not nearly as much as there was before. It used to be called 'anti-Zionism,' but it was really anti-Semitism dressed up as being against the idea of Israel as a nation," Filip said, happy to stop talking about himself. "As I mentioned earlier, more and more Poles around my age have recently learned of their Jewish heritage."

"How fascinating," Klara said.

"You know, it turns out that next week is the annual Jewish Cultural Festival in Krakow."

"What's that?" Klara asked.

"It's been going on for over twenty-five years. It celebrates Jewish culture and Jewish life in Poland through music, art, dance, and theater." Leaning in toward Klara, Filip said, "You should go, assuming you're still here. It's really something."

Klara rubbed her gold locket, hoping Filip might invite her to accompany him. Or did she dare to ask him?

"I notice you keep playing with your locket. Does it have some special meaning?" he asked.

She opened it and showed him the photographs inside. "These," she said, pointing to the boy and girl, "were my father and aunt just before the war started. "And these," she continued, pointing to her grandparents, "were their parents. It's particularly meaningful because it was the last thing my father gave me before he left."

"Where'd he go?"

"That's a whole other story, but I can show you what he looked like when he was older, and what I looked like as a young girl." Klara took out the photo that Rachel had given her earlier that day.

Filip studied it. "You look a lot like you did back then. The shape of your face and your lips are the same," he said, looking from the photo to Klara and back again.

Klara changed the subject. "Do you think you might be able to translate other letters for me sometime? I only have this one right now, but my aunt told me there are others too."

"Sure," he replied. "What are your plans over the next few days?" he asked, gazing directly into her face.

"I was hoping to visit the old Jewish Quarter on Thursday. Would you like to come?" Klara asked, again surprising herself with her boldness, which was quite unlike her.

"I'd love to." He smiled. "But I have to work until five on Thursday. I'm taking off from work next week for the Jewish Cultural Festival, so I have to get ahead on my work. If you want to stop by the cemetery at five o'clock, though, I can join you then and show you some sights. It's very interesting but also can be quite upsetting."

"Okay." Now it was Klara's turn to smile. "It's a deal."

# CHAPTER 11

A few days later, Klara awoke in the morning to a written invitation from her aunt, left for her at the concierge's desk, to help her make challah. By midmorning, she was knocking on Rachel's door.

Rachel greeted her with a warm hug, and Klara returned the embrace. "Thank you for asking me to come over to bake with you. I'm really excited to help, but I must confess that I truly have no idea what I'm doing. I'm not much of a baker or cook for that matter, and I've never made any sort of bread before, and certainly not challah," Klara explained sheepishly.

"Well, I guess this will be your first time, then," Rachel said, leading the way into the kitchen.

"Oh, I must remember to return the letter you lent me," Klara said. "Filip translated it." Rachel did not ask, and Klara did not offer more. Klara handed it to Rachel.

The two women then washed their hands and measured the ingredients. Rachel sprinkled some yeast into a small mixing bowl, adding water and a healthy pinch of sugar. It was clear from her expert manner that she had done this hundreds of times before. She didn't rely on a written recipe but knew the steps by heart.

"Klara, can you crack the eggs, dear?" she asked.

"Sure," Klara replied, promptly making a mess of even this simple task. Rachel came over to look. "I'm sorry, I really don't know what I'm doing. There are little pieces of eggshell in the yolk," Klara said, blushing.

"Don't worry. We'll just start again. Let me show you." Klara felt like a five-year-old in the kitchen, but Rachel was a patient teacher, taking her time to show her what to do.

"Now we knead the dough." Rachel demonstrated, throwing some loose flour on the wooden table and taking out two rolling pins, one for each of them.

As they worked, Klara asked, "Rachel, would you tell me about my father?"

Her aunt nodded as they both continued to knead at the table, side by side.

"Like when he was a boy?" Rachel paused. "Oh, your father was mischievous. He was very kind but so mischievous," she said, laughing.

Klara grinned. "Really? How so?"

"One time, when he was six years old, and I was eight, we were all sitting down having supper—me, your father, and our parents—and all of a sudden, we heard a *ribbit* out of nowhere." Rachel was smiling at the memory. "Dawid had put a small frog in his pocket and forgotten to take it out."

"What did your parents say?"

"First, they scolded him. My mother said, 'Dawid, we do not bring frogs to the supper table.' Then, when he went to put it outside, they laughed. He was too funny and sweet for them to stay mad at him.

"But that wasn't the end of the story. Later that night, I saw Dawid carrying a shoebox and was sure I heard another *ribbit*. He put his finger over his lips to shush me and whispered that the frog was hurt, begging me not to tell. Of course, I didn't. It mattered so much to him."

While Klara was rolling her dough into a ball and throwing it on the table, Rachel had finished kneading hers and had rolled it into three long, thin, even parts to braid.

"David liked to run around like all young children," Rachel continued, her hands busily plaiting the dough. "When we weren't at school, we used to play outside with the other Jewish children in our neighborhood. All the Jewish families lived in one area, even before the war. That's just how it was, but the businesses were more mixed. Your grandfather was a tailor, and everyone came to him—Jewish, Christian, young, old. He was known as the best tailor in the area. Your father and I used to walk to his store that was right on the border of the Mirow district, which was the Jewish section before the war. We'd bring him his lunch every day during the summertime. He always loved his cold, purple borscht, especially with sour cream." Rachel suddenly grew quiet, looking pensive.

"And then what happened?" Klara asked, glancing over at her aunt, waiting for her to continue.

Rachel's face dropped. "Then we all started to have to wear armbands with the yellow Gwiazda Dawida [Star of David]. If you were caught without an armband and known to be Jewish, you could get in bad trouble, even thrown in jail. Then it got worse. My father started losing customers, and his business suffered terribly. The Nazis said Jews and Christians couldn't mix at all, and that they could not shop in each other's stores or attend school together. Then Jews were fired from their jobs, and no one had money to pay a tailor."

Klara's fingers were playing with the dough, unsure of what to do next. She looked up at Rachel, whose hands were working while her eyes showed that she was deep in thought, remembering the past.

"My father came home one day and told my mother he couldn't go on any longer without customers, and he had to close his shop. That was the first time I ever saw him cry." She again became quiet. Both women stopped what they were doing and looked at each other sadly.

"I'm sorry, Rachel," Klara said, punching the dough, feeling anger at what had happened to her family and so many others.

"It was frightening and heartbreaking," Rachel said with tears in her eyes. "I'm also crying because even though it was such a long time ago, I still miss him. I miss all of them: my father, my mother, and Dawid. It never seems to get easier, despite so many years passing."

Klara threw the ball of dough on the table and put her arms around Rachel.

Just then the front door opened, and Hanna walked in, abruptly stopping once she saw Klara hugging her mother.

"What are you doing here?" she asked Klara tersely. Before Klara could answer, her aunt calmly replied.

"Hello, Hanna dear. I invited Klara to bake with me," her mother said, dabbing her eyes with a tissue. "You can join us if you want, but otherwise, we have work to do."

Hanna said nothing, turned on her heel, and went into another room. But a few minutes later, she joined them, washing her hands to help.

"We do this together every Thursday evening," Rachel explained to Klara.

"I didn't realize it was a special ritual between you and Hanna. I don't want to intrude," Klara said nervously. The last thing she wanted to do was to usurp Hanna's place and make an already tenuous relationship with her cousin any worse.

"It's a family custom, dear," Rachel replied. "Whoever's around joins us. Sometimes it's Hanna, sometimes it's Rebeka, and sometimes it's Alek, Hanna's husband. Today it's you. Hanna doesn't mind. Right, Hanna?" Rachel seemed to affirm rather than ask this, staring at her daughter who towered over her by several inches.

Hanna nodded, though reluctantly, making it seem like she minded very much. Klara noticed her cousin's irritation and punched the dough a little harder. *Hanna is so possessive of her mother*, she thought. *It isn't fair; she's had her mother all her life.* Klara knew she was being irrational since they had all just met, but she was getting a taste of what it was like to have some semblance of a close familial relationship and wanted to bask in it a little longer.

❋ ❋ ❋

When the women were done with their preparations, they set aside three raw braided mounds of dough to rise for a few hours before they would be put in the oven.

"They're beautiful," Klara observed, impressed with even her own novice handiwork.

"They'll be more beautiful once we bake them, and they'll taste better too," Rachel said, laughing.

"I'm sure they will be," Klara said, before glimpsing at her watch. "Oh, no, it's almost five o'clock. I need to go. Sorry, I lost track of time," she said, wiping her hands and brushing flour from her skirt.

"Where are you going?" Rachel and Hanna asked in unison, both surprised that Klara would have other plans or even know anyone else in Warsaw.

"To meet a friend I met at the Jewish Cemetery, Filip Jablonski," she said, trying hard to sound casual.

"Filip Jablonski?" they asked simultaneously, glancing at each other.

"Filip?" Hanna asked again, unable to keep her surprise to herself.

"Yes. He works at the cemetery," Klara replied.

"I know who he is and what he does," Hanna said with both hands on her hips.

"Well, I met him there, and we started talking. It turns out he knows Yiddish—how to read it—so he translated the letter you gave me from my father to you," Klara said, looking back at Rachel. "I hope you don't mind," Klara added, realizing perhaps she should have checked with her aunt first.

"It's fine, dear," her aunt replied.

"If you're sure. I was wondering if I could exchange it for another letter," she said, scrunching up her face. "I'd really like to hear more of my father's words." She was in a hurry and wished this conversation could just be over so she could gracefully leave.

"Not so fast," Hanna said. "Let me get this right. You have a date with Filip Jablonski?"

"It's not a date," Klara insisted. "He's going to show me around the old Jewish district."

"Is that all?" Hanna asked with a knowing look.

"Hanna, stop that right now," Rachel demanded. "Klara, come with me, and we'll go find the next letter. If you could just return the other one first," she added as she walked down the hallway, Klara following closely. "Oh right, you just did. I want to keep track of them. They're among the few things I have left from your father." Klara understood how hard it was for her aunt, and how much it opened old wounds, but she needed to know what her father had written all those years ago.

Rachel opened the light-blue box she had taken out a few days earlier and handed Klara the next letter. As they walked to the front entrance, where Hanna stood, to say goodbye, Rachel said, "Oh, and you should come over at six o'clock tomorrow evening for a Shabbat dinner. Maybe you could bring Filip too?"

"Filip?" Klara asked, taken aback.

"Filip Jablonski," Hanna replied, following them to the door. "The guy you're going out on a date with this evening. Come on. Admit it. It's a date, Klara."

"Right," Klara replied, ignoring the last comment, while blushing a deep shade of red. "Um, thank you, Rachel, but

I'm sure he has other plans, but if it's okay, I'd really like to bring him some challah tomorrow for Shabbat, maybe after our dinner here, if there's any left over. I don't know if he's ever had homemade challah before. You know, not from the bakery."

"Of course, dear," Rachel replied. "I always make extra." Hanna snickered. "Have fun," she said, waving her hand.

For the second time, Klara thought to herself, as she left Rachel and Hanna's apartment, *Is it a date? Am I going out on a date with Filip Jablonski?* She smiled, aware that something inside her was opening up. For the first time in a very long time, she felt excited. She, Klara, was going on a date.

# CHAPTER 12

Klara arrived at Cmentarz Zydowski just after five thirty that evening and knocked on Filip's office door. Her hair was windblown, and her face glowed with perspiration. She had played with the amber stone from her father the whole bus ride over to the cemetery, hoping it would give her the strength and confidence to be with this man.

"There you are. What happened to you?" he asked, staring at her from behind a desk piled with papers. "I was beginning to worry," he said, standing up.

"I was running late, so I rushed," Klara said, while attempting to smooth down her hair. She was kicking herself for not ducking into the restroom at the entrance to freshen up first.

"That was thoughtful of you, but you didn't have to rush that much," he said, putting on a suit jacket.

"I didn't want you to think I forgot."

He smiled. "That was kind of you."

The phone rang, and Filip looked at it, holding up one finger to Klara. "I'll just answer this, and then I'll be ready to go."

"Hello. Oh, hi, Natalia. No, I can't talk right now. Dinner? Tomorrow night? Um. No, sorry, that's not going to work for me. I'll give you a call back tomorrow, okay? Bye."

"Who was that?" Klara asked.

"Just a colleague."

Klara made a mental note.

❈ ❈ ❈

They took the bus to Twarda Street. Klara's guidebook explained that most of the old Jewish Quarter had been destroyed by the Nazis, except for memorials, remnants of what once was, and a few museums. Klara was grateful she'd have a "local" by her side to show her around and even more grateful that that local was Filip.

"I must warn you that there's actually not a lot to see, compared to what was once here," he said. "Much of what now stands memorializes what used to be here, before the Nazis bombed and burned it down. There are very few Jews who still live here today, and the old Jewish stores and blocks are long gone, but we will see memorials, some markers, and a few old buildings that are still standing. And there's Nozyk Synagogue, right down the street," he said, pointing to a discreet pale-yellow, nineteenth-century building.

"My aunt and cousin's family are members," Klara said, her eyes following his pointed finger. "Have you ever been?" she asked him, tilting her head.

"I went once. It was interesting. The whole service was in Hebrew, so I was able to follow along with the prayer book, but I didn't know any of the songs."

"Where did you learn Hebrew?" Klara asked.

"Oh, I guess working in the cemetery and then taking classes here and there. You know," he replied, as though it were no big deal.

"Why didn't you go back?" she asked.

"I don't know. I just didn't," he said, shrugging his shoulders. "Maybe I will sometime. Are you religious?"

"Religious as in observant, like Orthodox?" Klara asked with a small chuckle, poking fun at him, as she knew he knew she wasn't.

"No. I know you're not Orthodox. You'd be married with a brood of children, and you'd probably be wearing a long skirt," he said, smiling. "I just meant, do you go to synagogue regularly?"

"I wear long skirts sometimes," she said. "But no, honestly, I can't even read Hebrew. Growing up, my family only went to temple on the High Holidays, and I haven't been in years. I'm more of what you'd call a 'cultural Jew.' The traditions are important to me."

"It sounds like we should go." He was looking straight ahead, and she wondered if he was as nervous about asking to spend more time together as she had been.

"You mean now?" Klara replied.

"Sure, it might still be open, as it's summertime." He took her arm momentarily to lead her in the right direction.

Klara almost walked right by Nozyk Synagogue, as it showed little evidence of being a house of worship other than a discreet Star of David and a Hebrew inscription above its doors that Filip pointed out as they approached. She was trying hard to focus on their surroundings but felt butterflies in her stomach.

"It's the only synagogue still standing in Warsaw, although of course, it was restored after World War II," Filip explained as they climbed the steps. "Had the Nazis not used it to stable their horses, it probably would have been destroyed as well."

Klara turned her head to look at him. "A stable? Really?" They opened the dark wooden doors, walking into a small vestibule with an ascending staircase. There were two flights up before they arrived in a lobby with easy access to a late nineteenth-century, dark wooden chapel that seemed frozen in time.

Klara's eyes widened. "Wow," was all she could say. Filip gave her a knowing look and smiled.

This was the first nineteenth-century synagogue she had ever seen. Although she knew some existed in New York City, she had never been. Before her stood an imposing mahogany multi-pillared ark that held the sacred Torah scrolls and a giant candelabrum. There were several wooden pews on the first floor and, because it had been built as and remained an Orthodox synagogue, an upper balcony for the women, girls, and very young children.

Klara looked around the room, which appeared empty except for her and Filip, and sat down in one of the pews. She closed her eyes for several peaceful moments, absorbing the history and spirituality. When she opened them again, she could imagine the joyful, lively singing of others around her, praying in Hebrew during a Friday night or Saturday morning Shabbat service. She could have sworn she detected a faint horse smell from seventy years earlier, but it was undoubtedly the power of suggestion.

"Hello there," said a deep, friendly voice from behind her, first in Polish, and then in English. Klara, having assumed she was alone except for Filip, nearly jumped out of her skin. "I'm Rabbi Schoenfeld," he said.

Startled, Klara turned toward the sound of the voice and saw that a gray-haired, balding man in his mid-fifties wearing a yarmulke was approaching.

"Are you okay?" he asked, first in Polish and again in English, looking directly at her.

"Um," Klara replied, confused. "Yes, I . . . I'm okay," she managed to reply, still a bit shaken. She looked around for Filip, but he was nowhere in sight. "I should go." She got up quickly.

"But I interrupted you. I'm Rabbi Schoenfeld," the man repeated in English. "Please don't rush away on my account. Can I help you?"

"I guess I was just deep in thought. I'm visiting with my friend. He was just over there," she said, looking around again. "Thank you, but I'm fine." She paused a moment after noticing his accent. "You sound like you're from Brooklyn."

"I am. I first came to visit here in the late 1970s, well before Soviet rule ended, and to my surprise, I found that there were still some Jews living here, even after the Shoah," Rabbi Schoenfeld explained. "I returned after the Berlin Wall fell in the late 1980s and stayed. I've found that every year since, more Jews keep emerging, especially in the past ten years or so. How about you?" he asked, studying her. "You sound American; is this your first time in Poland?"

"I came to Warsaw to find my father's people, my aunt and her family, and to visit my father's grave. You probably know her. She's a congregant here—Rachel Lieberman," Klara said, waiting for his answer. "I mean, Sheinberg—Lieberman was her maiden name."

"Yes. Of course, I know Rachel, and her daughter Hanna and her family. So, you're Rachel's brother's daughter from America," he said, nodding. "I know he was buried here some years after the war, but before my time."

"Yes, in 1971, the year he died."

"The story of how he came to be buried here is quite a tale," the rabbi said with emphasis.

"Could you tell me what you know?" Klara asked, desperate for more information.

"I understand that your aunt spent her life savings to fly your father to Warsaw after his fatal accident and was even able to get around all the government bureaucracy—quite a feat forty-three years ago, given the great tension between the Eastern Bloc and the United States at that time." He sounded impressed. "From what I've heard, your aunt was very tenacious."

"Yes. I'm trying to take it all in—my personal history, Poland's history, and Polish Jewish history, all in one fell swoop."

"I understand. Maybe you'll join us with your aunt for Shabbat services sometime. I'm sorry, but you'll need to excuse me. I have a meeting to get to. It was very nice to meet you. Please send my best to your aunt," he said with a nod, taking his leave.

"Thank you, Rabbi." Klara could see Rabbi Schoenfeld and Filip passing each other at the rear of the synagogue and exchanging a few words before Filip walked back to where Klara was sitting.

"Do you know him?" Klara asked.

Filip smiled. "Of course, I know him. I work at the Jewish Cemetery, and he's a rabbi. Actually, he's not just the rabbi of this temple; he's the chief rabbi of Poland, which I'd say is ironic, don't you think? It used to be that the holiest rabbis traveled from Poland to America, but now, you see, it's the other way around."

They lingered in the synagogue for a few more minutes, then headed over to Prozna Street, the only former Warsaw Ghetto street with houses still standing. When they arrived, Klara couldn't stop staring. Before her stood a very old, bombed-out brick building with no windows. It looked as though it might completely crumble at any moment, but it had been left standing for fate to determine when its end would come. A life-size black-and-white photo of three young, fashionably dressed women from the 1930s hung prominently from it. The women walked with their arms linked together, wearing stylish period hats and dresses with smiles on their faces, a pre-war photo of happier times.

Klara turned to Filip. "What's this?" she asked, pointing to the life-size photo.

"It was the winner of a recent photo contest. Locals were asked to send family pictures from the pre-war years. There are more on some other pre-war buildings over there," he said, motioning across the street. The crowds of tourists were beginning to thin out as many of the sights were closing. Filip took Klara's arm and led her to Minerska Street, which she knew was where the infamous Warsaw Ghetto had been built under the Germans during World War II.

"Here's the beginning of the old Warsaw Ghetto," he said, pointing to a decaying wall next to a bronze plaque and a map.

The map read PLAN GETTA *Warszawskiego*, or Warsaw Ghetto Plan. Klara felt stricken, as though she'd been punched in the gut, as she continued her walk along the "Ghetto Trail." She placed a hand over her stomach.

"Are you all right?" Filip asked, with a look of concern.

"I'm not sure," she replied, feeling weak in the knees. She hadn't realized that visiting this site of so many atrocities—especially one where her own family members had suffered so—would affect her like this. Reading about the horrors of history was one thing; actually being there was quite another. At Filip's insistence, they sat down for a moment so Klara could collect herself before continuing to walk past several Ghetto boundary markers and memorial plaques on sidewalks and lawns marked MUR GETTA/GHETTO WALL 1943.

Somehow Klara's feet walked in tandem with Filip's and carried her forward to their destination on Stawki Street, close to the intersection with Dzika Street. She knew what awaited them there. Her heart beat more rapidly. *There it is*, she thought disdainfully. She had a powerful urge to spit, something she never did. Before them stood the former Nazi deportation site, where hundreds of thousands of women, men, and children waited to meet their end at the gas chambers of Treblinka just a few hours away. But now, instead of train tracks, there stood a memorial, the Umschlagplatz Monument, in all its bleakness, in their memory. As Klara stood in front of it with Filip, tears ran down her cheeks while she read the names:

*"Benjamin . . . Izaak . . . Judyta . . . Julian . . . Gabriel . . . Oskar . . . Rozalia . . . Roza . . . Rudolf . . . Sylvia . . . Wladyslaw . . ."* Without speaking, she anxiously searched for the names of her grandparents, Meyer and Sarah. Finding them, she wondered if these names belonged to her grandmother and grandfather or to someone else. As she allowed her fingers to slowly glide over the engravings on the smooth slate stone, her body suddenly felt weak as her thoughts ricocheted between anger, fear, and sorrow. She wondered if she might faint, and then her mind screamed out.

*You shouldn't have died this way! You shouldn't have been sent to your deaths when you were in the prime of your lives, or at any time! This should never have happened. Why did this happen?*

Her stomach dropped, as if she were on an elevator quickly going down several floors. She imagined her grandparents and all those around them holding two suitcases—the maximum allowed by the Nazis—each filled with warm clothes and their most precious worldly possessions. She could sense their fear and confusion.

The past and present blurred together in her mind: she imagined that this train platform where the memorial now stood was crowded with people carrying suitcases, mothers holding crying children and trying to shush them, and husbands trying to reassure their wives that all would be fine. It was 1942, and the Warsaw Ghetto deportations had just begun. "Move faster! Faster, I said," shouted the crisply outfitted soldiers in shiny polished black boots with large metal guns, as the scene played out in her mind's eye. Klara felt helpless. All she could do was watch as hundreds of exhausted, terrified, malnourished women, men, and children squeezed into the railroad cattle cars. She was having trouble breathing. She felt dizzy, and her legs were wobbly. She had experienced these sensations before and knew she was having a panic attack.

*Open your eyes, Klara. It's not real,* she told herself, realizing that they were tightly shut, as she had been deep in thought. She did and quickly remembered that she was in present-day Warsaw. There were no armed Nazis in uniform and no barking German shepherds ready to charge on command.

Filip was gently shaking her shoulder, peering down at her with concern. "Klara, are you all right? What is it?"

Klara stumbled over to a bench, sitting down while taking deep breaths of fresh summer air. She touched her pendant, pulling on it, and then reached into her pocket for her father's dark orange amber stone.

She turned to Filip and was sure from his pale complexion that he had spotted the fear in her eyes. She wanted to apologize and tell him that she was fine, but for the moment, no words came. A few minutes passed before she had a sudden thought; taking another deep breath, she pulled out the second letter Rachel had given her and handed it to him with a shaky hand. "Can you translate this for me? It's another letter from my father. I think it's the only thing that will calm me right now."

Filip put his hand on Klara's shoulder. "Just take a moment," he said gently. "You're not the only one who reacts to this place like that." He took the old, yellowed envelope from Klara, carefully examining it before removing its contents, a single page. Like the last one, it was written in Yiddish. He scanned it and, assuring himself that she was okay, sat down next to her, and slowly began reading aloud. "*Sixteenth of June, 1965 . . .*"

"That's a month after the first letter," Klara said, already calmer.

Filip continued reading.

*Dear Rachel,*
*  I wish you were here. Klara is so beautiful, but Bessie has been terribly depressed since her birth and doesn't want to hold her. I thought it would be better once she left the hospital, but instead, it's worse. Bessie sleeps much of the day and ignores little Klara.*

Filip paused.
"Keep reading," Klara insisted.

*  Bessie's mad at me and will only respond favorably to her father, Siggy. I've been getting up at night to feed the baby. I can't bear to be apart from Klara all day, especially knowing Bessie is not regularly holding her. I hold her from the time I get home from work until she falls asleep at night. This only seems to further annoy Bessie. I tried talking to Siggy, but he dismisses everything I say and tells me how lucky I am to be in this country with a job, a wife, and now a baby. I feel confused. What should I do?*
*  Love, Dawid*

Filip put the letter down. Klara sat quietly with tears rolling down her face.

"I'm sorry," Filip said, looking unsure of what to do.

"This just affirms what I already knew—that she never really loved me," Klara said, her voice trailing off.

"It sounds like maybe your mother had postpartum depression before anyone ever understood what that was, and she probably couldn't help herself."

"I'm not sure about that," Klara replied. Her mother had had years to get over it, which she never did.

"Let me take you home," Filip said, gently helping her stand and putting his arm around her as they strolled back to her hotel. Despite her emotional reaction to the Ghetto just moments earlier, her body tingled, and her heart softened. This felt right to her.

# CHAPTER 13

The next evening, Klara sat down to a family Shabbat dinner with Rachel, Hanna, Hanna's husband, Alek, and Hanna's daughter, Rebeka. From the moment she arrived at their apartment, she was calculating just how long she needed to stay. Although her aunt had prepared a delicious dinner of *kopytka* (potato gnocchi) with turkey and vegetables, and Klara was happy for the opportunity to get to know Alek—whom she was just meeting—and Rebeka a little better, she was too anxious about her plans to see Filip later on to fully concentrate on the conversation. Since she had been so out of sorts during their visit to the Ghetto the day before, Filip had suggested they get together after her Shabbat meal.

Rachel, in whom she had confided her plans, noticed how distracted she was and finally said, "Go," midway through the main course. Smiling as she handed Klara the third challah from the night before, which she had carefully wrapped in a cloth, Rachel kissed Klara on the cheek and shooed her along.

"Thank you," Klara replied, smiling at her aunt as she jumped up from her chair, adding the challah to her bag of picnic items—a cold bottle of white wine with three cups, some cheese and fruit, and a woolen blanket to sit on.

"Have fun," Hanna said a bit tauntingly. Her mother elbowed her, while Alek gave his wife a disapproving look.

"Don't tease her, Hanna," Rachel said. Looking again at Klara, she added, "You might want this too," and held out another letter from her beloved brother.

Klara took it from her gratefully, exchanging it for the previous day's letter. "Yes, thank you," she said. "Thank you for everything, Aunt Rachel," she added, thinking about how warm and welcoming Rachel had been these last few days, despite Klara's sudden appearance after all these years.

Rachel put her hand over her chest. "That's the first time you've called me that, *Aunt Rachel.*"

"Is that okay?" Klara asked, turning her head to check in with her, worried that she may have overstepped some imaginary line.

"It's perfect. I love it," Rachel said, hugging her as she sent her off. "Just have fun."

As she went on her way, Klara's mind shifted from the family warmth to the prior evening with Filip, when he walked her back to her hotel. Her stomach began doing backflips, and her heart felt like it might jump out of her chest.

❖ ❖ ❖

A half hour later, as the sun was beginning to set, Klara arrived at the Jewish Cemetery to meet Filip as they had arranged, but she found the gates locked. Confused and concerned that she'd misunderstood his invitation, she double-checked the cemetery hours listed on a plaque, noting that on Shabbat, today, it closed earlier than usual. But just then she saw Filip poke his head out of his office door, and he came over to unlock the gate so she could enter.

"I hope you haven't been waiting too long. I was just finishing a phone call. We're officially closed for Shabbat, so I didn't want to be disturbed by other visitors."

"Oh, I didn't realize. Would it be all right if I visited my father's gravestone?"

Filip looked at Klara with his head tilted to one side as though he were confused.

"I thought we could celebrate Shabbat with my father, if that doesn't seem too macabre or weird," she continued.

"I like that idea. Just give me a few minutes, and I'll meet you there," he said with a grin.

Klara walked the now-familiar path, laying out the picnic blanket in front of her father's gravestone when she arrived. She set out the challah, grapes, and cheese. She was struggling to open the bottle of wine when Filip appeared next to her.

"Can I help you with that?" he offered, holding out his hand for the bottle.

"Sure," she said, surprising herself, as she would usually dismiss any offer of help. She set down the three glasses along with two candlestick holders and candles on the picnic blanket.

"Who's the third glass for?" he asked, confused. "Expecting someone else?"

"My father."

Filip nodded. "What a nice idea," he said as he poured three glasses of wine while Klara set out the challah and two white Shabbat candles, getting them ready to light. She said the Hebrew blessings over the candles, then over the wine, and finally over the challah, from which she tore a piece for Filip and one for herself.

"*L'chaim!*" Filip pronounced, raising his wine glass and clinking it against hers. "You know all the blessings?"

"I do." She smiled, saying the one over the wine. "L'chaim," she said back to him, still holding up her glass of wine, laughing a bit. "L'chaim, Papa," she said, raising her glass toward her father's gravestone.

Filip raised his glass toward her father's gravestone as well and smiled. After a second glass of wine, Klara felt a pleasant buzz and became much chattier.

"I'm so glad we're doing this," she said as she sat back, resting her head on her hands as she unfolded her legs straight in front of her. Filip joined her in doing the same. "So, what do you do for fun?" she asked.

"I play in a klezmer band with some friends," he said as he sipped his wine.

"A klezmer band, like music from the old Jewish *shtetls* [small Jewish villages]?"

"Exactly."

"Which instrument do you play?" she asked. "No, don't tell me," she said, closing her eyes and putting her index fingers on her temples as though in deep concentration. "The accordion? No, the violin," she said with emphasis. "Am I right? The violin?"

"You are," he said, surprised. "How'd you guess?"

"I have special powers," she replied with a twinkle in her eye.

"I guess you do. Do you know what I'm thinking right now?"

"That you want me to come hear your band?"

"Hmm. I'll be right back," he replied, getting up.

"Where are you going?" Klara asked playfully.

"I want to show you something. I'll be back in two minutes. Don't go anywhere," Filip said as he got up and ran in the direction of his office.

While she waited for him to return, Klara lay back on her blanket with her knees facing up to the sky, completely content for the first time in ages. Dusk was turning to darkness, and several bright white stars appeared above. She began wishing on one aloud: "Star light, star bright, first star I see tonight. I wish I may, I wish I might, have the wish I wish tonight." As she finished, she began to hear the faint sound of a violin playing klezmer music, first in the distance and then nearby. As she sat up, she spotted Filip walking toward her, playing the violin while he rhythmically moved his arms and body.

Klara closed her eyes, listening to the music. When Filip was finished, he sat next to her on the blanket.

"That was beautiful," she said, smiling. "Thank you for playing for me."

After a few minutes of chitchat, she took out the envelope her aunt had given her earlier that evening from her bag. "I have another letter," she announced, shoving it in front of him.

"What?" he asked.

"I have another letter from my aunt," she persisted. "Do you think you can translate it for me?"

He took the envelope from her hand and opened it. Using the Shabbat candles for light, he began to translate the Yiddish letter, first in a matter-of-fact tone, and then with more emotion, caught up in Klara's father's words from decades ago.

*Seventh of September, 1965*

*Dear Rachel,*
*Klara is now three months old. She's lost much of her dark hair, and it is now growing in reddish, like yours. She coos and smiles, and I coo and smile back at her. The weather in New York is beautiful this time of year. It's in the upper sixties here, nice and mild. It's almost fall, although the leaves are still green. Even in the city, there is lush greenery in the parks. Soon the leaves will begin to change color. My favorite thing to do is to take Klara for a walk*

*in her carriage when I get home from work in the evening. Bessie is still depressed. She is starting to become a little more active but is still always in a bad mood. I worry for Klara when I'm gone during the day, that she is not being taken care of the way she should be. I know she is being fed and changed, but I think Bessie does these tasks in a cold, efficient manner, rather than lovingly.*

Here, Filip paused, taking a breath and looking at Klara. She nodded to him as if to tell him to keep going. He continued.

*Bessie and I are increasingly arguing. She is never happy with me and seems to be turning more and more toward her father. This is not at all what I imagined marriage and having a family would be like. Recently, she accused me of only caring about the baby and not her. That's not true, but she makes it hard to get close to her, and the baby is so easy to love. Things are not going very well. I wish you were here.*

*Love, David*

Filip handed the letter back to Klara. "I'm sorry," he said.

"Thank you, but you don't need to be," she said with downcast eyes.

He looked at her. "I'm sorry that you had to go through what you went through."

She shrugged it off. "I don't remember any of it anyway, at least not when I was that age. It's no big deal."

"But it is. It is a big deal, and it must have felt very confusing. You didn't deserve that. No one does," he added sympathetically.

"I guess not, but I'm not surprised. That's just how my mother is, and it gives me some insight to know that's the way she's always been," Klara replied, shrugging.

"Your father, though, he cared a lot about you," he said as he gently put his hand on her shoulder.

"Yeah, I guess he did," she said, unable to shake the sadness of knowing that her mother did not.

Filip picked up on Klara's mood shift, which had turned from playful to studied to sad in a matter of minutes. She looked down and remained quiet until she said, "Maybe we should think of packing up."

Although Klara had just suggested going, Filip clearly didn't want the evening to end yet.

"What do you think about coming to the Krakow Jewish Cultural Festival with me on Sunday?" he asked. "My klezmer band is playing at a café there on Monday night. I'm taking off time from work for the week. It's going to be amazing. There'll be great music, dance, art, and lectures from Jewish groups and authorities all over the world. You have to come—you'll love it! It's been going on since 1988, about a year before the Berlin Wall fell. It's for Jews and non-Jews to celebrate all things Jewish in our Polish culture. In fact, the director of the festival is a self-described 'Shabbos goy.' He's a non-Jew who helps keep the Jewish culture alive."

"I don't really know," Klara said, staring off into the darkness, shaking her head. The cold, harsh reality of her mother's anger and rejection of her, as described in her father's letter, had hit her like an ice-cold glass of water in the face. She felt utterly defeated. And then, Jacob Herschler's pasty white face flashed through her mind. *Will he never leave me alone?*

"C'mon, Klara. You should come. You'll get to hear from people with degrees in Hebrew studies and the Holocaust who've helped to revive Polish Jewish culture and teach about the past. These are people who have helped to build monuments, restore cemeteries, conserve archives, as well as establish Holocaust education curricula and whole academic departments in Polish universities." He gently tried to cajole her. "This is right up your alley, and your visit to Poland wouldn't be complete without it."

"How is it you know so much about Holocaust education and university departments?" Klara asked, intrigued despite herself.

"It goes with my job. I meet all kinds of people," he replied. "Anyway, it would be nice if you came. Nice for you, and nice for us to spend some more time together. You know, to hang out. You'll get more of a feel for the history of Polish Jewish culture, and you'll get to see Krakow, which is a beautiful, unblemished city."

"I'll think about it," she said noncommittally, feeling the need to get up and run away.

"Are you upset with me, Klara? I don't understand. I feel like I'm on the defensive somehow."

She blew out the candles that had melted halfway down and stood up. "No, I'm just not sure of my plans right now." She hadn't intended to be so abrupt, especially given how kind he had been to her, but the discussion of her mother in the letter had triggered her trust issues. Rationally, she knew she shouldn't take it out on him, but she couldn't help it.

Filip stood too, following Klara's cue. He reached out and tried to hold her hand, but she turned away as if she hadn't noticed.

"I like you, Klara. I enjoy spending time with you, and you're obviously quite a smart woman. I thought you might like spending time with me too," Filip said gently, but it was clear he was confused by her mood shifts.

Klara just stood there, not knowing what to say. All she could focus on was that her mother had never really cared for her, something she always had known.

"We should go," she finally said.

"That's it?" he asked, staring at her.

"What about Natalia? The woman who you were talking to on the phone at your office?"

"Natalia? What made you think of her? We're just colleagues. She knows that. I'm not in a relationship with anyone. What about you?"

Klara pulled her chin close to her neck, as she was taken off guard by Filip's straightforwardness. "What? No," she answered honestly. Regaining her composure, she said, "Look, I really appreciate your spending time with me translating the letters and showing me around Warsaw. I've learned a lot from you. I'm not sure about going to Krakow. If I do, I may go on my own. That's how I generally like to do things, by myself," she said as she folded the picnic blanket and packed the food. "You should take the rest of this," she added, handing him the challah that she had wrapped up for him.

"No, that's okay," he said flatly. "It's yours."

"But I made it for you," she said before she could stop the words from coming out.

"What? You made it for me? Then why are you rushing off? I thought we were having a nice time together. Did I offend you in some way?" He threw his hands up. "Please help me understand."

"No," she said, shaking her head, holding her bag tightly, ready to bolt. "You've done nothing wrong. I just need to go back to my hotel room."

They walked in silence to the front of the cemetery, where Filip stood with Klara while she waited for her bus. She knew that he was confused, but she couldn't help it. She just couldn't let him in. She couldn't let anyone in. Her father's letter was a reminder that she would only get hurt.

"Would you like me to take you back to your hotel?" he asked in the same flat tone.

"No thanks. I appreciate it, but it's pretty close, and I'll be fine."

"All right, if you're sure."

When the lights of the bus approached, he turned to Klara. "Good night."

As she boarded the bus and sat down, Klara watched Filip walk away with his hands in his pockets and his head down. Even though she had just told herself that she was safer alone, a competing voice in her head was reprimanding her. *Once again, you messed it up. You always mess things up. You'll never learn. Stupid girl.* It was her mother's internalized voice. She did her best to ignore this voice. It was the one that liked to criticize her when she was already feeling down on herself. Instead, she took out the piece of burnt-orange amber from her pocket, rubbing it the rest of the way home, as she tried to soothe herself. But she couldn't stop thinking about how she pushed Filip away, and what had been raised in her father's letter. She'd always known that her mother was disappointed in her, but to hear in such clear words that she didn't pick her up and play with her, even as a baby, was inescapable proof of her rejection.

By the time she returned to her small, dark hotel room, Klara's sadness had turned to anger. *Of course, my mother never gave a shit about me. Tell me something I don't know,* she thought. And now Filip knew. *He knows what a sad, unlovable sack I am. Why would he ever want me? Forget it, I don't need him. I don't need anyone.*

Tears running down her cheeks, she crawled under the covers, too exhausted to undress. She would leave Warsaw first thing the next morning, after saying goodbye to Rachel. Who did she think she was? She thought she could take a leap of faith and trust someone, a man, no less. Well, she just couldn't do it.

She'd go to Krakow by herself for a day or two and then head back to her solitary life in Maine, researching other peoples' cultures, while cocooning herself away. She finally cried herself to sleep, but her dreams were even more unsettling than usual. They were full of faces—those of her mother, her grandfather, and Jacob Herschler, their "family friend." But there were other more comforting ones, too, with images of Rachel, Filip, and her father. Her father's face from when she was a young child was the most soothing. Ultimately, however, the visions of her mother won out. She startled a few times, feeling upset, but mostly at herself.

Early the next morning, the phone woke her. It was Rachel.

"I couldn't wait to call you, Klara. How was your date with Filip?"

"It wasn't a date," she replied too strongly.

"Of course, dear, sorry. How was your time with him? Did he like the challah?"

"Yes, Rachel, thank you again, he liked the challah. It was fine, but I don't expect to see him again any time soon." Klara was aware of the note of sadness in her voice.

"I'm sorry, dear. You didn't have a good time together?"

"No, that's not it. I . . . I just need to be on my own right now. I'm thinking of going to Krakow, to the Jewish Cultural Festival early on Sunday."

"You'll love that, but maybe you can wait another day or two, and Hanna and Alek can go with you. Then you would have company. It would be so much nicer with company."

"Thank you for your concern, but I'll be fine. I always do everything by myself. This will be no different," Klara insisted, still in the same flat voice she had used with Filip the night before. Anyway, while Alek was nice enough, the last thing she needed right now was Hanna's judgment and barely concealed scorn.

"Okay, Klara, if you're sure." Rachel sounded hesitant and a little concerned. "Please just call me when you get there."

"I'll call you when I get there," she said, and ended the call.

Klara knew she wasn't sure of anything right now except for her need to flee as quickly as possible. That she understood. She had done it often enough.

# CHAPTER 14

Klara slept in for the day, leaving the Hotel Novotel Warszawa on Sunday, the following morning, this time with her backpack and suitcase in hand, along with her handbag, wearing comfortable clothes: a peasant blouse, jeans, and flat sandals. She was planning on boarding the local bus to Warsaw's downtown train station when she spotted Hanna and Alek waiting for her in their small gray Fiat outside the hotel.

"Hi, Klara," Hanna said, waving from the car window.

"What are *you* doing here?" Klara asked, taken aback by their presence.

"Alek is driving us to the train station. I'm going with you to Krakow," Hanna replied casually.

"Hi, Klara." Alek waved, getting out of the car to open the trunk for her bags.

"Hi, Alek," Klara replied, befuddled. Turning to Hanna, she said, "No, I'm going to Krakow alone. I'll be fine." She tried to sound forceful, but she knew Aunt Rachel was behind this.

"I know you'll be fine, but my mother thinks otherwise," Hanna explained. "She wants me to accompany you, and I want to make her happy. She worries way too much."

"What about your job?" Klara asked a bit too sharply. She guessed that Hanna was no keener to accompany her than she was to have Hanna babysit her.

"Today's Sunday, so it's not an issue. It's just three hours each way. I'll stay until Monday evening, and go back to work on Tuesday."

Klara stood outside the car, settling her suitcase on the curb, while Alek waited by the open trunk.

"Come on," Hanna said, clearly irritated. "Get in the car."

Klara took a deep breath and, against her better judgment, gave Alek her suitcase and got in. A moment later, he pulled away from the curb.

"What did your mother tell you?" Klara found herself asking, after they had driven in silence for a few minutes.

"That she wouldn't forgive me if I let you go to Krakow by yourself, and that you weren't in any frame of mind to be alone."

"I'll be fine. I'm *not* a child," Klara replied with emphasis.

"Yes, I know, that's what I told her," her cousin responded. "But as you get to know my mother, you'll learn she doesn't take no for an answer."

"I know she means well, but I'm quite self-sufficient," Klara declared.

"It's not all about you," Hanna said. "You have a lot to learn about Holocaust survivors and an old woman who lost most of her family. My mother worries about everyone she loves when they're out of her sight. She worries if they will ever come home again. She spent my childhood looking out our apartment window, waiting for me to return home from school every day, and then doing the same for my father until he came home from work at suppertime each evening. I'm not going to let her wait and wonder when you're coming back from Krakow, checking the window for you and jumping every time the phone rings," Hanna said in a flat tone.

"Come on, Hanna," Alek interjected, trying to calm his wife. "Be nice. Klara doesn't know how your mother is."

"*No,* she most certainly *doesn't,*" Hanna replied, then turned to face Klara, who sat in the back seat. "You just waltz into our lives, wriggling your way into my mother's good graces until she trusts you, and then you think you can just waltz right out again, and everything will be okay? You have no idea what you're dealing with, and I'm not going to let you hurt her."

"She's not trying to hurt your mother," Alek replied softly to his wife, placing his hand on her arm.

"She doesn't know what she's doing," Hanna barked.

"What am I doing?" Klara asked, truly bewildered. "I came to find my father's family, and now I'm going to take a trip to Krakow. Why arc you so upset? I'm not trying to hurt your mother."

"You haven't been listening to a word I've said. My mother *cares about you.* You got her to care about you. I guess that's what you wanted—not just money, like I first thought. But now that she cares, you can't just ignore or forget about her feelings," Hanna said.

"I wasn't trying to ignore her feelings. I care about her too," Klara insisted. "I didn't realize that my leaving for a few days or so would upset her," she said, as Hanna glarcd.

Until that moment, Klara hadn't considered Rachel's perspective as a Holocaust survivor—that she would be hypervigilant about her family's whereabouts because of her experience during the war. She also recognized, with some surprise, that Hanna had begun to come around and believe that she might not have underhanded motives and was maybe even starting to accept her. Mentally kicking herself, Klara realized that she was being selfish and short-sighted. Wasn't this the kind of family connection that she had wanted all along?

"Fine," Klara said.

Alek tried to make pleasant conversation for the rest of the drive, talking about what a beautiful city Krakow was. "It wasn't destroyed by the Germans like Warsaw. It retains much of its original beauty," he said.

Klara appreciated his efforts to engage her, but she just didn't have it in her to make small talk. As she had only experienced Hanna's wrath, bitterness, and sarcasm, she couldn't help but wonder what such a pleasant man like Alek saw in her cousin. She was bewildered as to how these two seemingly opposite personalities had gotten together. In all fairness, she knew she was reacting to Hanna's rudeness toward her; Hanna must possess some positive qualities that she hadn't seen yet.

❁ ❁ ❁

The two women caught a train to Krakow about an hour later, finding seats together in a stifling, six-person compartment. The air-conditioning was broken, so the compartment door had been left ajar, giving easy access to the train's narrow passageway directly outside it.

"So, Klara, tell me, how exactly is it that you decided to come to Warsaw now?" Hanna asked as she dabbed her cheeks and neck with a handkerchief and drank some water before fanning herself.

"I've told you before," Klara said.

"You told me some, but I still don't fully understand."

Klara had to catch herself from overreacting to Hanna's question. She was sure she had told her before exactly why she had decided to come to Warsaw at this point in time, and so was annoyed at the interrogation. Was Hanna being nosy, or did she still not believe her? She reminded herself that she had come to Poland for just this kind of family connection, so she needed to be more patient and accommodating if she wanted to build a relationship with her cousin.

"I really want to know," Hanna continued with apparent sincerity. "I'm not trying to bait you. I want to know more about why and how it is you came to find us after so many years."

Klara took a deep breath, looking intently at her cousin for several moments. She wanted to trust her but could not easily forget Hanna's initial rude treatment of her. "It's so hard to tell when you're being sincere. I want us to be friends, but it feels like you're always waiting to pounce on me," Klara finally said. "I'm not trying to steal your mother, if that's what you're worried about," she added, a bit too defensively.

"I don't think you're trying to steal my mother," Hanna replied. "I just don't think you're being sensitive enough to her feelings, or mine, for that matter. I could be at home with Alek, Rebeka, and my mother, going to the park for a picnic this weekend, but instead, I'm here with you to make sure you're not alone. And you don't seem all that appreciative." Klara took a few moments to absorb what her cousin was saying. Despite herself, she found that Hanna was making a valid point.

"Okay, I'll tell you more of the background, if you really want to know. Of course, you know about the letter my mother received from the Polish government about my father's portion of land restitution, stating that the country was paying former Polish Jewish and non-Jewish citizens back for land that had been seized from them during the war. Until my mother wrote me about it, she had never actually told me of my father's death. But then she had no choice."

Hanna shook her head. "I can't believe she would hide something like that from you. Don't get me wrong; I believe you, but that's just mind-boggling."

"It was something she never spoke of," Klara continued. "When I was six years old, my father went to Philadelphia to look for a job, and that was the last I heard of him. My mother made it seem like he just disappeared after that, and the truth is that, although I tried asking at first, I think I ultimately didn't want to know." Klara's head dropped to her chest for a moment; then she lifted it. "To some extent, it was more comforting to believe he might still be out there somewhere, just waiting for the right time to come get me. I was also angry with him for leaving me, but I think the hope that he was out there was stronger than the anger. So of course, as soon as I learned he was dead and buried here, I had to come here. I made immediate plans."

"That makes so much sense. I'm really sorry I questioned your motives earlier," Hanna said, again fanning herself.

"I understand why you did," Klara replied, looking down at the floor. "Also, I think I was already primed to come, from an experience I had on an archaeological dig in the Yucatán, several months ago. There, I met a Mayan healer named Rosario. She asked me why I was so interested in learning about other peoples' cultures, particularly when I didn't seem to know much about my own family. Rosario and the other Indigenous Mayan people I met there had such a strong, palpable connection to their ancestors and history. It made me much more curious about finding out about my own."

Hanna nodded.

Klara continued, "For them, their history is their lifeline. I know it sounds strange, but I never thought to question my own family history. I was taught not to. Once I got back to the States, this curiosity was a constant nudge for me. So when my mother's letter about my father arrived, I had no doubt that I would come. The money was secondary. My father and a possible connection to his family has always been first and foremost."

"That must have been a huge shock to learn of his death through your mother's letter," Hanna said, putting a hand on Klara's shoulder. "I'm really sorry about all of it. It must have been terrible finding out that way. And I'm sorry for how I treated you at first."

"It was a shock," Klara said with tears in her eyes. She wasn't sure if they came from unburdening herself of the story or from her cousin's sudden kindness and understanding. "Thank you for apologizing. I really appreciate it. But if you don't mind, I think I'm going to take a break from this heat and go stand by a window out there." Klara stood up. She couldn't help herself; she felt overwhelmingly sad and needed to be alone.

"Sure," Hanna replied. "Take your time."

As Klara walked out to the aisle where the windows were open, she felt the wind on her face. As she gazed outside, they passed one small village after another, each with five or six homes situated near the train tracks. All looked alike, neat and tidy with clean laundry hanging on drying lines in their backyards. Klara wondered about the people who lived in those houses and wore those clothes. She wondered how aware they were of what their country must have been like seventy years earlier during the Nazi occupation, when all of Poland was engulfed by unimaginable horror.

After some time passed, Hanna tapped Klara's back, making her jump at being snapped out of her reverie.

"You're so touchy," Hanna said, but smiled. "I just want to let you know that we'll be in Krakow in about a half hour. We should talk about what you want to do and what you'd like to see."

Klara thought that Hanna sounded genuine and welcoming and was grateful for the turn their relationship had taken.

"How about you? Aren't there things you'd like to see?" Klara asked, trying to mirror Hanna's sincerity. "You are kind enough to accompany me, so let's do what you'd like to do."

"Of course, but I've been to Krakow many times before, including to the Jewish Cultural Festival. If you want to see

Jewish sites, though, I'd recommend we start with Krakow's Jewish Quarter, known as Kazimierz. There are still a handful of synagogues there, along with cemeteries and Jewish-style restaurants, mostly for the tourists." Hanna started listing some of her favorite dining spots, but Klara interrupted.

"Why have you been here so many times?"

"Well, first, Krakow is a beautiful city. It wasn't destroyed during the war like Warsaw, and Alek, Rebeka, my mother, and I love coming here for long weekend visits. Also, there's a good amount of Polish Jewish history that's been preserved here, so I've also come out of professional interest as well. Did my mother tell you that I now work at POLIN, the Museum of the History of Polish Jews? I was involved in its official opening last year." Hanna tilted her head toward Klara.

"She said you were connected with its opening, but I didn't realize your regular job is there. For some reason, I thought you were at the Jewish Historical Institute."

"I actually helped to curate as well as research some of the historical exhibits at POLIN," Hanna said with pride.

"That's so interesting. I will have to go and visit it. Doesn't it celebrate over a thousand years of Polish Jewish life?" Klara asked.

Hanna nodded. "It does. You know, speaking of celebrating over a thousand years of Jewish history, we'll probably run into Filip Jablonski if you're planning to stay for the Jewish Cultural Festival," she said with a twinkle in her eye.

Klara could feel her face get red. "Why are you bringing him up?"

"Alek and I got to know him a bit while we worked on some of the research for the historical exhibits at POLIN. He's a good guy. You really don't have to act so secretive with me. I know you went to see him the other night, and I know you like him." Hanna smiled conspiratorially. "He is—how do you say it?—*a catch*."

"How do you know I like him?" Klara asked.

"Because you just told me so." Hanna chuckled.

"I never told you anything of the kind." Klara folded her arms.

"You just did a moment ago, by your response." Hanna smiled. "Come on. Why not just admit it?"

"There's nothing going on. I don't like him like that, and I definitely don't plan to see him. I just won't go to the restaurant his klezmer band is playing at while we're here."

"Okay," Hanna said, but Klara had a feeling that this was not the end of the discussion.

# CHAPTER 15

They arrived at Krakow's train station, Krakow Glowny, a half hour later, as Hanna had predicted. Their station was just northeast of the Old Town where the famous Main Square, Rynek Glowny, was. Before walking the ten minutes to Kazimierz, the Jewish Quarter, they stored their overnight bags in a train station locker. Once they arrived, Klara noticed that some of the buildings looked like they could use a fresh coat of paint, but the town was bustling with people, mostly tourists. There were multiple cafés and bars with Jewish food as their specialty, and some restaurants featured klezmer music as well. The streets were narrow, with a mixture of three-story buildings, including a number of art galleries and antique shops with wooden shutters to go along with the historical sites. It was different from the other areas; there was a distinct bohemian feel, and Klara noticed there were no spires or churches here.

"Wow," she said, looking all around. "You weren't kidding—this really seems to be a fascinating place."

"It's quite special," Hanna replied, following Klara's gaze. "It's probably the best example of pre-war Jewish culture in all of Europe, but it was in disrepair for so many years until it was rediscovered in the 1990s. It came to life again with the fall of the Communist regime, then the annual Jewish Cultural Festival, and, of course, from its exposure through Steven Spielberg's movie *Schindler's List*. Remnants of Schindler's factory are still here. We can visit it if you'd like."

"I remember that movie well," Klara said quietly, taking in the scene around her, trying to imagine the horrors that had taken place in these now beautiful and vibrant streets.

"I'm hungry," she heard Hanna say.

"Me too."

"There's a bagel shop down the street," Hanna said, pointing.

"Really?" Klara laughed. "Just like in New York City. I can't wait to try one."

"You know, of course, that bagels were first created in this part of the world before they were ever made in New York City."

As they walked inside the shop to order, Klara heard many different languages being spoken: Slavic, German, French, Spanish, and some English and Polish as well. They were waiting in line when Klara heard herself ask her cousin, "How well do you know Filip Jablonski?"

Hanna seemed surprised. "I know him a bit professionally, like I said. Why?" she asked, eyeing Klara.

"I'm just curious about him." Klara tried to sound casual.

"He always struck me as quite decent, although a bit mysterious. And he's not at all hard on the eyes. What really happened with him, Klara? Did you scare him off?"

"No. It was the other way around," she said, shaking her head vigorously.

"Did he come on too strong?" Hanna asked.

"No." Klara now regretted bringing him up in conversation.

"So, what's the problem?" Hanna stared at Klara, but she didn't answer. She was thinking back to the other night with Filip, and how quickly she had shut down emotionally the moment they began getting closer to one another. Really, what was she so afraid of?

After eating her first Krakow bagel, Klara noticed there was something different in its taste compared to its New York counterpart. She couldn't quite put her finger on it. With a full stomach, she was now ready to see the sights, and Hanna offered to show her around.

"There are two Jewish cemeteries, six synagogues, three museums, and an active market square, Nowy Square, all within a few blocks of here," Hanna explained as they walked on Szeroka Street. Traditionally the center of the Jewish Quarter, it looked more like a square filled with tourists than a street. Klara nodded, her head swiveling left and right, taking in the sights and smells. They made their way to Barotsza Street, finally arriving at Stara Synagoga, also known as the Old Synagogue.

"This is the oldest surviving Jewish building in all of Poland," Hanna continued, looking up at the facade. "It was originally built sometime in the beginning of the fifteenth century. It's now a museum of Jewish heritage and culture, displaying Jewish items from another time—torahs, menorahs, wedding contracts," she said in a low tone that sounded sad.

As they got closer, Klara's eyes were drawn to a black plaque written in Hebrew, Polish, and English, placed on the peeling white exterior wall. It read:

> IN MEMORY OF THE JEWISH MARTYRS OF
> CRACOW WHO WERE ANNIHILATED BY THE NAZI
> GERMANS IN THE TERRIBLE PERIOD 1939–1945.
> EARTH DOES NOT COVER THEIR BLOOD.

Klara again felt the weight of history descend upon her shoulders as they entered the building.

The feeling continued inside, where Klara felt like she was viewing cultural artifacts from a people who were supposed to be extinct, but who had, against unfathomable odds, managed to survive and carry on their traditions. There was a *ketubah*, a Jewish wedding contract, like those still used today. There were descriptions in Polish and English of the Jewish holidays still celebrated: Passover; Rosh Hashanah, the Jewish New Year; and Yom Kippur, the Day of Atonement. Even the terms *Shabbat*, the Jewish Sabbath from Friday evening to Saturday evening each week, and *synagogue* were explained. Nearby was a nineteenth-century *bimah*, made of black wrought iron and covered in a dark red carpet, where the rabbi would have stood.

"It's like we're studying a vanished culture, but these people were our ancestors, and we're still here," Klara said to Hanna.

"You're right, but many Poles grew up never knowing any Jewish people or anything about our customs and rituals. We haven't been part of Polish mainstream culture for many years, since before World War II. Perhaps we never were. This is a way to educate people, and even for Jewish people to remember that all this was once here: that we were here, sharing a vibrant community with one another." They stood quietly, silently paying tribute to the previously lost Jewish culture.

Klara felt a connection to her religion and traditions that she hadn't felt in years.

❀ ❀ ❀

As they headed to Krakow's only presently active synagogue, Synagoga Remu, also known as Remuh Synagogue, Hanna tentatively asked Klara, "Can you tell me more about what your mother is like?"

Klara paused for a moment, looking at Hanna, again trying to judge her sincerity. She pushed her distrust aside. "In a nutshell, she's a very self-serving person, not warm or loving, and *very* controlling. She's completely different from your mother in every respect. You have no idea how lucky you are," she said, looking straight ahead. "The way she's always acted toward me . . . made me put up a wall, keeping me from really getting close to anyone, including myself. She's probably a lot of the reason I'm still alone."

"That's pretty sad." Hanna sounded genuinely sympathetic. "I'm sorry."

"Thank you," Klara replied gratefully, feeling like Hanna really meant it. For once, she tried to just take in her cousin's comforting words without immediately dismissing them, as she would normally do when someone said something supportive or complimentary. Fortunately, Hanna did not ask any further questions about Klara's mother or family, at least not for now. Klara figured her cousin could tell that this was a difficult and loaded subject for her. Maybe she'd be able to share more with her later.

"Here we are: Remuh Synagogue," Hanna announced, as they approached a series of two-story connected stone buildings with a red Mediterranean roof and black wrought-iron fencing. "It was originally built in 1553 and has been renovated to look similar to its original state."

"It still has an active congregation?" Klara asked.

"Yes. There are approximately two hundred congregants. They hold regular Shabbat and High Holiday services," Hanna said as she pushed open the heavy wooden doors.

"How do you know the exact details? From your job at the Jewish Museum?" Klara asked.

Hanna held up a guidebook, and they both laughed.

Klara felt as if she were walking into a palace, awed by the synagogue's high, elaborately painted ceilings in bold, colored patterns with multiple exquisite candelabra hanging above. The overall effect was breathtaking. Klara was craning her neck to fully take in her surroundings when Hanna joined her.

"This isn't even the most interesting part. There's a famous Jewish cemetery in back, and Jews from all over the world, particularly devout, observant ones, come to pray by the graves of famous Krakow rabbis and scholars."

Klara was surprised to hear about a synagogue and cemetery existing side by side. "That's quite unusual, right?"

"For the most part, but in some medieval Jewish ghettos, like here and in Prague, space was very limited, so the cemetery was placed behind the synagogue, with a high wall erected."

"It's amazing that all this survived," Klara said, looking around at the elaborately painted ceilings and walls.

"Not exactly," Hanna replied, staring ahead. "The Nazis used this synagogue to store rubberized sacks for corpses during their occupation, and they stole all the valuable ceremonial objects. The antique *bimah* and most of the furnishings were destroyed. It was later restored by the Jewish community."

Klara shook her head gloomily, then walked over to a nearby pew where she sat, taking in the atmosphere. In the center of the room was a rectangular *bimah* with wrought ironwork constructed to replace the original display. While appreciating the surroundings, she was also considering Hanna's enthusiasm for and overall knowledge about these historical sites. *We actually have quite a bit in common*, she thought.

As they walked outside to the celebrated cemetery, Klara saw a man in traditional Orthodox dress—a long black coat and black pants, a white dress shirt, and a black hat, with a substantial beard and *payos*, or sidelocks, hanging in front of each ear—praying over what Klara expected was a highly revered rabbi's tombstone. A black wrought-iron fence surrounding the metal roof–covered gravestone encased it.

Klara looked around at the rows of five-hundred-year-old tombstones, each covered by a metal roof to preserve and protect it. Her attention was drawn to a multi-shaded gray mosaic wall of broken gravestones that stood about twelve feet high and approximately one hundred feet wide.

"What's that?" she asked Hanna, pointing to the magnificent wall.

"People call it the 'Wailing Wall,' like in Jerusalem, because it represents the destruction of the Krakow Jews by the Nazis, just as the Wailing Wall represents the destruction of the Israelites. About ten years or so after the war, the cemetery was cleaned up, and an archaeological excavation was begun. This is what they found," Hanna replied, pointing to the wall. "Hundreds of complete tombstones, along with tens of thousands of broken pieces were discovered not far below the ground. People decided to put them together to construct this wall."

"We are stronger together than any of us are on our own. Together we are unbroken," Klara replied, her voice ringing out clearly from a place deep in her belly.

"Excuse me?" Hanna said.

"To me, this wall screams of our strength as a people. Each fragment is like a broken life; in itself it is sad and tragic, but bound together with others, it is fierce. It is like the Jewish people. We are *unbroken.* Hitler and his Nazis tried to annihilate us as a race, which of course we're not. We're an ethnicity, but he spoke of us as an 'impure race.' The Nazis rounded us up like cattle and then sent us off to be gassed to death and then burned in the crematorium. They killed six million of us, but they did not eradicate us. You and I are standing right here. Over fourteen and a half million Jews around the world are very much alive today, and Poland's own Jewish Cultural Festival, which has been going on for over twenty-five years, is about to start tomorrow.

"We've survived!" Klara raised her fists in the air, surprised yet exhilarated by her own outburst.

She walked over to touch the wall, followed by Hanna.

Closing her eyes, she spoke in a whisper. "It feels coarse and jagged in some parts, and smooth in others."

Hanna stared at Klara. "You're right. We survived, but we're like the tombstones that were dug up. We're each damaged in our own way, and still somewhat shell-shocked. It will take a long time before we can rebuild ourselves into a strong Jewish community again."

"How many other Polish Jewish cemeteries have undergone this type of resurrection?"

"I really don't know. There were hundreds before the war. Some were completely razed, while others were at least partly destroyed. There hasn't been enough money available to clean up and excavate so many of them. Why do you ask?"

"I'm thinking that excavation is my specialty," Klara replied. "Unearthing old broken things is my area of expertise— old broken Mayan artifacts, but old broken shards, nonetheless."

Klara suddenly felt the presence of someone else behind her. She turned around to see Filip Jablonski. "Filip? What are you doing here?" she asked, not able to hide the shock in her voice, despite the fact that she knew he would be in Krakow. He seemed less surprised to see her.

"I'm here for the festival. Remember, I told you my klezmer band would be performing?" he replied, sounding far more composed than she felt. "The same as you, I suppose." He looked past her, recognizing her cousin. "Nice to see you, Hanna," he said with a smile.

"You too, Filip." Hanna returned the pleasantry. "I guess you never know who you'll run into here."

"I guess not," he replied, forcing a grin as Klara began inching away.

"We were just about to leave," Klara said, barely looking at him, as she grabbed Hanna by the arm. Embarrassed and awkward, given the circumstances of their parting two nights earlier, she couldn't leave fast enough.

"Well, I hope to run into you again," he said. Hanna looked at him, and then back at Klara.

"Maybe," Klara said, practically running out of the cemetery.

# CHAPTER 16

Klara was so flustered from her run-in with Filip that she didn't even notice the bustling neighborhood around them. Finding herself babbling about it, she felt uncomfortable as she and Hanna made their way to their hotel in historic Kazimierz.

"What are you, a child?" Hanna finally asked, throwing her hands up in the air as they made their way through the throngs of people.

"No. Of course not," Klara declared, feeling that Hanna was no longer on her side.

"Well, you're acting like you're ten years old, and the boy you like just showed up uninvited to your bowling party."

"I never had a bowling party," Klara mumbled.

"That's not the point. The point is that he's allowed to be in a public place, and you knew he'd be in Krakow. You're acting really silly," Hanna said with exasperation. She looked over at Klara and asked more gently, "C'mon, what's really wrong?"

"Nothing." Klara opened the map of the old Jewish Quarter as they stood on a busy street corner.

"It's like you've never dated a man. Have you? Have you ever dated anyone, for that matter?" Hanna asked, peering at her cousin.

"Yes, of course I have," Klara replied sharply, tucking her hair behind her ear and folding the map. "I've dated men before."

"For how long?"

"I don't know. Maybe a month or two."

"A month or two?" Hanna asked, leaning in.

"Yes," Klara replied, starting to walk again. She hoped Hanna would drop the subject but found herself opening up more than she had planned to. "Well, they were mostly long-distance relationships or just flings, because I used to travel so often due to my work. I dated a colleague for a while. We were on a dig together in the Yucatán last year, just professionally, but we had dated some years earlier. He turned out to be more in love with himself than he could ever be with me or anyone else, and unfortunately, he didn't believe in monogamy," she added, irritated at the memory even after all these years.

"I really don't get it, Klara. You're almost fifty years old. You're smart. You're interesting. You're attractive . . . a bit uptight, but not completely. What's wrong with you that you won't allow people to get close to you?"

Klara's face turned red as she stared down at the cobblestones. "I don't like it when you talk to me that way, and frankly, I don't know that I want to discuss it any further."

An image of Jacob Herschler flashed before Klara. She knew that it had something to do with him, but she couldn't bring herself to explain it to Hanna now, if ever. Just thinking about him made her head hurt, and she said little for the rest of the trip to the hotel. Hanna took the hint.

By the time they had retrieved their luggage and arrived at the charming four-story townhouse that was Hotel Kazimierz, it was early evening. Klara was exhausted, and her head was now pounding. She wished that she could afford her own room, but it was cheaper to share one with Hanna, especially since the rates were higher than usual because of festival week. The only somewhat reasonably priced room they could get at the last minute was one with a queen-size bed. Klara was dismayed; not only would she have to share her room with Hanna, she would have to share a bed too. The hotel was not unlike Hotel Novotel Warszawa—a bit dark and dated, but with nicer details like ornate lamps, and bronze chandeliers on the ceilings. On the way to their room, they each picked up a Jewish Cultural Festival program in the lobby.

Klara set down her suitcase in the corner of the room, pulled back the mustard-yellow brocade bedspread, and fell onto the crisp white sheets, while Hanna went to wash up in the bathroom. While sitting up resting against the pillows, Klara flipped through the festival program. There were all sorts of Jewish music events from around the world—contemporary and traditional klezmer, Central Asian, Turkish, Persian, Israeli, jazz, and big band—combined with more well-known Jewish and Hasidic music fused with improvisational music. There were workshops focusing on klezmer, Jewish folk dances, and Yiddish songs; exhibitions and installations; graffiti workshops; and Jewish paper-cutting tutorials, among many other exciting and unique activities.

As Klara read about the tour to Remuh Cemetery, also known as the Old Cemetery, that she had just visited, her heart skipped a beat. Right there on page 23, under the heading "Jewish Cemetery Tours," Filip's name was listed: *Filip P. Jablonski, PhD*. It said he would be leading tours of the two Jewish cemeteries, both old and new, that had survived after the war: *Both cemeteries contain rare and beautiful models of sepulchral art. The art itself, the forms and the gravestones, and, most importantly, the way the deceased were buried can be traced through their transformation over the years. As such, one gets a unique view into the strong intellectual life of the Krakow Jews, states Dr. Jablonski.* Klara stopped reading and sat straight up on the bed, staring at the pamphlet.

"*Dr. Jablonski?*" She paused. "Hanna!"

Hanna ran out of the bathroom, still holding a towel.

"What's wrong?" she asked.

"Why didn't you tell me Filip has a PhD in Jewish and Holocaust studies?"

"I figured you knew. Why are you so upset?" Hanna looked relieved; the way Klara had screamed would make anyone think something was terribly wrong.

"Well, I didn't know. It would have been nice for some- one to have told me. He certainly didn't." Klara knew she was again being silly, even unreasonable, but she felt deceived.

"Why? Because if you'd known he was your cerebral and professional equal, you would have given him more of a chance?"

"That's not fair," Klara said, as she strewed her clothes all over the bed.

"Why in heavens are you so scared of him?" Hanna asked, genuinely bewildered. "He's a great guy, and no matter what you say, I can tell you like him."

"I'm not scared of him. He just makes me a bit nervous." She began pulling out her toiletries.

Hanna refused to let it go. "What is it about him that makes you nervous? He's not a scary guy. Quite the opposite— from what I've seen, he's a pretty gentle person. But whenever you're around him, you get so jumpy. Is it something about him, or is it about all men?"

Klara realized she was not going to get off easy this time. "I guess a lot of men make me nervous. I'm actually surprisingly comfortable around him, but the thought of him, and where things could lead, makes me very anxious."

"I don't understand why you wouldn't think you deserve a good man. I just don't get it, Klara." Hanna slipped her feet into a pair of ballet-style slip-ons and walked over to the mirror to apply some lipstick.

"You wouldn't get it. You grew up with two loving parents for much of your life. I'm sorry your dad passed away then, but you had him for all those years before that."

"You say that like it's a crime. Yes, I did have both my parents, but it seems to me there's something more here than your difficult mother and absent father. You're not being fair to either Filip or yourself because you don't know what you want. Don't waste your time, or his."

Klara stared at her blankly. Everything Hanna said was right, but it was forcing her to confront things she would rather avoid, and that was quite unsettling.

"I'm going to get a cup of coffee downstairs in the outdoor café," Hanna said. "You can come join me when you're ready, if you'd like."

After Hanna closed the door, Klara sat down on the hotel bed and shut her eyes.

Unbidden, Jacob Herschler's sweaty face appeared. She was vaguely aware that whenever she had to deal with issues related to getting close to a man, his face would suddenly pop into her head. Alone and exhausted, the terrible memories came flooding back. Her chest was tight, and her breathing became labored. Klara put her hands on her forehead and her elbows on her knees as the unwelcome memories pushed forth.

He was wearing a white button-down shirt with the collar open over an undershirt tucked into his black dress pants. He had taken off his tie earlier that evening and was patting his forehead with a pristine white handkerchief. Flinging off his laced shoes, he sat on their living room couch. "Oh, I could really use a good foot massage," he said, holding his back with one hand.

"Klara, go rub Jacob's feet," her mother said. Eleven-year-old Klara stood still, too terrified to move, while her mother pushed her in the direction of the couch where he sat. As she moved slowly, her stomach twisted and turned. She sat on the living room floor, reluctantly rubbing Jacob Herschler's damp, socked feet. They smelled like rotten eggs.

"Ahh," he exhaled. "That feels so good, Klara. You don't mind if I take off my socks, do you?" he asked in a syrupy voice that made her skin crawl.

Klara said nothing. She began to rub the dry, scaly skin of his heel, and then the arch, and finally his sole, trying to conceal her disgust and building nausea.

"How about the other one." It was a demand, rather than a question. "You're young. You can do it," he said, displaying a bone-chilling smile.

She was sure she detected a knowing "just between us" look when he said, "Thank you, Klara." Of all the things she had been forced to do for and to him, this was hardly the most demeaning. She suppressed a shudder.

At that thought, Klara forced herself out of her unbidden memories, determinedly banishing the disturbing memories by stroking her locket, which had become something of a talisman. Despite her fatigue, she got up from her hotel bed, washed her face, and changed into a loose, printed cotton blouse and a gauze peasant skirt. Resolving to live in the moment and not the past, she went outside to find Hanna.

Her cousin sat alone at a small outdoor café table, wearing sunglasses and drinking coffee. Klara joined her, motioning for the waiter to bring her a coffee too.

"Hi, Klara. I'm really glad you decided to come down," Hanna said. "I'm looking through the festival program and thought it would be fun to go to the concert at the Galicia Jewish Museum tonight. It's the opening of the festival. Did you know that it's now in its twenty-sixth year?" she asked, shaking her head. "I can't believe it's been that long."

"Sure, that sounds great," Klara replied, taking a deep

breath before continuing. "Look—let me explain something from earlier. There are some things in my past that are really hard for me to talk about. You're right. There is more to my story. I just don't like to discuss it, and one of the few people I tried to talk to was my mother, who simply dismissed what I had to say." Klara gazed at her coffee.

"I would never dismiss whatever you want to tell me about your life," Hanna said softly. "But you have to understand that getting to know each other and becoming a part of our family needs to be a two-way street. You can't just expect *us* to open up to *you*; you need to be prepared to do the same."

"I know, and you're absolutely right. I do appreciate your kindness, especially given our rough start. Please understand that it's really hard for me to discuss personal things." Klara took another deep breath. "There was a creepy man in my childhood, a friend of my mother and grandfather. His name was Jacob Herschler.

"They thought he could do no wrong. It was as if he were a god to them. He was the person responsible for getting my father out of Poland during the war, oddly enough. I'm not sure how much your mother has told you," Klara said, backtracking in her narrative to fill in some of the blanks for Hanna. "Your mother probably shared the basic gist. During the war, Herschler bribed Polish officials so that twenty young Jewish men could escape. My father was one of them. Jacob's payback was community honor, and for these young men to work for him at his factory in New York for years. That's how my parents met—my grandfather was Herschler's good friend, and he introduced my parents. He also supposedly tried to rescue some German Jews as well, but I don't know as much about that."

Repeating this history aloud made Klara angry, and her voice suddenly rose in the small courtyard. "He was slimy and horrible!" she exclaimed, furiously shaking her head.

"Are you okay?" Hanna reached across the table and put a hand on her shoulder.

"I'm okay," she replied. "I just don't like thinking about or talking about him." She shrugged and cradled her head in her arms.

"We don't need to talk about it any further right now, if you don't want to," Hanna said gently, putting a hand over Klara's. Klara didn't need much convincing; she had already revealed more about her past than she had to anyone, except her wise and trusted Mayan friend, Rosario, from her time in the Yucatán.

The bright orange sun was slowly setting, although there was still perhaps an hour of light left. "Let's go somewhere," suggested Klara. They quickly finished their coffees and stood. "Maybe we can talk more later, but now I just want to see more of this beautiful city."

After again consulting the festival program, they decided to go to the Israeli music concert closing a service at the Galicia Jewish Museum, following a quick dinner. On the way there, they passed a phone booth with a life-size black-and-white poster advertising the festival. It showed an Orthodox man dressed in a white shirt tucked into black slacks, a black hat, and sporting sidelocks and *tzitzit*, specially knotted tassels hanging from the waist worn by highly observant men.

"Look at that." Klara laughed. "It's wonderful—bold and unapologetic." Revealing even that small part of her story had taken somewhat of a load off her shoulders, allowing her to appreciate this experience and recognize the freedom that Jews, who were once oppressed, now enjoyed in Poland.

When they arrived at the concert, the room was crowded, with a group of casually dressed Israeli teens sitting on the floor, and many others seated in folding chairs. Before long, Klara and Hanna were swaying to the rhythm with the rest

of the crowd. Both the service and singing were primarily in
Hebrew, and although she knew very little of the language, she
hummed along. Hanna told Klara that the red-haired woman
leading the congregation in song was a rabbi from Russia, by
way of Israel. She sang as they moved their heads to the beat
of the music played by three male instrumentalists.

Klara smiled as her body gently swayed to the music.
She felt free and unburdened, and it felt good, although
unfamiliar. She was moved that so many people had gathered in this rather small section of the city for the same
purpose—to celebrate Jewish life—and here she was with
her newfound cousin doing the same. Although she wasn't
alone, it was still hard not to keep a wall up between herself
and everyone else, but she was consciously trying to just be
in the moment.

Following the crowd leaving the service, Klara stopped
at the gift shop, promising Hanna that she would only be
a few minutes. She picked out four silver necklaces bearing
the Star of David, one for each new female relative—Hanna,
Rachel, and Rebeka—and one for herself. She stuffed the
paper bag in her pocketbook, smiling on her way out the
door. After she found Hanna, they headed toward the door,
but just before they reached it, she saw Filip out of the corner
of her eye, surrounded by friends. He waved, and she waved
back. Klara realized that she did want to talk to him, but this
was clearly not a good time or place. Her conversations with
Hanna had made her recognize that she was being childish,
and that she at least owed him an apology for a few nights
earlier. That was what she told herself, but a thought had
lodged in the back of her mind: What if Hanna was right,
and she should give him another chance?

When she got back to the hotel that evening, Klara
thought of her good friend and Holbrook College colleague,
Sheila, and recalled that she owed her another email.

*Hi, Sheila,*
*I just wanted you to know since I last wrote to you I've met my father's sister and her family. I'm actually now in Krakow with my cousin Hanna. I also met a man I really like, but it's confusing. I'm not sure how long I'll be staying for, but I'll tell you when I know more.*
> *Talk soon,*
> *Klara*

# CHAPTER 17

Klara awoke early the next morning and lay in bed obsessing over the fact that Filip was giving a tour of Remuh Cemetery in a few short hours. She thought again about her discussion with Hanna the day before and was confused. *Am I really afraid of all men? And what about Filip—am I afraid of him too? Afraid he might like me? Afraid I might like him too much, and then he'd reject me?* It dawned on her just how silly she was being. It was time for her to confront him, if only to answer her own questions.

"Hanna, wake up." Klara put her hand on Hanna's back and nudged her.

"What time is it?" Hanna grunted.

"The tour at Remuh Cemetery is in an hour. We need to hurry if we're going to make it." Klara wanted to see Filip, but not by herself.

"Maybe you can go without me. I think I'm going to sleep in," Hanna mumbled, rolling over.

"You can't. I need you there," she said, shaking Hanna's shoulder. She had already pulled out clothes—both hers and Hanna's—from the closet and tossed them on the bed.

"Why can't you go by yourself? I can meet up with you afterward."

"Filip's giving a tour of the cemetery, and I need you there for moral support. Please?"

With half-opened eyes, Hanna asked, "Are you begging me to come?"

"Yes, I'm begging you to come," Klara replied, her hands together in prayer position. She sat on the edge of the bed next to Hanna, who was still lying down. "Please come. I can't do this without you."

Hanna sat up, brushing her disheveled brunette and gray curls away from her face. "You *can* do this without me, but I'll go with you. If I go with you, though, you *have* to talk to him. You can't play games. He deserves better than that, and so do you," she added, throwing off her blanket and standing up.

"I know," Klara said, biting her lip. "Thank you."

"Look," Hanna continued as she started getting dressed. "You'll take one step at a time, and you'll see how it goes. You're both good people. It will be okay, whatever happens."

After dressing hurriedly and grabbing coffee from the hotel café, they arrived at Remuh Cemetery at exactly eleven o'clock, when the tour was to begin. About fifty people were already there, and standing before them was Filip, in front of the mosaic Wailing Wall and the five-hundred-year-old tombstones. The crowd's murmuring ceased as he introduced himself.

"Good morning, everyone. Thank you for coming. I'm Dr. Jablonski, and I will be giving you a tour today of Krakow's oldest cemetery. It's quite special and has a tremendous history, starting with the wall on my right, built from former Jewish tombstones."

Filip continued relaying many of the interesting facts that Hanna had told her yesterday, but Klara found that she was having trouble concentrating on his words. Rather, she watched him speak, clearly displaying his expertise. He had a confident but relaxed air, and the crowd listened attentively. She surreptitiously examined him from the back of the group; she had never seen him dressed up before, and as this was a professional occasion, he'd taken more care with his appearance than she was used to. Instead of looking a bit disheveled as was usual, he was neatly dressed, and his slightly long, light-brown locks were neatly brushed to one side and placed behind his ears. He wore a tailored navy-blue blazer over a white button-down shirt, tucked into dark jeans with a black belt and black-laced boots. His green eyes were congenial and welcoming, but she felt they could pierce right through her. Standing there, she could take in his full six-foot height and broad build.

Klara smiled. Once again, she noticed his good looks. *He's handsome*, she thought, not for the first time, as her stomach jumped. Something was different this time. Klara felt a definite attraction to him. *Maybe he's too handsome. He probably thinks I'm plain.* She knew she shouldn't think that way, but she couldn't help it.

After a fifty-minute tour of the cemetery, Filip took questions from the crowd. Once the last tourist had drifted away, he walked over to Klara and Hanna.

"That was a really interesting talk," Hanna said after they'd exchanged greetings.

"Thank you. I love this cemetery. Of course, there is much sadness here," he said, pointing to the Wailing Wall. "But there is much rich history too."

"I know," Klara said, unable to stop herself. "I was telling Hanna just yesterday that this wall is amazing. To me, it symbolizes our unity as a Jewish people. It tells the world that even if they break us, we will emerge stronger through our bond together." Her nerves were causing her to speak very quickly.

Filip looked at her. "Yes," he said, "that's right. That's how I see it too. I'm really glad you both came," he added, glancing at Hanna as well.

Klara asked him some questions about sepulchral designs on specific gravestones, which he took his time to answer. "These pictorial designs are specific to the six-teenth-century period." He pointed to the carefully engraved motif, but his explanation was cut short when a few friends approached him.

"Filip, there you are," a tall dark-haired man said, pat-ting him on the back. "Good job. We're going to get some lunch, and then we have practice for tonight."

"These are the other members of my klezmer band," Filip said by way of introduction to Klara and Hanna. "Hey, why don't you come with us for lunch?"

His friends agreed, one saying, "Sure, why don't you join us?"

Hanna looked at Klara, who nodded in agreement. The two women joined the group at the café, where Filip's band-mates were friendly and talkative. Everyone was drinking beer and joining in, and Klara felt herself relaxing.

Filip turned to Klara. "So, can you come tonight, you and Hanna? You could watch us perform and maybe dance a little."

"I'd love to," replied Hanna, "but I really need to catch a train back to Warsaw this evening. I have to work tomorrow."

"How about you, Klara?" Filip put her on the spot.

"I don't know," she replied, her nervousness returning as she looked at Hanna. Filip frowned.

Hanna regarded the two of them. "What the heck!" she exclaimed. "I'll call Alek and tell him I'm staying one more night. I'll leave early tomorrow, and get to work by noon."

"Great," Klara and Filip said in unison.

"By the way," Klara began, lowering her voice. "I'm really sorry about how our last outing ended. I just wigged out on you. It wasn't fair."

"You're forgiven," Filip said with a smile.

She had made an active decision not to question him about why he hadn't mentioned his PhD to her. The timing was wrong.

❋ ❋ ❋

When they returned to their hotel room, Klara thanked Hanna again, as she had done on their walk back. "That was really nice of you. You didn't have to do that for me."

"I thought I could help, and *now* you owe me," Hanna said with a wink.

But Klara knew that was just her way. She really did feel very grateful to Hanna and was beginning to feel more and more that she could trust herself. She had thoroughly enjoyed this morning with her cousin and meeting up with Filip. She was excited about seeing him again later this evening.

As she lay down on her side of the hotel bed to rest for an hour, wondering if she was ready to open herself up to someone, she fell into a deep, dream-filled sleep . . .

In this dream, she was very young, and her father still lived with them. She felt light and happy. She wore a red, flouncy dress with a big bow on the back, and shiny black patent leather Mary Janes. Oh, how she loved her shiny black Mary Janes! Her father had just come home from work and still wore his suit and tie. He put down his fedora and looked at her, laughing. "There's my girl," he said as he opened his arms wide, squatting down to her level. As soon as Klara saw him, she gave him a big smile and ran into his arms. She loved his hugs, which were warm and firm. He gave the best hugs. "Papa!" she squealed with joy.

When she awoke to the sound of the alarm clock at five o'clock, she was smiling but couldn't remember anything except her father's hug. Her arms were wrapped around her chest, and she was rocking herself back and forth, recreating the feeling of warmth, love, and security.

"Klara, it's time to get up if we're going to get a bite to eat before the concert," Hanna called from behind the partly closed bathroom door. Klara could hear the sink water running.

While Hanna showered, Klara sorted through her clothes, finding little except for jeans, shorts, and the one skirt she had already worn that morning. She looked at her tops and knew exactly what this occasion called for: the huipil blouse given to her by Rosario and the other Mayan women as a parting gift before she left the Yucatán many months before. She had thrown it into her bag when she packed for Poland but hadn't yet worn it. With its bright colorful yarn and geometric patterns, her date of birth woven into the fabric, it was the most special garment she owned. Maybe wearing it tonight would give her the additional courage she needed. It had been months since she'd said goodbye to Rosario and her family. A part of her felt melancholy, as though she had left a piece of herself behind in the Yucatán.

Instead of dwelling on her sadness, she stared admiringly at the blouse. Realizing it was getting late, she quickly showered and got ready, paying more attention to her appearance than usual. She brushed out her long, wet hair with care, allowing it to hang loosely, and put a touch of perfume on her wrists and behind her ears.

She looked in the mirror and studied the image staring back at her. She saw a somewhat plain but not unattractive woman with slightly hunched shoulders. She forced herself to stand straighter, something her mother was always yelling at her about, noting that she then looked her full five feet, seven inches. Her dark, wet, temporarily straight hair would soon dry to a wavy light brown. She generally refrained from analyzing her appearance too closely, but noted her high cheekbones, smooth, creamy skin, and large blue eyes.

Noticing the laugh lines around her eyes and mouth, Klara could not deny the fact that she was aging.

"What a beautiful blouse!" Hanna exclaimed, finishing her own preparations.

"It was a gift from Rosario and some other friends in Mexico."

"Would you like to borrow some lipstick, since we're going out for the evening? It would brighten your face a bit."

"I'm not really the makeup kind," Klara demurred.

"I've noticed. Maybe you could just try it and see what you think?"

Klara accepted Hanna's offer and applied a light coral color to her lips, which picked up the colors in her blouse.

"Now I have something for *you*, Hanna," Klara said, remembering her purchases from the other day. She took out one of the silver chains with the Star of David pendant she had bought at the Galicia Jewish Museum's gift shop the other night. She was already wearing hers, along with her longer gold locket, and pointed to it as she handed the gift to her cousin.

"I love it!" Hanna exclaimed as she opened the clasp and placed it around her neck.

"I have one for your mother and one for Rebeka too," Klara said softly. "I saw them and thought they symbolized our finding each other and our connection."

"That was really thoughtful of you." Hanna smiled and hugged her cousin, and they walked arm in arm out the door.

As they left their hotel, Klara noticed they each had their own individual style—while Hanna was dressed simply, in a tailored above-the-knee skirt, short-sleeve blouse, and a scarf, Klara wore her beautiful loose-fitting handmade tunic and light, unstructured pants.

After sitting down to dinner, they raised their glasses in unison with the chardonnay the waiter had poured for them.

"To us," Hanna said.

"To us," Klara repeated, smiling.

"I have to say, I never thought we'd get to this point in our relationship. And so soon! You surprised me," Hanna said.

"And you, me!" Klara agreed. They both laughed.

"Honestly, I didn't know if I could trust you about why you suddenly showed up when you did, but I was also jealous of you."

"Why would you be jealous of me?" Klara's eyes opened wide, as this was the last thing she would have expected her cousin to say. If anything, it was the opposite.

Hanna looked into the distance for a moment before responding. "For years, my mother wistfully talked about the day she would finally meet you, her brother's daughter. I knew she loved me, but I also knew you had something I could never have— a direct connection to the family she grew up with and lost far too soon."

Klara let the words sink in, finally understanding Hanna's initial mistrust and curtness. She realized she had only been thinking about what she personally had been missing all those years, rather than considering her aunt's tremendous loss and what the sudden appearance of her brother's daughter would mean for all of them. Of course, Hanna would have mixed feelings toward her.

Hanna looked back at her. "Don't get me wrong. I'm honestly glad you came—glad for my mother, and now even glad for myself," she added with a grin.

"Why did you decide to stay in Krakow tonight?" Klara asked as she looked directly at her cousin.

"Because I wanted to be here for you. I think maybe you could have a nice thing with Filip, and I want you to give him a chance. I was worried you'd run away again if I left, and I figured a little moral support couldn't hurt. Either way, I now know you'll be okay on your own. You're much stronger and tougher than I originally thought. I guess you have to be, to do all the solo traveling you've done. More importantly, you're much stronger than you think you are."

Klara exhaled. "I guess I am." She laughed. "But I still have a lot to learn. You've made me think about a number of things in a different way and confront some really difficult issues — like trusting others, especially trusting a man. I can't thank you enough for that. Thank you again for coming with me to Krakow, even if it was your mother's idea." She touched Hanna's elbow.

They both giggled and hugged one another.

By the time they finished dinner, it was dark, and the streets were filled with people heading to bars, restaurants, and clubs. They walked the few blocks to the club where Filip's klezmer band would be playing. Once inside the crowded room, they were escorted to a table in front that Filip had saved for them. But when the band started playing, the patrons pushed the tables to the side, creating a makeshift dance floor where couples and small groups eagerly gathered to dance. Filip had a few solos on his violin, as did the clarinetist, trumpeter, and flutist. He couldn't have looked happier, clearly in his element.

At one point, he took a break from playing, jumped off the stage, and grabbed Klara's hand, twirling her around the dance floor. Before she could think, she joined in, focusing on the beat as Filip took the lead. For the moment, she didn't have a care in the world.

# CHAPTER 18

Hanna had returned to the hotel well before Filip and the others had finished performing, as she needed a good night's sleep before traveling back to Warsaw and work the next morning. As Klara had no plans for the following day, she pushed aside any anxiety about being alone with Filip and stayed until almost closing time, enjoying listening and dancing to his klezmer band at the local café-turned-nightclub. She was finally all right with Hanna leaving, even though she didn't believe she could have gone without her earlier that evening. After he finished the performance, Filip quickly packed up his violin, steering Klara out the door before she could protest. The two walked the busy streets of Kazimierz together, accompanied by other late-night pub crawlers still out having fun.

Klara's long, wavy hair blew in the breeze, along with her huipil blouse. She felt unfettered, like she could do anything, maybe even stay in Poland. She was smiling more than usual, and if asked, would actually have said she was happy. It felt good being with Filip on this warm summer night; she was relaxed and comfortable in his presence. She glanced over and observed that, in the light of the full moon, he looked very handsome in his well-fitted black jeans and rolled-up shirtsleeves.

And he was staring at her. "That blouse you're wearing looks very special. The embroidery is beautiful."

"It was a gift from a group of Mayan friends of mine in the Yucatán, particularly one special friend. They made it for me as a parting gift using my birthday symbols and their village's colors and geometric patterns," she explained, pointing out the details. "It's very meaningful to me," she added, gently rubbing the fabric with her fingers.

"I can see why. They must have really wanted to show you how much you meant to them."

"Yes, I think they did," she replied, glowing as she thought of Rosario and the others. This was the first gift someone had given her in a long while, and it was certainly the most special one.

"Do you think you might go back there sometime?" he asked.

"I think so. If you had asked me a year ago, I would have said definitely. At that point, I was seriously considering settling there in the near future, and getting a teaching job at a Mexican university, but the timing didn't seem right, so I went back home to Maine to continue teaching there. I love the place and the people. I was beginning to really feel at home there, but being here makes me question all that. This feels like a place I truly belong." Klara realized she was speaking out loud the thoughts that had just taken root in her mind these last several days.

"How so?" Filip asked.

"I don't know how to explain it in words. It just does," she said, looking up at him. He smiled.

The conversation was getting heavy, and Klara wasn't ready to go any further—at least not yet. Changing the subject, she said, "Enough about me, I want to hear more about you. When did you get your doctorate in Holocaust studies? Was it after you learned your mother was Jewish?"

"It was," he replied, looking into her eyes. "When I finally learned, I had only a short time left with my mother before she died. I longed to be closer to that part of her and to know more about her family's experiences as Jews. I quit my day job and dove into a doctoral program. It was like a switch inside me was suddenly turned on."

"Why didn't you tell me before?"

"I'm not really sure. Maybe I didn't want it to matter either way. It was silly of me. I should have."

Filip's intense gaze was too much for Klara. She looked away and turned the conversation back to the cemetery they had visited earlier that day. "Are there other Wailing Walls made of broken tombstones like the one in Remuh Cemetery?"

"We hope to build more like it," he said. "There are certainly many uncared-for Jewish cemeteries in disrepair with broken stones, just waiting for someone to rebuild them. Why, do you want to help?" he asked, both teasing and curious as he dangled the handle of his violin case from one hand.

"Well, now that you mention it, I'm starting to feel like I might want to stay here longer and see more. It feels like the broken tombstones are somehow calling to me. Does that sound weird?" she asked, pausing for his response.

Before he could answer, a man and woman in their mid-thirties passed them, arguing loudly. They stopped, appearing lost, the man slightly off-balance and slurring his words. "You stupid bitch!" he screamed at the woman. "You don't know how to read a map. We're just walking in circles."

Klara stopped too; the man was tall and large, while the woman was petite and no match for his anger. Klara's stomach lurched, and before she could think, she heard herself speaking. "Excuse me," she said in a strong, clear voice to the woman in English, ignoring the man. "Do you need help? Are you all right?"

The woman, whom Klara guessed was a tourist, seemed to understand her. Clutching her map, she replied in English nervously, "Thank you, but I'm fine. Our hotel is right up the street. My boyfriend just had a bit too much to drink," she added, grabbing his hand.

"What did you say?" the red-faced man yelled at her. "I didn't have too much to drink, you bitch. You're just too stupid to know how to get back to the hotel."

"Are you sure you are all right?" Klara persisted, staring at the woman, trying to ignore the man.

"Who the hell are you, girly?" the man demanded, attempting to approach Klara but instead swaying from side to side, as though he might fall down.

Stepping between Klara and the man, Filip yelled, "Don't talk to her like that!" He dropped his violin case and grabbed the man's arm, his temper flaring. The man tried to free himself from his grip, but Filip wouldn't let go.

"No, really, we're fine. Our hotel is just that way," the woman insisted, pointing up the street. "We'll be fine. Thank you. Really," she said quickly, taking her boyfriend's other arm and dragging him off before things could escalate further.

As they walked away, Klara heard the man protesting, saying something incomprehensible. She stood still by the side of the dark cobblestone street, watching until the couple was out of sight, as though her sandals were glued to the sidewalk. Filip's violin case lay open on the ground from the force of being dropped so quickly.

"Klara," Filip said softly, gently putting his hands on her shoulders and looking into her eyes. "Are you okay?"

She didn't immediately respond, standing like a frozen statue for a few moments. He began to rub her shoulders with his hands, as if to help thaw her. She took a deep breath and shivered. "They're gone," she said, as though confirming that fact, looking down the road for any sign of them.

"They're gone," Filip replied reassuringly.

Her eyes watered. "I hate nasty men. They make me physically ill. I feel sick," she said, holding her stomach, overwhelmed with how she reacted to the strangers' altercation and worried about what Filip might think of her. *The situation was bad, but it didn't warrant this intense a reaction. What must he think of me? He doesn't know about my ugly history. If he did, he'd understand.*

But Filip surprised her. Under a streetlamp, he put his arms around her, embracing her. "You're safe now. That guy was a mean drunk, and you were trying to help the woman. You did a good thing by speaking up. Now it's over," he said, rubbing her back gently as she started to tremble. It wasn't yet over for her; sometimes she thought it never would be. He hugged her tighter. "It's okay. They're really gone. It's okay now."

"But it's not okay," Klara said, shaking her head back and forth. "It will never be okay."

"What do you mean?" he asked, dropping his hands to her arms so he could face her. He seemed confused at the intensity of her reaction and concerned about just how upset she was.

"There will always be men like that who treat women badly and make us feel afraid. I've known men like that," she replied. Her mind jumped to the memory of Jacob Herschler's abuse, and she began rubbing her gold pendant between her fingers.

Filip took Klara's hands gently. "Well, I'm not one of them," he said, looking directly into her eyes. He put an arm around her shoulders.

"I know," she replied, tears running down her cheeks, her body folding into his. As he embraced her again, Klara allowed her muscles to release into the comfort of his strong, firm arms. In that moment, she felt like she was home. She turned her face to his; as their lips brushed, her body tingled, and she tugged him closer, kissing him fiercely.

"I don't want to go back to my hotel yet," she whispered, surprised by her audacity and sudden passion, especially after what had just occurred.

He pulled away and looked at her, in a soft voice asking, "What do you want?"

"I want to be with you right now. Just the two of us."

"Okay," he said, smiling, as he picked up his violin case, checking that the instrument was still in one piece and closing the cover. He took her hand, holding it firmly in his own. "Are you sure you're okay?" he asked, clearly concerned. "We can keep walking or go back to my hotel. No one's there."

Klara squeezed his hand in response, allowing him to lead her back to his hotel. Although she'd felt shaken minutes before, her body had experienced a complete turnaround. Her heart thumped, and she felt as though she were one with the night, becoming more attuned to its darkness and distinct sounds. She heard an owl hoot in the distance and could feel the warm summer air on her skin as she lightly perspired. The stars looked brighter, and the moon appeared to be a more intense shade of yellow. She knew that right now, she wanted more than anything to be with this man. She could let her guard down with him, at least for tonight. Desire took over, and she would deal with the consequences tomorrow.

As soon as they entered his room, they began passionately kissing and undressing one another. Hours later, Filip fell asleep first. Klara put her hand on his warm chest, feeling the rhythm of his breath. She sat up on her elbow, leaning her head in her hand, and began outlining his naked body with her fingers. He smelled like sweat, sex, cologne, and cigarettes. She thought that in the darkness, he looked a little like Michelangelo's *David*, with beautiful lines and well-defined muscles.

When was the last time she'd lain in bed beside a man she really liked? It had certainly been a while. And now here she was, lying beside this man.

She wondered if she was capable of doing this, of having a relationship with him. As she lay back down and drifted off to sleep, she couldn't stop thinking how he was everything she wanted: strong, caring, smart, interesting, and good-looking to boot.

A few hours later, Klara woke up, immediately realizing that she had forgotten to call Hanna. *Shit. She's going to be worried about me.* Filip heard her moving about the room and sat up. "What's wrong?" he asked.

"I'm so stupid. I forgot to call Hanna. She's going to be up soon and wonder where I am," she said with panic in her voice.

"Come back to bed," he said soothingly. "I already called her hotel's front desk last night and left a message for her that you're with me. You don't need to worry."

Klara relaxed, pulling Filip's button-down shirt over her naked body before lying down again. He reached over, gently guiding her back under the covers with him and holding her in his arms. "And you are the furthest thing from stupid . . . you're perfect. You're perfect for me."

Klara instinctively softened with him, aware that, for once, she wasn't protesting or trying to leave. Instead of second-guessing his words or motives, she pressed her back against his muscular chest and happily fell back to sleep.

When she next awoke, the first rays of sunlight were pouring into the hotel room through a gap between the heavy brocade curtains. Filip was nowhere in sight, but he walked into the room just as Klara was starting to get dressed, carrying two cups of coffee.

He smiled as he placed hers on the dresser.

"Good morning to you," he said with a slight appreciative grin, trying not to openly leer but enjoying watching her dress.

"And to you," Klara replied, also smiling.

Filip set his coffee cup down as well, reaching out to Klara, and embraced her while kissing her lips. He made her feel like this wasn't just a one-night fling, like he cared and wanted to be with her. *Just enjoy it*, she told herself.

A few moments later, Filip said, "If you're really interested in learning more about the artifacts of the Polish Jewish people, especially what's left of the synagogues and cemeteries, then you have to see the photographs hanging on the walls of the Galicia Museum where the concert was held on Sunday night."

"Weren't parts of southeastern Poland and southwestern Ukraine, where a lot of Jews used to live, called Galicia?" she replied, searching under the bed for her left shoe.

"Yes, the Jews were the third-largest ethnic group living there before the Second World War. The museum's photographs are a must-see. They make me think about what life must have been like for my mother and her parents—going to synagogue and living in a *shtetl* [a small Jewish village], and then how they were not only murdered, but never even given a proper burial."

Filip continued talking, growing more animated as he shared his knowledge. "There are photographs of decimated synagogues and Jewish cemeteries, most with only a few broken walls or tombstones left over. They depict a mixture of beauty and destruction—something that was once sacred, annihilated by unspeakable horror. They are haunting, to say the least," Filip explained with intensity.

"I'm so sorry, Filip. I'm sorry for you and I'm sorry for me, and for all those like us whose family members were massacred."

He stood there in silence, deep in thought. Klara reached out and put her arm around his neck. He still said nothing but nodded. She could see tears in his eyes, and her eyes began to tear as well.

They fell back onto the bed, holding each other tightly.

"You know," Klara said between kisses, "last night you said something that stuck with me. You said I was perfect. But I'm not perfect," she said adamantly, looking at him while waiting for an answer, but wishing he'd say it again.

"No one's perfect, Klara," he replied as he stroked her side.

He buried his face in her neck, inhaling her scent.

"You seem pretty perfect. You seem so sure of yourself," she said defensively.

Looking surprised, he stared straight at her. "I am sure of myself in some ways. I know what I want, and I try to follow that, but I still have a lot that I'm figuring out. You, actually, are fierce."

"Fierce?" Klara queried, echoing the word, as though she were trying it on for size.

"You could have walked away last night when that couple was arguing, but you stood your ground instead. I'd call that fierce."

They were seated next to one another on the bed now. She leaned over to the bedside table and took a sip of her coffee. "I don't like seeing women being pushed around. I never want to be pushed around again, and I will never just stand by or keep my mouth shut when I see it happening to someone else," she said, louder than she had intended.

He leaned over, putting his hands around her face and kissing her before pulling back to gaze at her. His stare was almost too much for her. She began nervously rubbing the gold locket hanging from her neck, mindlessly opening and closing it.

Standing up, Filip opened the curtains for more light. "Can I take another look at the photos inside?" he asked, coming closer to Klara and squinting in order to see better, as he held the locket in his hand.

He looked back and forth from the small black-and-white photos to Klara. "You look like him," Filip said, looking up at her and affectionately touching her cheek. "You have similarly shaped eyes and lips and the same mischievous smile as your father."

"Mischievous smile, huh? My aunt Rachel just said that to me the other day, but she was the first. Nobody has ever said it before," she replied, jokingly elbowing him.

"Maybe that's because we bring it out in you," he replied with a huge grin. She smiled, but even as she did, she could feel the light, carefree atmosphere slipping though her fingers. Her mind wandered back to last night when the drunken man had verbally accosted her. It made her uneasy and nervous now, just as it had then. But instead of feeling overwhelmed and frozen by these emotions, she was able to soothe herself by focusing on Filip.

"You do," Klara replied. "You really do." She wasn't alone anymore, she reminded herself. She had people in her life who cared about her—like her good friends Sheila and Rosario, and now Rachel and Hanna, and perhaps Filip too. She knew it would take a while for this new truth to sink in, but for the moment, she would allow herself to enjoy it. That reminded her to call Hanna, as she would be returning to Warsaw that morning. But that could wait until later.

# CHAPTER 19

K lara's hotel was on the way to Dajwor Street, the home of the Galicia Museum. They stopped there so she could shower and change. Hanna had left a note for Klara that she grabbed so only she could read it.

> Dear Klara,
> Hope you had a good evening. I had to leave first thing this morning to catch an early train before dawn. Call me in the next day or so.
> Enjoy yourself! I'm happy for you.
> Hanna

Filip discreetly asked no questions.

The Galicia Jewish Museum was essentially a large, spacious room that had once served as a Jewish-owned furniture factory. The permanent exhibit was titled "Traces of Memory." Klara was immediately struck by photograph upon photograph displaying the remnants of a forgotten world that had once existed but was now only remembered in the minds of a few and captured in these pictures as evidence of what was formerly there.

There were many photographs of long-forgotten synagogues and old Jewish tombstones, along with photographs of present-day visitors marching in memory of those who perished in the gas chambers of Auschwitz. It was all a tribute to the region's strong Jewish heritage and the many Jewish people who were killed on its soil, simply for being Jewish.

Klara was drawn to a particular photograph of traditional Jewish gravestones in an unusually well-preserved Polish Galician cemetery. It was located in a small southeastern town near the Ukrainian border called Lubaczow. The gravestones were elaborately carved, displaying a rich Jewish tradition. They contained highly literary, poetic texts in elegant Hebrew lettering praising the moral virtues of the deceased, along with pictorial images of animals, birds, flowers, fruit, and ritual objects. Klara felt drawn by the carvings, as though she were being mystically beckoned to another time and place. Her pulse beat faster, and she knew she must discover more about the people who designed these intricate tombstones and those they were made for. When she realized they were somehow her people, she felt a rush of emotion, and without thinking, reached for Filip's hand, squeezing it tightly. Once she loosened her grip, he raised her hand to his lips and kissed it.

"The lion is evocative of strength of character and commitment to moral virtue," Filip said, pointing to the tombstones' details. "It's commonly found on Jewish tombstones of this period and represents the human face. The candlestick represents female virtue as women light the Sabbath candles. It also symbolizes the tranquility women bring to the home," he explained.

"The animal and nature symbols look so much like some of the symbols on many of the Mayan vases I've studied. It's like we're all drawn to the same things when it comes down to it. Whether you're Jewish or Mayan, or probably any other culture, animals and nature represent an everlasting connection with the universe," Klara contemplated aloud.

She leaned closer and studied the photograph further, analyzing its detail. "You know, it's amazing how people today, and over many hundreds and thousands of years that preceded us, are so much more the same than they are different. And yet the Nazis led a crusade of destruction based on highlighting all our differences."

Filip listened, nodding his head in agreement. They continued to look at more photographs, holding hands through the gallery. There were multiple photos of dark gray, cracked and weathered gravestones, either partly or fully slanted on what appeared to be desolate hilltops, and others with only a handful or no tombstones left standing, with just stumps and foundation remaining. Klara stared at the images, feeling sad and horrified by the destruction and desolation.

"Here is more evidence that Jews once lived in these small villages and market towns in Galicia," Filip said, leading Klara to other photos depicting better-tended gravestones. "It's actually quite surprising that some of these cemeteries are in unusually decent condition, despite not having any local Jewish community to care for them."

Klara stopped in front of a photograph in which a field of orange-brown dirt encircled a small group of green trees clumped together, with a blue sky in the background. "What's this?" she asked, pointing to the picture while turning to Filip.

"There are areas like this around the Galician countryside where a few trees are left to grow by themselves in the middle of farmland a short distance from a village. The trees mark the site of the former local Jewish cemetery. Even though all the Jewish gravestones disappeared a long time ago, in the minds of the local villagers, it remains a burial site, and they leave it undisturbed," he said, looking from the photo to Klara, who was enthralled by his explanation.

"I'd like to visit this place," Klara said, continuing to stare at the photo. It says it's called 'Stary Dzikow.' I want to see it for myself," she repeated, closing her eyes tightly as though she were trying to burn the image into her mind. She couldn't explain it to Filip, or even to herself, but she somehow felt that this was the reason she was meant to stay in Poland. "I feel like it's calling to me to come witness it, and then to do something more, like maybe put up some kind of memorial plaque. Does that sound crazy?" she asked, staring at him.

"No," Filip said, gazing at her. "It doesn't sound crazy at all. We can go. It's about two and a half hours away by car."

Klara wrapped her arms around Filip, hugging him tightly. "Thank you," she said, again marveling at his kindness and how he had walked into her life. And that much to her surprise, she had let him stay, at least for now.

❖ ❖ ❖

In the museum's gift shop, Klara noticed a hardcover book with the photo of the elaborately carved tombstones that she had just seen. It was titled *It Is the Stones That Tell the Story*. Lifting the book from its display, she shivered. It somehow represented the embodiment of her personal and professional journey, as an archaeologist, a Jew, and a woman with her own history of personal suffering and pain.

"It is the stones that tell the story," she said aloud.

"What is it you're saying?" asked Filip, walking over to her.

"It is the stones that tell the story, just like in other fallen cultures we study as a part of history. It's as though these are the recovered stones of a lost people, but many of these stones were never buried. They were left here in fairly recent history. There was no need to unbury them, as the people who watched over them were killed in the light of day only seventy years ago." Tears began rolling down Klara's face, the sadness of the Holocaust overwhelming her. Filip carefully wiped her tears away with his thumbs, remaining quiet as she digested all that was in front of her.

"These photos are all so sad," she continued, looking around at the exhibit after regaining control of her emotions. "They seem to say that this is all that's left of the Jewish Galician people who once lived here. They were here for hundreds of years, until they were systematically murdered, practically over just a few short years. Now they're gone, with no family left to care for their gravestones or even remember them. We must be the ones to care for what's left of their culture, Filip, their stones and what's left of what were once well-tended cemeteries. It's our duty—we must be the ones to take on this task," she repeated.

"Yes, we must," Filip agreed, surprising Klara. "Let's see. Today is Tuesday. We can go to Stary Dzikow on Thursday. I just have to give another tour tomorrow, and then we can go."

"How do you do it?" Klara asked, stopping in her tracks and gazing at him in wonder.

"How do I do what?" he replied, confused.

"Work in the cemetery day after day, logging the dead and looking up genealogical information for visitors. How do you work among all those gravestones? Doesn't it ever bother you? Doesn't it depress you?"

"No, actually, I feel the opposite effect. I feel a strange sense of peace, along with a driving purpose each day when I go to work. Much like what you just said, I feel like I'm keeping the names of those who were buried there alive through their memory and paying respect to their tombstones by making sure the weeds are taken away," he explained with a pensive expression. "Like you said," he repeated, "I feel like it's become my duty to keep their memory alive, especially since there are so few others willing or available to do so."

"But doesn't it bother you? The memories that lie there,

like the anonymous mass graves of so many Jews who were killed during the Holocaust?"

"It bothers me every single moment of every single day, but it would bother me more not to be involved in perpetuating their memory. Isn't that how you feel as an archaeologist when you dig up people's pasts? Like you're helping to pay homage to a people who were once here, through sharing their artifacts with the world? Otherwise, what's the point? We would all just forget about who and what came before us and live only for ourselves, without understanding where we fit in history." Now he was the one who sounded fierce.

"And where do you fit?" Klara asked, pressing.

"Right here with you," he said unexpectedly, putting his arm around her.

❊ ❊ ❊

They had an early dinner that evening, laughing and chatting while they polished off a bottle of merlot. Neither could get back to Filip's hotel room fast enough. When they arrived there, they peeled off each other's clothes, spending the next several hours in bed making love and discovering one another.

That night, as she rested her head on the pillow next to Filip's, Klara thought about Hanna's advice to her. "Be honest with him," her cousin had said. While she knew what these words meant intellectually, she didn't have much experience with how they felt emotionally. Honesty on a personal level wasn't something she'd had much of in her life, until she'd met Rosario in the Yucatán. Rosario had pushed her to be honest with herself, which ultimately allowed her to be honest with Rosario. While letting herself trust someone else was a very unfamiliar and even uncomfortable feeling, the benefits she had reaped in return were great. Now, here she was, on the way to making real, honest relationships with her father's family—Rachel and Hanna. Although it was a bit scary, it certainly felt good. It made her feel a part of something greater than herself, and it made her feel a whole lot less alone. Could she be honest with Filip? Could she trust him? Looking at his face, she thought she could.

As Klara closed her eyes, ready to fall asleep, she imagined being back on the top of the mountain in the Yucatán with Rosario and the other women villagers, dancing around a burning fire as she inhaled earthy incense and beat a tambourine on her hip in sync with the rhythm of the deep, drumming music. For the first time she could recall, she had felt a full sense of peace, of belonging. She was hopeful and knew she had made the right decision in coming to Poland. She had made this decision by trusting in herself and felt she could trust in Rachel and now even Hanna in a similar way. And Filip? In her dream, they held hands and took a flying leap off a giant boulder into the vast blue ocean.

# CHAPTER 20

The next day was Wednesday, and Klara and Filip had a full day of Israeli dancing, lectures on Jewish culture and literature, and an architectural tour of Kazimierz. They turned in early that night, as they planned to rise before dawn. Klara had checked out of her hotel and was now officially staying with Filip in his. Both exhausted, they slept soundly.

The following morning, they left before sunrise, driving east toward the Ukrainian border in Filip's royal-blue, four-seat Skoda Fabia. There was room for just the two of them, as the back seat was full of junk—papers, wrappers, and a gym bag, among other items. It was a clear, sunny day with few clouds in the sky. They were visiting Stary Dzikow, the former Jewish cemetery now marked by just a few trees.

"What are you thinking about?" Filip asked.

Klara, who had been watching the green scenery from the two-lane highway go by, replied, "I'm thinking about how normal this all looks and seems, like we're taking a pleasant trip to the countryside, with no cares in the world. But that's not the case. How about you? What are you thinking?"

"That life is full of contradictions. That we're visiting a decimated Jewish cemetery, but I'm doing it with you," Filip said, smiling and putting a hand on Klara's knee.

After about two hours, they drove into Jaroslaw, an old city with renovated sixteenth- and seventeenth-century buildings.

Modern signs hung over many storefronts, along with some traces of black-and-red graffiti. Filip stopped at the market depot, an old gray stone building seemingly built a few centuries earlier; it was now a general store, and a few men stood out front, chatting.

"This doesn't look like the photo in the museum," Klara said, looking around, confused. "There's no farmland here. Why did you stop?"

"I've never been here before," Filip replied. "The cemetery is outside the city, and from my experience, it's probably not well marked or easy to get to. GPS won't be able to help us. I just need to ask for directions." He opened the car door and jumped out, approaching the men outside the store and introducing himself in Polish.

Klara couldn't understand their conversation, and she wasn't sure why, but she noticed her right foot tapping as her stomach lurched. It occurred to her that she was about to visit a completely desecrated burial site of people who could have been her ancestors, some of whom had been buried less than a century ago. What was it that she needed to witness so badly? Maybe it was about experiencing her awe that even without headstones, the townspeople respected this area as sacred burial ground. They remembered that their Jewish neighbors were once buried here and kept their memory alive by planting a few trees and leaving the land alone. But what would happen once this generation and the one before and after it were gone? Who would remember what this land had been set aside for and the people who were once buried here?

Klara thought about her professional work up to this point. It was through digging and excavating that the past was remembered and memorialized, just as she had done some months ago in the Yucatán. But now in unearthing her own history, there were no stones to uncover, just trees that, while beautiful, belonged to nature. She needed to do something. She took out the burnt-orange amber stone that had belonged to her father, that she had carried in her pocket since Rachel had given it to her the week before. Now she placed it between her palms, transferring it from one hand to the other, feeling its smoothness with her fingers. She understood stones; they were something tangible that she could touch, and that inexplicably brought her both solace and a feeling of connection to the past. She pondered what her father would think about her chasing after desecrated cemeteries and old gravestones, which to many others would sound either crazy or just plain strange. But she knew, somehow, that he would understand. *How can I make a difference?*

"We need to drive close to another hour north to get to Stary Dzikow," Filip said as he opened the car door, settled behind the wheel, and started the engine.

Klara was shaken out of her thoughts by the sound of his voice. "What else did they say?"

"Just that they did their best over the years to leave the cemetery ground alone, so it could stay peaceful," he replied as he pulled the car back onto the road. They were both quiet. After a few moments, he added, "They also told me there is a former synagogue that's still in pretty decent shape that we could visit on the way to the cemetery. Of course, there is no congregation, and no one staffing it."

"Let's go," she said, fascinated that a synagogue had been left standing and thrilled that they would be able to visit. Filip smiled, seeming to know that would be her response.

Before long, they came upon two stone synagogues with stained glass windows, one built at the beginning of the nineteenth century, and one at the end, according to the plaques that hung on them. Both were in surprisingly good condition, the larger one now serving as an art school.

After walking around the outside and looking in through the windows, Klara said, "It's nice they're using it for educational and artistic purposes if it can't be used for its original intention."

"Yes," Filip replied, taking hold of Klara's hand and leading her back toward the car. "It's better than what many of the other old synagogues are now used for."

"Like what?" she asked, noticing some students being dropped off for class.

"There's one that houses a swimming pool, and others that have been utilized as warehouses over the years," he explained, sounding irritated at the mundane uses of these former houses of worship. But then he brightened. "There are also some, though, that have been beautifully restored."

"I'd love to see them sometime."

They got back in the car and continued to drive for another half hour. The main road ended, and ahead was a badly rutted dirt road with a small wooden sign that read STARY DZIKOW, and an arrow pointing left. Filip stopped the vehicle.

"She's not going to make it," he said, gently tapping the steering wheel of the Skoda. "We need to walk." He opened the trunk and took out reusable water bottles for each of them, as well as his wide-lens camera, commenting that it was fortunate they'd both worn comfortable shoes. They walked about a half mile through unused farmland, Klara leading the way, until they arrived at a spot where a few large, full trees stood alone in a vast field of dirt.

"This must be it," Filip said, pointing to the thick, leafy branches, while wiping the sweat off his face and neck.

"How can you be sure? Nothing's marked," Klara replied, still wandering around, looking for some sort of signpost.

"It's the same with most of these sites. There's been so little government money available to maintain and mark them, and obviously the Jewish community that was once here is gone, with no family left to care for it. Once in a while, there are some private funds," Filip explained, his tone defeated. "But this looks like how it was described."

"What's the first thing that needs to be done to get the government to do more?" Klara asked, her interest now piqued.

"It would need the money and incentive to identify this area and many others like it as sacred burial grounds."

Klara took a sip of water, scanning the area with a hand above her eyes like a visor. "Just like with lost ancient cultures, and their tombs and artifacts," she said, following his logic.

"Yes," he replied, his face brightening at the parallel connection.

"How many sites like this do you think there are around Poland?" Klara asked, an idea starting to germinate.

"Just over a thousand that were once Jewish cemeteries, although many look like this today, totally barren or with just a few headstones. Less than half contain at least one gravestone," he said, momentarily removing his sunglasses to take in the site.

"How do you know?" Klara asked, surprised by such an exact number.

Filip combed his fingers through his thick locks. "I came across a 1993 research survey that documented the number of Jewish cemeteries once existing in Poland. It was sponsored by the American government in cooperation with the Jewish Heritage Institute in Warsaw."

"That's impressive," Klara said. "Do you know what's been done with the information?"

"Well, the Polish government, a few Jewish organizations, and some private individuals abroad, mostly Holocaust survivors, have sponsored particular projects, but there is so much work to be done," Filip said as he walked around, surveying the area while taking photos.

"What are you planning to do with the photographs?" Klara asked, watching him as she stretched her arms and legs, cramped from the car ride.

"They're for my research."

Klara nodded, but felt embarrassed that she hadn't asked more about his work before. She made a mental note to do so later.

By now, it was 11:30 a.m., and the summer sun was beating down on the dirt. After Filip finished photographing the area, they stood side by side under one of the tall oak trees for shade. They held hands, standing in silence for a couple of minutes, to remember those whose tombstones had been destroyed, along with all those lost in the Holocaust. Finally, they each put a small stone on the protruding roots of the largest tree, as there were no headstones, to pay their respects, as Jewish law required. Klara took out the amber stone from her father. She bent down, ready to set it next to the two small stones they had just placed, but Filip grabbed her hand and pulled her upright.

"No, Klara, not that. Your father would want you to keep it. It's yours," he said firmly. She agreed, nodding and returning the stone to her pocket.

As they walked back to the car, some teenagers they passed extended their arms straight and shouted, "Heil Hitler!" breaking the afternoon serenity before running away.

"What the hell was that?" Klara cried out, turning to Filip.

"Wow. What a bunch of delinquents," he said angrily.

"Why'd they do that? How'd they know we're Jewish?" Klara asked, very upset and wildly flustered at the same time.

"They guessed, I suppose, because we're visiting this old Jewish burial ground," replied Filip. "Not many people have cause to come out this way."

"How ironic," Klara said. "The Nazis never loved the Poles either. I guess they don't think about that."

"I guess not."

"Do you know Pastor Niemöller's writing?" Klara asked. "You know what I'm talking about, right?" Filip nodded silently, and they both recited it together in unison while standing there looking at one another:

*First they came for the socialists, and I did not speak out— because I was not a socialist.*

*Then they came for the trade unionists, and I did not speak out—because I was not a trade unionist.*

*Then they came for the Jews, and I did not speak out— because I was not a Jew.*

*Then they came for me—and there was no one left to speak for me.*

# CHAPTER 21

Beginning their ride back to Warsaw, with the potential for a few stops along the way, Klara and Filip rode around the green, hilly countryside, stopping to investigate a few more towns and Jewish cemetery grounds. Klara started to think more and more about remaining longer in Poland. Perhaps she could finagle a sabbatical through the fall, so she would have more time here to consider where she belonged. Maybe she could somehow arrange to work on the 1993 report that Filip had mentioned, to identify and renovate the forsaken Jewish burial grounds. What if she had finally found a place that felt right, with a new purpose? What if she didn't have to keep running—from her mother, her own past, and her self-imposed solitude? What if she could stay here in Poland and help to further memorialize the once-vibrant Jewish community, bringing those who perished their proper recognition in death, which had been denied them in life? What if—and this was the part that scared her the most—what if she had found someone to open up to and perhaps share her life with?

It was all still quite fresh, but possible.

Pushing these thoughts aside as they drove in companionable silence, Klara felt as though these cemetery sites were crying out for someone to restore them. They were all that was left of these villages' previously active Jewish communities. And she had the training for it, even though there were no pots and pans or vases and vessels to dig up. What was left from those killed now sat in museum showcases in Auschwitz, along with thousands of suitcases, shoes, and kitchen bowls. *If not me*, she thought, *then who will be the keeper of these precious memorials? Who will hold the memories of these people, their very existence?* Deep down inside, she felt strength she hadn't known before, a will to really make a difference to what could otherwise soon become a completely forgotten people in Poland.

Wasn't she an archaeologist? What was so different between tombstones and artifacts? They were both evidence of a person's life. Were her Mayan digs and these burial sites so dissimilar? This was her battle to fight. She convinced herself that she needed to stay in Poland, at least for a while, to help resurrect the little that was left of Jewish burial grounds.

But really, who was she kidding? Yes, she could tell herself that she had discovered her professional calling, which was not untrue. But she knew deep down that she wanted to stay in Poland because she needed more time with Filip. He had awakened something in her that she had thought dormant, if not dead. It was hard enough to admit this to herself, let alone to Filip. She felt hopeful, but, as always, lacked the courage and confidence that her feelings would be reciprocated.

Her head fell back, and she let out a long sigh.

"Are you okay?" Filip asked, looking over at Klara while squeezing her hand.

"Yeah, thanks." She glanced out the car window, noticing how dark it had become. "Just tired." She wasn't ready to tell him what she was thinking. She knew it was too soon, and she was afraid of falling for him. She was even more afraid of letting him know her true feelings without first knowing how he felt about her—for she would then once again be that young, vulnerable girl of her childhood who felt alone, afraid, and confused. Her optimism of a few minutes earlier waned; whatever the cost to her now, she needed to shield the hurt child within from any further pain. So, she remained quiet. In any case, she knew it was too soon to start talking about "us." Instead, it occurred to her how little she knew about his previous life.

She turned to him. "Can you tell me more about how you and your ex-wife met? I don't think I even know her name," she said, clearing her throat.

"Nina. We met in secondary school, what you Americans call high school. I was friends with her brother, who was in my grade, and she was two years younger—fifteen to my seventeen. She was chatty with lots of energy and had a way of bringing me out. I was a bit quiet and brooding, even back then."

Klara gave a knowing smile. "What a surprise," she said. But it occurred to her just how insecure she felt hearing about this other woman, even as a teenager—that she had been happy, sociable, and bouncy. Nina was nothing like Klara, who was quiet, serious, and sullen. Perhaps she had no chance with Filip.

"We hung out in a big group with other teens, and by Christmas, we had all paired off," he continued. "We weren't the most natural couple, but we balanced each other out—she'd get me to go out more than I normally would, and I helped her to mellow out. It worked. By the time I went to university, it was a fait accompli that we were a permanent couple. We hung out every weekend, were welcomed into one another's families, and shared the same friends. I think both sets of parents expected we'd marry by the time Nina completed university. I guess we did too. It seemed to be our life's path. She was from a 'good Catholic' family, as was I, or so everyone thought, and we shared a similar educated, middle-class family background."

Filip became quiet, drifting off into his own private thoughts. Klara wondered what they were, willing herself to read his mind, but of course, she couldn't.

"Is that what happened? Did you and Nina stay together, and marry after she graduated from university?" she asked, curious to find out what happened next.

"Not exactly," he said. "She started dating another boy behind my back in her senior year of secondary school. He was in the same grade as her and was a well-liked athlete — a popular guy, the life of the party — kind of like her. At first, she didn't tell me about him. She said she was sick one weekend, had to be with her family the next, and had some school project to work on with friends after that. Then her brother inadvertently spilled the beans. I felt so hurt at first. My heart ached." Filip took one hand off the steering wheel, putting it on his chest. "I must sound like a naïve, heartsick boy, which I was." He shook his head.

Klara put her hand on his shoulder and rubbed it. "I'm sorry that happened to you. You were so young, twenty maybe? The heart is so tender at that age. Then we all learn to toughen up. Don't we?" she added, looking away. She was surprised and impressed by how vulnerable he was with her. She certainly could never be so with him, or anyone, for that matter.

"Well, that's a lesson I would have been happy to miss. I really thought I would be with Nina forever back then."

"What happened after that?" Klara asked.

"What happened after that?" he repeated, staring ahead, but looking like he was somewhere else. "I met Julia. She was a PhD graduate student in economics. Believe it or not, that was my major at the time, and she assisted the main professor. She was four years my senior, and I was shocked when she came on to me."

"I bet you were," Klara said, nodding, trying to suppress a laugh. Shocked and intrigued, she did her best to play along, but was feeling more than a little jealous of both this graduate student and of Filip's easiness in getting involved with someone new, as if these two young women had just fallen into his lap. *Is that what I'm doing?* she wondered. *Falling into his lap?*

"What? Is that so shocking to you that an older woman would be interested in me?" Filip asked, feigning hurt feelings.

"Not at all," Klara replied, shaking her head. "Kind of like me and you. How old did you say you were, forty-six? I'm forty-nine, or didn't you know?" The words had escaped her mouth before she could catch herself.

He smiled, looking at her. "Kind of like me and you." Klara returned his smile, but she was busy worrying about whether she was making things too easy for him. For her, nothing ever came easily.

"About a month later, Nina called me, begging to get back together. The athlete had dropped her for his next conquest. She pleaded that she'd made a huge mistake, and that we were meant to be together, and that everyone makes mistakes sometimes."

"What did you do?" Klara asked.

"Eventually, I broke up with Julia, which was messy, and got back together with Nina. She'd called my mother, asking her to talk to me about how we were meant for each other, and how everyone deserved a second chance. I think my mother thought I'd be happy with her—that she just needed to mature a little but was generally sensible, had a good head on her shoulders, and would ultimately be good for me—because *my* head was in the clouds much of the time. I'm grateful she wasn't alive to see Nina emotionally torture me when I started to embrace my mother's family's Judaism. It would have broken her heart."

"How old was your son then?"

"Jan was seven when my mother died. They were so

close. He was still young enough to let her hug him in public or tousle his hair without being mortified. He took it really hard. My father had died the year before." Before Klara could ask another question, Filip turned the conversation around. "What about you?"

"What about me? I'm an open book," Klara said, tucking her hair behind her ear, as she slouched.

"Seriously, you're an open book? Then tell me about your dating life, your past relationships."

Realizing she couldn't skip over this part of her life, Klara pushed herself. "There's not much to tell," she said, intermittently biting her three middle nails. "Relationships and I don't do well together. I tend to go solo. That's what's worked best for me. No heartbreak, thank you very much." She realized she sounded contrite and even silly, rather than mysterious and sophisticated, which was what she was going for.

Filip glanced at her face for a moment, and his next words surprised her.

"Do you really believe that's what you want—a life by yourself? That sounds a little sad to me," he said, staring at her.

Klara looked away. *He has no right to judge my life,* she thought. "Well it's not like I haven't had relationships. They were just fairly short-lived. I could have gotten back together with Arthur in the Yucatán last year if I'd wanted to. But I'd already been through that with him in the past and knew it would be just another fling." Klara said this hurriedly, followed by an uncomfortable silence.

"I'm sorry if I hit a sore spot. I really didn't mean to sound critical," Filip said softly. "I just can't imagine what that must feel like." He was looking at her, trying to catch her eye, but she turned away.

Klara didn't want to hear what Filip had to say. She certainly didn't want his pity, although he did sound genuine. After a few moments passed, she decided that he was trying to get closer to her, and that she need not be so defensive. But still, it was easier to ask about him than to talk about herself. "Can you tell me more about Jan? Are the two of you very close?"

"We are, and I'm glad to report that we've gotten closer since he's become an older teenager." Filip seemed happy to tell her more about his son. "After Nina flipped out about my 'obsession' with Judaism and being Jewish, as she called it, we separated and ultimately divorced. Jan was confused and quite upset with both of us, but more with me because I was the one who physically left. It seemed natural that he should live with his mother. Eventually, he began spending every other weekend with me, and then a couple of evenings during the week as well. Nina remarried a relatively decent guy, and Jan grew up and developed his own opinions about Nina, his stepfather, life, and me in general. The last few years we've become a lot closer. Of course, he wishes we could have stayed together as a family, but he understands why I needed to pursue my identity, and that his mother couldn't live with my doing so.

"'Who are you?' Nina demanded one day. 'You're certainly not the man I married. So, your mother was Jewish. She hid it from you throughout your childhood. Why as an adult do you have to embrace it, and make it your whole life? She didn't tell you until just before she died. She wouldn't want you to do this. I'm sure of that,' Nina said, gesturing at me with her hands." Filip demonstrated by throwing his hands in the air.

"I told her, 'I'm sorry if you can't understand, Nina. I don't know that I even fully understand myself, but it's just something I have to do.' Soon after that, I quit my job in finance, enrolled in a PhD program in Holocaust studies at Warsaw University, and then started working at the cemetery. Other than not getting to see Jan all the time, I don't regret a moment of it." He grew quiet for a minute and then continued.

"I always felt there was something different about me from the other kids, even when I was young. When I was in church, I said all the prayers like everyone else, and I took Communion, but it felt like I was just going through the motions. I felt like there was something else out there, waiting for me to find it."

Klara nodded. She knew what he meant—not about Judaism, but about there being more to life than what was right in front of you.

"So, what happened with Arthur?" Filip asked.

"Excuse me?"

"You know, Arthur, that other archaeologist you were in the Yucatán with. Is he still in your life?" Filip said.

"Are you serious? Absolutely not." Klara pursed her lips and shook her head. After a moment, she said, "You must have dated other women over the past ten years. What happened to them?"

"How are you so sure there's a 'them'?" he asked. "I could say touché to you."

"Answering a question with a question is not polite."

"It may not be polite, but you've told me so little about yourself, Klara, after I poured out my heartbreak to you. There must have been someone, either before or after Arthur," he said, trying to goad her.

She let out a long exhale. "If you must know, there have been a few someones, but they were short-lived relationships and one-night stands. I'm not proud of it, but that's just the way it is. Sometimes you find yourself lonely and just want physical comfort." Klara was surprised by the words flowing from her mouth. She certainly hadn't intended to share that much.

"I know what you mean," Filip said gently, which was the sweetest thing he could possibly have said. At that moment, Klara felt an invisible wall come down, and she reached out to squeeze his hand. He smiled. He could have become judgmental and distant, but instead he understood. She decided not to ask further about any relationships he may have had since his divorce, knowing she had already asked many more questions than she was prepared to answer.

# CHAPTER 22

By now the sun had fully set, and the moon glowed high above them. They were driving in comfortable silence until Filip interrupted Klara's inner musings.

"I thought we could stay at a local inn tonight," he said, cutting into her thoughts. "It's a two-hour ride back to Warsaw from here, and it would be easier to drive back during daylight tomorrow. What do you think?" he asked tentatively. "We could spend another night together." It was something between a question and a statement.

Klara couldn't quite tell which, but heard herself replying, "I'd like that," as Filip put his hand over hers, giving it a squeeze. She squeezed his back. Her body certainly wanted him, and more time spent together might help convince both of them of a possible future.

The inn they found was a former stable, and although supposedly insulated, it was cool even on this July night. After finishing a bottle of riesling, they lit a candle, undressed, and snuggled naked together under a fluffy goose down blanket, making love by the light of a slow-burning flame. Afterward, Klara lay in Filip's arms as he stroked her long, thick hair.

"I'm beginning to get used to this," he murmured against her head. "How about you?" he asked, stroking her back.

"Me too," she replied, trying to stay in the moment, copying his cadence, though her thoughts swirled around her head, taking her elsewhere.

Filip noticed, as he pulled back and looked into her eyes with concern. "Are you okay?" he asked.

She nodded. "Perfect." But her fear of getting too close to him and being hurt was again sprouting from her subconscious like an unwelcome weed, reminding her of how unloved and scarred she had been as a child. She imagined running away in the middle of the night but successfully pushed that thought away.

❖ ❖ ❖

The next morning, they left the countryside early to head back to Warsaw. While driving, they passed acres and acres of farmland, spotting horses, cows, and chickens as they drove. Both were silent, but something had shifted in Klara.

"You've been very quiet this morning. What's on your mind?" Filip asked, turning toward her.

She took a deep breath before speaking, knowing that she was about to take a brave leap of faith. Her eyes sparkled brightly as she smiled. "I've decided I'm going to stay in Poland for now."

"That's amazing!" Filip cried out. "I was hoping you'd want to stay longer, beyond a couple of weeks, but I didn't want to push you. What are your plans?" Klara had to admit she was thrilled by his reaction.

"I'm not really sure," she said, recognizing that she needed some concrete direction. "I was thinking I'd like to learn more about the 1993 project you mentioned, to study and perhaps even work on refurbishing some of the Jewish cemeteries in disrepair." Klara continued to talk about her professional reasons for wanting to stay, without realizing she hadn't mentioned her interest in Filip as a factor. "First, I need to figure out where I'm going to live. Maybe I can stay with Hanna and Rachel for a little while," she said, looking away from him.

Filip was silent for several beats before responding. "You know, you didn't mention me at all when talking about your reasons for staying. I'm confused. I thought we were starting to have something nice together," he said, looking straight ahead at the road.

Klara realized her error. "Yes, we are. I've loved every minute we've spent together, and I want that to continue," she said, smiling. She reached over and took his hand, trying not to choose her words too carefully, while ever mindful of protecting herself. "I'm sorry, I should have said that first. I want to keep spending time with you."

"What about your job at the college back in the States?"

"Good point. Well, I have the rest of the summer off, and I could inquire about taking a fall sabbatical. I've been there for seven years and have never taken one. I don't think it will be that hard. I hope." She took the amber stone from her pocket and held it in her hand. "Thanks again for encouraging me to keep this rather than leaving it at the burial site," she said, holding it up in the light. "I know I can be impulsive at times." The stone made her think of her father, which gave her a sense of comfort. She'd have to figure out how to get Rachel to translate the rest of her father's letters. She didn't know why, but she wasn't sure she wanted Filip to translate any more of them.

❈ ❈ ❈

Around noon that day, Filip dropped off Klara at Rachel and Hanna's apartment. She had called them when she regained a signal on the cell phone as they approached Warsaw, and they had invited her to stay with them now that she was back from Krakow. Filip said he would be spending some time with his son over the next few days before returning to work.

They kissed goodbye, and he helped her with her suitcase. She suddenly felt like she couldn't get away from him fast enough and wondered if he could sense it. Fear of intimacy was overtaking her thoughts and actions. She knew she was sending mixed signals.

"Bye," Filip said, waving with an expression she couldn't quite read.

❖ ❖ ❖

It was lunchtime on Friday when Klara arrived at Hanna and Rachel's apartment. Rachel answered the door after buzzing Klara into the building.

"How was it?" Rachel asked with unmistakable anticipation, in lieu of a proper hello.

"Hi, Rachel. It's nice to see you too," Klara replied, seemingly cheerful, but the stiffness of her face betrayed her.

Rachel smiled and hugged her, pulling her inside while raising an eyebrow, as if to ask, *Is everything all right?* Instead, she just welcomed Klara in. Grabbing one hand, she said, "It's wonderful to see you, dear. Put down your bag. I wasn't sure exactly when you'd get back, but I'll put on the coffee now that you're here. You must be hungry; let me get you something. Hanna and Alek are at work, and Rebeka's at school." Rachel put away her knitting from the living room couch and hurried into the kitchen to make a fresh pot of coffee.

As Klara entered her aunt's warm, welcoming apartment, she wished she had a place like this that she could call home. She followed Rachel into the kitchen, sitting down at the table, as Rachel took out some home-baked pastries and two cups for the soon-to-be brewed coffee. Her forced cheeriness now gone, Klara looked pale, and she said little. She was again consumed by her own thoughts, obsessing over what Filip might really think of her. Despite having spent the past four days with him in Krakow and the countryside, she again experienced crippling self-doubt.

Rachel could tell something was wrong from the moment her niece walked in. She leaned over and put a hand on Klara's back. "Dear, what happened? Why do you look so forlorn?"

Klara took a bite of a buttery pastry and put her head in her hands. "We had a nice time, and I told Filip I want to stay in Poland for now," she said, wiping her nose with a tissue.

"That's wonderful news," Rachel said jubilantly. "So, what's wrong?" she asked as she sat down. "And why are you twisting your locket back and forth like that?"

Klara looked down at her locket. "Aunt Rachel, I'm so confused," she said, unexpectedly starting to cry. "I'm so scared of getting closer to Filip. A part of me really wants to, but it's so hard for me to trust people, especially a man I'm interested in and who's interested in me." She sobbed. "I'm not good at relationships. I've never been able to make a long-term one work. If I let him get too close, then maybe he won't like me anymore, or he'll get bored with me, and then I'll get hurt. How do I begin to trust him? As much as I want to, I don't think I can do it."

"Does he know how you feel?" Rachel asked softly. Klara shook her head.

"I see." Rachel moved her chair closer to Klara's. She rubbed Klara's shoulder and put her arm around her. The two sat there like that without speaking for a few minutes, until Klara's sobs had settled into sniffles.

"I have something to show you," Rachel said. She slowly stood up and left the room. When she came back, she was holding the pale blue box of letters. She took out her glasses, setting them on her nose. "I finished translating them," she said proudly.

"Really?" Klara replied. It was almost as if her aunt had read her mind, as she was hoping for just this. "I thought you couldn't make out some of the words."

"I spent more time deciphering them," her aunt replied, "using a magnifying glass. And a lot of Yiddish and German came back to me with the help of an old dictionary," she added with a smile. "Let's go into the sitting room, where it's more comfortable." Rachel took the box of letters, and Klara brought the coffee and pastries.

"Tell me when the last letter Filip translated for you was dated," Rachel said as she opened the box.

"I believe it was September 1965. It was the third letter you gave me. My father was describing how happy he was to have me in his life, while my mother was depressed and irritable, wanting little to do with me. It sounded like she only wanted a boy."

Rachel sat down, shaking her head. She finally said, "Your father wanted you more than enough for the both of them." She put on her glasses and leafed through the letters. "Okay, here we are, May 1966."

As Rachel began reading the letter aloud, Klara wrapped herself in a woolen blanket she'd grabbed from the armchair.

*Sixth of May, 1966*

*Dear Rachel,*
*Klara just turned a year old a few days ago! She is walking all by herself and starting to say a couple of words, which are a little hard to understand, but she is beginning to talk. We had a birthday cake for her, and I helped her blow out the candle. She is such a happy baby! Bessie and I have gotten into a routine*

*where we talk about what is necessary, but the love
I once thought was there is lost. She looks at me as
though I'm beneath her and no good, not as though
I'm her husband and the father of our child. I go to
work, come home, spend time with Klara, and try
to ignore Bessie and her father as much as possible. I
miss you so much! I am including a photo of Klara.*
    *Love, Dawid*

Attached was a black-and-white photo of Klara with a short wavy brown bob, wearing a little white dress, and with a big smile on her face.

"Look at how adorable you were," Rachel said, handing Klara the photo. Klara stared at the happy little face looking back at her. "That's me?" she asked in disbelief. "I can't believe that's me. I've never seen this photo before." She realized that she wouldn't have, as it was mailed to Poland shortly after it was taken.

Staring at the photograph, Rachel repeated, "How adorable you are," as she smiled.

"Then why didn't she love me? What was wrong with me that she didn't love me?" Klara asked.

"It wasn't you," Rachel said soothingly. "It was *her*. There was something wrong with her, but she made you feel like there was something wrong with you. It's not you. It never was," she said, hugging Klara tightly.

"Why did he have to be the one to leave?" Klara asked aloud. "Why didn't he take me with him? My life could have been so different if he'd been the one to raise me."

"Yes, it very likely would have been," Rachel agreed, looking at Klara sympathetically.

"My poor father," Klara said, blowing her nose and wiping her face of tears. She sat there shaking her head. Finally, she said, "I'm exhausted."

"I'm not surprised," Rachel replied. "Why don't you lie down in Rebeka's bed? She won't be home from university until much later today," Rachel said as she put a hand on Klara's shoulder.

Klara agreed, feeling like she hadn't slept in days.

# CHAPTER 23

Klara was fast asleep. In her dream, she was back in the Yucatán. She heard voices speaking around her.

"How sick is she?" one woman asked.

"I'm afraid she might not make it," said another. "Her fever isn't breaking."

"We must keep praying," said the first, who was praying in a Mayan dialect Klara didn't recognize or understand.

Klara felt as if she were in another world. She wondered what she had to live for, and why these women were praying over her. She tried to tell them she was okay, that she didn't need their help.

"Shh," one woman said. "Don't try to speak. Drink this." She held up Klara's head to pour a hot liquid down her throat and set it down again. The hot liquid felt good on Klara's sore throat. The woman put another blanket over her, wiping her forehead with a cloth as she continued to pray over her body. Although Klara felt horribly sick, she also felt cared for.

She heard another woman ask, "Who is she?" referring to Klara.

The first replied, "She is a foreigner, but she needs our help. Her body and soul are both sick, and crying out to be healed. She came here in search of our culture, but she needs to regain her strength to go in search of her own, so she can find out who she is. We must help her in the meantime."

"But why do you care so much about her?" the second woman asked.

"She took care of my child. I will take care of her," the first answered.

Klara recognized the voice of the first woman; it was Rosario's.

In another dream, she saw her father's face. He was a relatively young man, maybe in his mid-thirties. He held a young girl of perhaps two or three years.

"Aren't you wonderful," he said. "Aren't you smart and special? I can't wait to see who you will grow up to become. I know you will be someone great. Never forget how much I love you, Klara."

But then her father faded away, and she was playing on the floor by herself as a young child, while her mother and grandfather sat in the living room, ignoring her while they talked among themselves.

When Klara awoke, she felt disoriented. She looked at her watch; it was five o'clock in the evening. She lifted the window shade to see that it was still quite bright outside and felt a light summer breeze blow through the open bedroom window. It was time to get up and face her life. She could hear voices in the kitchen.

Klara got up to join them, first stopping in the bathroom to splash cold water on her face. Entering the kitchen, she unexpectedly spotted Hanna sitting next to Rachel. "Aren't you home early?" she asked her, suspecting Rachel might have called Hanna because she was worried about Klara.

"I finished my work and came straight home," Hanna replied casually, as she looked up from chopping vegetables in preparation for dinner. "Welcome back from Krakow. What did I miss?"

Klara sat down at the kitchen table, eyeing Hanna, assuming Rachel had already filled her in. "You really don't know?"

"I know you and Filip went to the countryside surrounding Krakow and planned to visit former Jewish cemeteries," Hanna responded, busying herself at the sink to avoid looking at her cousin. "I assume you enjoyed each other's company."

The conversation was interrupted when the phone rang. Rachel walked into the kitchen with the receiver, holding her hand over it, while she whispered in Klara's direction, "It's Filip."

Still groggy from her dream-filled nap and not prepared to talk to him at that moment, Klara whispered back, "Tell him I'm not here," making exaggerated gestures to accentuate her words with her hands. She didn't know what she wanted to say. There was still so much to process. Did she want to be with him? Did she just want to be friends? It was clear to her that she just didn't know at that moment.

She felt embarrassed as she overheard Rachel say into the phone, "I'm sorry, but she's sleeping right now. I'll tell her you called when she wakes up. Nice talking to you too." After hanging up, Rachel turned to Klara. "You know, I really don't like to lie. You're putting me in a very awkward position. He's a nice man. Why are you avoiding him? Did something unpleasant happen between the two of you?"

Hanna piped up, "What's going on?" and threw her hands in the air. "I thought you two had a nice time together. You just spent the last three or four days with him. I thought you were happy." She sat down across from Klara, who was crossing her legs, first one way, then the other, while her dangling foot shook back and forth.

Klara exhaled a long breath, put her head in her hands, and leaned on the table. "I just need some time. Maybe I'm a bit confused."

"You're confused?" Hanna repeated, as though throwing a dart at a board, and the board was Klara.

"Hanna, why don't you put on some fresh tea, dear," Rachel said, sensing that Klara was not yet ready to confront her feelings about Filip. "Klara, come join me in the living room, dear." She took Klara by the hand and stood. "Let's look at some more of your father's letters in there. I translated them into German so you could read them yourself, but I'd be happy to read them with you."

Rachel and Klara spent the next half hour reading through the rest of her father's letters to Rachel from so many years ago. They continued the story of the sorry situation that her father was in, attempting to hold his ground with his wife and father-in-law while trying to put his daughter's best interests first. Hanna had joined them with the tea but sat quietly on a separate couch, responding to her mother's glare that told her to stay out of it.

Rachel took out a yellowed envelope from the light-blue box. "Before we read your father's final letter to me, I found another one from him; it was from before you were one year old. I must have misfiled it. I'm not sure how to share its contents with you, other than to just read it. It may explain some things. I'm just sorry for all of it," Rachel said, her voice breaking. As she held out the letter, Klara took it, and began reading the German translation aloud.

*Fifth of January, 1966*

*Dear Rachel,*
*It's cold, and all the leaves have fallen from the trees. Bessie's mood has not improved as I hoped it would. She's still irritable, distant, and depressed and has not yet bonded well with Klara.*
*There's something I never told you, but it will*

*explain things further. You know that we tried to have a baby for a while. The truth is that Bessie was pregnant before. She kept telling me not to say anything because it was bad luck, so I respected her wishes and kept quiet. She had a miscarriage at seven months. The baby was a boy. We would have had a baby boy. Bessie couldn't get over the miscarriage, and the grief over losing a male baby. Of course, it was devastating for both of us, and it took time before she became pregnant again, four and a half years, actually. When she finally did, she was convinced she was having a baby boy, like last time. She had picked out a name for him too. When Klara was born, she was in disbelief, thinking it was a mistake. I was so thrilled at seeing our new baby daughter, but Bessie refused to hold her. She was convinced the doctor had switched the baby with the male baby she was supposed to have. I thought things would improve, but they haven't.*

*I love Klara more than anything, enough for both of us, but I fear that if Bessie doesn't overcome this, she will never be able to fully love our daughter.*

*What can I do?*

*Your loving and distressed brother, Dawid*

Klara let the letter drop from her fingers as her body fell against her aunt's, her head landing on Rachel's shoulder. Rachel rubbed Klara's head. "I'm so sorry, Klara. I'm so very sorry."

Klara spoke, although she didn't connect the words coming out of her mouth to her being. She didn't feel real, and it was as though her words were someone else's. "She never wanted me. My mother never wanted me. She only wanted a boy, and I wasn't a boy. She hates me because I wasn't a boy. I never had a chance with her." She cried as the tears broke through. All Rachel could do was to hold and rock her, while Hanna sat with her lips pressed together.

After giving Klara a handkerchief, Rachel said, "Your father loved you more than words could ever express. He loved you enough for both of them. Your mother had what is now understood to be postpartum depression, which was further aggravated by her fantasy that there was no doubt she'd have another boy. It had nothing to do with you, Klara."

Klara sat up and blew her nose hard. "But it had everything to do with me, because I was her daughter, and she was my mother. I had no way of understanding her hurt, and no way of knowing why she couldn't love me. I thought it was all my fault. It's like she took it all out on me. How could a parent do that to her child? How could she do that to me?!"

Hanna handed Klara a hot cup of tea, which she slowly sipped.

"No wonder I can't trust being in a relationship with anyone. No wonder I can't trust what it means to enjoy my time with Filip. Am I doomed to always be alone? Is that my fate?" Klara said to no one in particular.

"No," Rachel answered firmly. "No. Your father loved you and made sure you knew it. He would have done anything for you. In fact, he did. He tried to go to another city, to make a life for both of you there, but sadly, it didn't work out. I don't seem to have the letters from the in-between years, when you were a toddler and a little girl. However, I do have your father's final letter to me a few years later, but I'd like to be the one to read it, if it's all right with you. I think it's best you hear it this way." She started reading:

*Fifteenth of June, 1971*

*Dear Rachel,*
*I've decided I must leave Bessie, as there is no changing her mind or behavior in how she treats me, and even more importantly, how she treats Klara. Jacob Herschler, who as you know is my boss and Sigmund's best friend, has blackballed me in the industry, as the Americans say. I am going to Philadelphia, where a friend has secured a job for me, with plans to start a new life there, and then come back and get Klara. It's a major city, just a couple of hours from New York. I'm hoping that, as Bessie treats Klara as a burden, she will allow this without a fuss, but if not, I will fight her in court. At any rate, I need to establish myself first, in order to show I can care for her. For the first time in many months, I feel free, although I also feel terribly guilty for having to leave little Klara behind. In the end, it will all be worth it.*
      *Wish me luck, and I will be in touch when I have a new address.*
      *All my love, Dawid*


"When did you say he wrote that?" Klara asked, looking over Rachel's shoulder.

"The fifteenth of June, 1971," Rachel replied, pointing to the date.

"He died only a few weeks later," Klara noted with widened eyes.

"Yes," Rachel replied with a frozen expression.

"Oh, my god, that must have been when his train crashed," Klara said, sitting back on the couch, doing the mental calculations while trying to absorb what she had just heard. "Right after he left New York to go to Philadelphia. My mother only recently wrote to me about it, telling me what really happened forty-three years ago. I was around six years old. At the time, however, she left out that he was planning to start a new life and then come back for me."

"Yes," replied Rachel. "That's exactly what he set out to do—secure a job, and come back for you. That was his plan all along," she proclaimed, grabbing Klara's hands. "He never intended to abandon you."

Klara shook her head as she repeated what Rachel had just told her. "He never intended to abandon me. He always wanted to come back for me." She was trying to process this new information that would take time to sink in. She was dumbfounded at hearing her father declare how much he loved her, and that he intended to give her a better life, until fate had so cruelly intervened, taking him away from her. She looked up at Rachel for a moment. "This fundamentally alters everything! He didn't abandon me. He intended to come back for me!"

"Yes," Rachel said, nodding emphatically. "He always intended to come back to get you."

Klara pulled over a crocheted afghan from the couch, curling up in it. "I believe you tried to reach out to me, Aunt Rachel, but my mother made sure it never happened. I wish it had. How I wish you could have made contact with me," Klara said, with her knees to her chest and her chin resting on them.

"Me too, dear. Me too," Rachel replied, rubbing Klara's back. "I tried many times, but your mother refused to allow me to talk to you, and she stopped speaking to me altogether after some months passed. Then, later on, I had no idea where you went to college, or how to track you down once you left home. I'm so sorry, dear, so very sorry." She continued to rub Klara's back, tears welling up in her eyes. "We lost so many years together." The two women embraced.

Rachel looked into the light-blue box with the old letters. There was one final envelope. She held it up.

"What's that one?" Klara asked with a furrowed brow. "It says 'from Bessie' on the envelope."

Klara and Rachel looked up at the same moment, locking eyes.

"Yes, it's from your mother," she said to Klara. "She sent it to me after your father passed, briefly explaining the circumstances of his death to me. It was quite shocking at the time, so much so that I immediately called her, and she took my call, thank goodness."

"What did she say?" Klara asked, with pressure in her voice.

"I'll read it to you, but I regret to have to share it."

Klara sat up tall, crisscrossing her legs in front of her on the coach. She wrapped her hair into a temporary bun, rolled her head a few times to get the kinks out of her neck, and said, "I'm ready."

Rachel picked up another envelope, took out a single sheet, and began reading.

*Thirtieth of June, 1971*

*Dear Rachel,*
*I regret to have to tell you that David is dead. I'm sure this will come as a shock to you. It did to me. He died in a train crash on his way to Philadelphia, where he apparently went to find a new job. I'm not sure how much he told you about our marriage. I tried so hard to make it work, and still, he left us. Money is tight right now, as David has been out of work for a while, so I won't be able to pay for his funeral. Actually, we were separated and planned to divorce. If you wish for a proper burial, you must*

*arrange it yourself. If you choose to have his body*
*flown to Poland, I will not stand in your way.*
    *Sincerely, Bessie*

Klara placed her hand over her mouth. Even though she knew some of the details from Hanna, it was still overwhelming to hear her mother's words written in her own voice.

"Upon receiving this letter, I immediately put my life savings together and reached out to underground American contacts and those within my own government about having your father's body flown here. I buried him in Warsaw's Jewish Cemetery. It was not easy, but I knew some people who helped me get him back where he belonged, with his family."

Although Klara had also learned these details from Hanna, she was still shocked and shaken by the coldness of her mother's words. She stared straight ahead. "My mother always looks at everything from her own point of view, never taking responsibility for her actions or showing empathy for others, like my father."

"I imagine she had her own reasons for doing what she did," replied Rachel, "like keeping you and me apart. But yes, she behaved terribly."

The tears began to flow down Klara's face once again. Finally, after all these years, she felt vindicated, and yet terribly cheated at the same time. This new knowledge that her father had intended to return for her was bittersweet, given the tragic ending to his life. She had always questioned the truth of her mother's frequent reminder, "Your father left us. He didn't care about us anymore," which was so contradictory to her vivid memories of her father twirling her around in the air and expressing his love for her.

After a while, when Klara had regained her composure, Rachel said quietly, "Perhaps you'd like to give Filip a call soon and tell him you woke up from your nap."

"I think I will," Klara said.

Hanna, who sat quietly the whole time, stood up and gave her cousin a big hug.

# CHAPTER 24

After dragging her feet for a while, Klara went into the kitchen and picked up the phone, unsure of what she would say to Filip. Feeling jittery, she dialed his number, telling herself, *You can do this.* When she heard his voice on the other end, she tried to sound casual. "Hi, Filip. I heard you called earlier, and I wanted to get back to you."

Klara sensed through his tone that Filip was pulling back. *I'm the one who was supposed to have mixed emotions, not him.* Perhaps he had picked up on her apprehension; she couldn't help it and realized she was being irrational in blaming him. She would need to be more encouraging if she wanted him to keep reaching out to her.

After he explained that he had called earlier to check on her, she thanked him. She must have encouraged him enough because he asked if she wanted to have dinner the next day so they could talk things through. That made her nervous, but she agreed, and in doing so, she realized that something deep inside her had begun to shift. She suddenly didn't feel quite so afraid to trust him as she had been before she'd heard her father's loving words from over four decades earlier—that he had planned to come back and get her. Trusting someone, without having her guard up, was certainly new for Klara. She would meet Filip at the cemetery the next day.

❀ ❀ ❀

The following day was perfect—clear, sunny, and not too hot. Klara felt as though a huge burden had been lifted since her aunt had read her father's old letters to her, explaining how much she meant to him. Until then, she hadn't known how heavy a burden she had been shouldering, or even that she'd been carrying it in the first place.

As she approached Filip's office at the cemetery, she saw him talking to a slender blonde woman in her thirties, who was giggling and standing too close to him. *Of course, I'm jealous*, she admitted to herself.

Seeing her approach, Filip stepped back from the woman and said, "Oh, hi, Klara. This is Natalia. We were just finishing some work. Natalia helps me research families' genealogy."

Klara caught Natalia looking her up and down. She tried to be the bigger person, extending her hand in greeting. As they shook hands, she said, "It's nice to meet you."

"You too," Natalia replied with a forced smile, looking as stiff as Klara felt.

"So, we'll talk again in a few days," Filip said to Natalia. Klara noticed that she touched Filip's arm for just a moment too long in parting.

Klara knew better than to act possessive, but she couldn't help herself. Following Natalia's departure, she asked, "Is there anything you want to tell me?"

Filip looked up from the papers on his desk. "About what?"

"You really don't know what I'm talking about?" She found this hard to believe. *Can he really be that dense, or is he playing with me?*

"No. You'll have to be clearer. I've been busy working all day, and I don't have it in me to second-guess you." He looked tired as he waited for her answer, and he sounded a bit irritated. She wasn't expecting that. In the short time she'd known him, he had never sounded annoyed with her. She was boxed in and would have to spell it out.

Klara felt herself blushing. "About Natalia?"

"Natalia? I told you, she helps me with research." He said this casually, as though he were pointing out where the coffee pot sat. Klara was beginning to feel a little stupid but persisted nonetheless. "You haven't noticed that she's interested in you?"

Now she'd caught Filip's attention. Looking her squarely in the eyes, he said, "We work together. She has a boyfriend; that's just how she is. She's at least fifteen years younger than me, probably only ten years older than my son."

Klara could tell he was exasperated. "Okay," she replied, trying to sound appeased, but she wasn't convinced. The awkwardness of their parting the day before felt too raw, despite the fact that it was due to her uncertainty about him.

❖ ❖ ❖

Filip washed up, changing into a clean, white-collared shirt and a pair of well-fitting black jeans. He smelled good too; it must have been his musky cologne. They ate at a casual outdoor restaurant. Over dinner, Klara did an about-face, from being a jealous lover to focusing solely on business. She talked about her plans to stay in Warsaw, given her desire to restore the desecrated Jewish cemeteries. She had begun to strategize how to make it happen, and wanted to hear what he thought.

"What about the research you mentioned that the American Preservation Committee funded twenty years ago?" she asked excitedly. "Maybe they'd consider updating it. Maybe we could convince them that it's worth updating." She leaned forward on her elbows, eager to hear his response.

"Slow down for a moment, Klara. Do you mean, you and me working on this project together?" Filip held up his hands. "Don't get me wrong, it's a good idea but a huge undertaking, and I don't have much extra time right now. Between my work at the cemetery and making time to spend with my son . . . and how do you propose to fund it?" he asked, looking up at her.

"I was thinking I could write to the American organization and talk to the Jewish Heritage Institute in Warsaw, to see if they'd be interested in getting behind the project," Klara replied. "It couldn't hurt to ask, and I figure that would be the best starting point. Would you help me contact the necessary people?"

Filip paused for a moment, trying to compose himself as he fidgeted in his seat. "Honestly, Klara, you confuse the hell out of me. First, we had what I thought was a wonderful time together in Krakow. Then you gave me a tepid goodbye. Next you act like a suspicious girlfriend, and now you're talking to me like a business partner. I don't understand you." He ran his hands through his hair but stopped midway, grabbing his head. He was the most straightforward man Klara had ever been involved with, and she wasn't used to it, unsure of how to respond. She didn't like it when men played games, but Filip's directness made her quite uncomfortable.

What *did* she want?

"I'm sorry," she said, touching his shoulder, but to her surprise, he pulled away. "I'm not good at this—at relationships. I don't know how to make things work. I've never been good at it." She felt like she was going to cry.

"It's all right," he said more calmly, touching her hand. "We don't need to get into it now." He paused, and Klara could tell he was thinking—deciding whether to share his thoughts perhaps. "I do know some people who work at the Jewish Historical Institute," he finally said. He sat forward, tapping his hand on the table. "Doesn't Hanna work there too?"

"I believe she used to."

"In fact," he said, finishing his appetizer, "I know the two people who worked on the original survey, Glenia and Michal."

"Can you introduce me?" Klara asked without taking a breath. She couldn't believe her good luck.

"Yes," he replied, nodding. "I can do that." But his voice sounded strained. Klara thought perhaps he was speaking in a measured tone to quell her enthusiasm, in case things didn't work out. Despite the fact that he had just told her how confusing her behavior was, she was still only focused on her intellectual interests as the reason to remain in Poland—never mentioning him as an important factor. She ignored his tone, relieved he was open to the idea of this project, and was looking forward to meeting the original researchers. Maybe they'd agree to oversee a new research undertaking all these years later, or at least share their older findings with her.

Although she had a nagging feeling that perhaps Filip wasn't quite as excited about pursuing all of this as she was, she ignored it. Taking a sip of wine, Klara realized that she had been going on about her own interests without asking about him.

If there was any future for them, it had to be a two-way street.

"I'm sorry," she said for the second time in the last few minutes, reaching out and placing her hand over his. "I've been so self-absorbed with my own agenda that I'm getting ahead of myself with this project idea. How's your son? Did you have a nice time with him?"

"Jan stayed with me last night and spent time with me at work today, helping me clear some of the overgrowth around the gravestones," Filip said, his face brightening. "It's good to have time with him, especially since he'll be starting classes at university this fall. I just wish I could have been there for him more than I have these last few years, but I feel like he's starting to let me in—that he wants to be around me more than he had. Of the three of us—my ex-wife, him, and me—he's lost out the most from our breakup. He's almost a man now, and I really want our relationship to get stronger."

"Of course, you do." Klara put her hand on Filip's arm.

"You understand?" he said, looking up at Klara.

"Of course, I understand. Why are you so surprised?" she asked, pulling her hand away.

"I don't know. Please don't be defensive. I'm just happy you feel that way," he said with a half-smile. "You confuse me, Klara." He shook his head. "I'm not sure what's more important to you—you and me, or reviving Poland's lost Jewish cemeteries. You finally seem more interested in my personal life," he added. "I think you know how much I'd like this to work—you and me—and I'm happy that today you seem to want the same thing. But what about tomorrow; will you feel differently then?"

"I'm sorry," Klara said, looking down. "Why can't it be both? Look, I know I've been sending mixed signals. I can't seem to help it. I really like you, but I haven't had the best of luck trusting men, and because of that, I'm not very good at relationships. I'm kind of learning how to do this as we go along, and I'm also learning the truth about how strongly my father felt about me, from the letters he sent my aunt." She twirled a lock of hair between her fingers, and then continued.

"I did have a really good time with you in Krakow, when we got to spend a few days alone together. I mean it," she said, looking into his eyes. "I just think I need to be a little cautious in not completely getting swept away." Reaching out and holding his hand, she said, "I *really* like you, but I'm pretty terrible at making emotional commitments. Trusting someone in a relationship is not my strong suit. I hope we can continue our friendship and see where it leads." Klara immediately regretted the use of the word *friendship*.

"I get that, Klara, but I think what we have is clearly more than a friendship. Don't you think?" he asked, gazing into her eyes.

She nodded. Taking a sip of coffee, she pondered what he'd just said. Knowing he had spoken the truth, there was nothing more to say, but she said it anyway. "You're right."

# CHAPTER 25

Over the next few days, Klara was busy moving forward with plans to establish her new life in Warsaw, at least for the next several months. She also needed to tie up loose ends back in the States, such as letting the college know she wouldn't be returning for fall term. She was hoping to start with a sabbatical. As Holbrook College owned her house and even some of the furniture in it, she didn't have to worry about selling or renting it. She'd ask Sheila to pack up her personal belongings. She knew it was a lot to ask but pushed herself to write the email.

*Hi, Sheila,*
*How are you, Jack, and the kids? I hope you're all doing well.*

*It's now been about two and a half weeks since I first arrived here in Warsaw. This may sound crazy, but I'm going to try to apply for a sabbatical for this September so I can stay here. I know it's late in the season, but perhaps I'll get lucky, as I haven't taken a sabbatical in the seven years I've been at Holbrook.*

*I met someone I really like. I think I mentioned him before in my last email to you. Also, there's some historical research I'm very interested in here as well, relating to decimated Jewish cemeteries from the Nazi era. In addition, I've gotten close with my aunt and even my cousin, and I'm not ready to leave yet. In fact, I feel like I only just arrived—like my life is finally beginning.*

*This is the part where I need to ask for your help. If I do get the sabbatical, I'm going to have to move out of my college-owned house for the semester. I know it's a big ask, but would you mind packing up my things? You know I don't own a lot—just some clothes and lots of books. In fact, it would be great if you could please send my fall clothes.*

*Please think of something really nice I can do for you. I'll give it some thought too.*

*Your eternally indebted friend,*
*Klara*

And then there was her mother. She'd write her a short note by hand, telling her of her plans to stay in Poland for the foreseeable future. Klara didn't believe she deserved more than that. She hadn't contacted her in a few weeks, not since she first arrived.

*Dear Mom,*
*I wanted to let you know that I'm still here in Warsaw. I've had a change of plans. I'm looking to stay here for the next few months or so and am hoping to take a sabbatical from my job. I will be renting my own apartment, but the best address to contact me at, if you'd like to write to me, is Aunt Rachel's, which I know you have. You also have my email address. I will make sure that the Polish government sends your portion of my father's inheritance to you.*

*By the way, Aunt Rachel and her daughter
Hanna are lovely people. It's too bad you never got
to know them.*
*Klara*

Klara could only imagine her mother's reaction to her
letter. She knew she'd be livid. *What comes around goes
around.* There was so much her mother had kept from her, not
to mention that she'd never wanted a girl to begin with. That
was something Klara could never forgive—not wanting her
as a baby, or as a child, for that matter. The list of things she
couldn't forgive her mother for had grown longer; rejection
of her as an infant was just the latest injury. There was her
omission that Klara's father had died in a terrible train accident
when she was six, that he planned to come back to get her, and
that he truly loved her. There was also the nagging memory of
her mother shutting her down and contradicting her whenever
she'd tried to tell her about Jacob Herschler.

It occurred to Klara that if she was going to live here for a
while, she'd need to learn to speak Polish, at least rudimentarily.
She was glad that she'd always had an ear for language. She
would also need to find a place of her own to rent; she wasn't
used to living with other people and didn't want to impose on
Rachel, Hanna, and their family any longer than necessary.

Over breakfast in Rachel's kitchen one morning, Klara
spoke to her aunt about her plans. Rachel clapped her hands
together.

"That's so exciting that you will be renting a place, but
you know you can always stay here with us," her aunt said.
"But if you are going to find your own place, do you need
money for a deposit and rent, Klara dear?" she inquired in
Polish, something Klara had requested in an attempt to pick
up basic phrases. Rachel repeated the question in German to
make sure Klara understood.

"No, I'm fine for a while at least, but thank you for asking," Klara responded, playing with the ends of her hair as she sipped her coffee. She had been financially independent since the day she left for college and wasn't used to having anyone help her. As kind as her aunt's offer was, it felt too uncomfortable to start now.

But Rachel didn't drop it. "We're family, Klara. I want to extend any help to you that I would have given to your father. I hope you know that you can come to me if you need anything," she insisted. "I'd really like to be able to do something for you, if only to try to make up for all those lost years." Rachel smoothed her apron as she looked down at the kitchen floor. Thinking for a moment, she took out a plain white envelope and tried to hand it to Klara.

"What's this?" Klara asked, looking up at Rachel with surprise, without taking the envelope.

"It's some money from your grandparents' property investment from many years ago, the one that your mother wrote to you about, asking you to come to Poland to collect. I just started receiving payments from the Polish government. It's not a lot yet, but it will help you get started, and much more is coming. It belongs to you, Klara—to me and to you."

"No, Aunt Rachel. I can't take it. It's yours," Klara said, handing it back, recalling Hanna's suspicion that this money was the reason she'd come to Poland in the first place. "I'm good. Really. I think I need to do these things for myself— find an apartment, sign up for a Polish immersion class, and maybe take a Hebrew class too."

Rachel extended the envelope back to Klara. "Please make an old lady happy."

"Okay," Klara conceded awkwardly, sensing Rachel's stubbornness and knowing she would not win this battle. But she swore to herself that she wouldn't use the money unless it was absolutely necessary. She hadn't yet begun to receive her own government payments. She planned to use at least a good chunk of them toward a restoration project. She had already decided she would let her mother get her portion from the Polish government, despite her aunt's protests that Klara should get it all, and that she was certainly under no obligation to share it with someone who had abandoned Klara's father, but Klara didn't want to deal with her mother's resentment. This was what she'd decided, despite the fact that Klara's grandfather had left Bessie a handsome inheritance when he passed away seven years earlier.

"Don't you ever think of yourself, Klara? You need to save money for later, when you can't work anymore. You need to think about these things," Rachel said.

"Thank you for thinking about my future. I really do appreciate your concern," Klara said, smiling. The truth was, she had always lived one day at a time, and she never thought about her future. Maybe she should start now.

Changing the subject, Rachel asked, "So why do you want to learn Hebrew?"

Klara explained her idea of restoring the desecrated cemeteries. "Well, in order to read and understand the gravestones, many of which are in Hebrew as well as Yiddish, which uses the Hebrew alphabet, it would be really helpful to study Hebrew."

"I can teach you some Hebrew and Yiddish for now, while you take Polish lessons. And I can speak to you more often in Polish. That way you'll have lots of reasons to come and spend time with an old lady in her upper eighties," Rachel said, smiling from ear to ear.

"I don't need any reasons to come and spend time with you, other than genuinely wanting to see you. And stop saying you're old." Klara smiled and hugged her aunt.

"That's sweet of you, dear, but I'm sure you'll be busy with many things. It's good for me to be needed, and for you to have reasons to come visit me often," Rachel said, getting up to clear the dishes. "And Hanna can help you look for an apartment. You don't have to do everything yourself, Klara. You have family now."

Klara's eyes welled up. Other people's generous offers of help were quite unfamiliar to her. Her aunt's easy manner in suggesting it unexpectedly touched her heart.

"By the way, may I ask how things are with you and Filip? You haven't said much, and I was just wondering."

Klara wiped her eyes. "We're figuring things out," she said, realizing she was speaking in code.

Rachel said no more, simply nodding.

❖ ❖ ❖

Rachel was right; Hanna was more than happy to help out. Over the next week or two, they investigated several apartments around Warsaw, all of which were relatively close to both the family's apartment and Warsaw University, where Klara had registered for a Polish immersion class. She settled on a modest one-bedroom apartment in a two-story walk-up that she could move into on August 1, just a few days later. Despite her worries that she was jumping into this too quickly, Klara chose to trust her gut and forge ahead.

She was so busy setting up the apartment and focusing on her upcoming studies that she didn't have as much contact with Filip over the next couple of weeks. They chatted a number of times by telephone, and he stayed true to his word, introducing her to Michal and Glenia, the researchers behind the 1993 survey of Jewish cemeteries. The four of them met for lunch one day at a local café. Klara had imagined them as perhaps being ten years older than her and was surprised to meet a white-haired man and woman in their upper seventies. In talking to them, she soon learned they were not just professional colleagues but had been married for over fifty years.

"It's wonderful to meet you both," Klara said, as she shook their hands. "I've read your full report from 1993 on the forgotten Jewish cemeteries. I so want to continue the work you've started."

Filip had explained Klara's interest in their previous research, along with her personal and now professional interest in Poland, its Jewish history, and the newer Polish Jewish renaissance. He also spoke of her background as an archaeologist and academic. Both Glenia and Michal were fluent in English.

"For a while now, we've been hoping there would be more money and interest from the American Preservation Committee, and also from Poland's government, to sponsor an updated survey," Glenia explained. "You know," she continued, "to fund further research and perhaps even rebuild some of the one thousand former Jewish cemeteries. So much has happened here since 1993 in terms of a Jewish renaissance. While some work has been done on particular sites, there's still an enormous amount to do. But in order to pursue a new research survey and memorialize and clean up these sites, we need money."

Michal nodded. "Yes, we need money in order to do the work."

"Klara has a proposal to raise funds," Filip replied, launching into a brief description of an idea Klara had shared with him on the phone. "We've been visiting several of the Jewish cemetery sites, and I've been taking photographs. Klara came up with the idea of traveling to the United States to meet with Jewish Community Centers and Jewish organizations under Federations of North America to present your findings from twenty years ago. She can also share her own eyewitness findings and photos, with the hope of raising awareness and funding."

Glenia and Michal were intrigued by these ideas but cautious, having had difficulty obtaining funding in the past. Glenia exchanged a look with Michal before responding. "Filip, this is all so fast, and we just met Klara. It sounds like an amazing undertaking, but if it was to work, there's a lot we would need to go over with both of you."

Filip cleared his throat. "Of course I'd want to work on the project, but it would be Klara who'd be traveling to the United States to present these plans."

He and Klara had in fact not discussed that part yet.

"So, you wouldn't be going with her?" Michal looked at Filip and Glenia in surprise. "We just assumed you'd be going too. You'd make an important contribution to any talk," he said, gesturing with his hand. "You're a Polish Jew with a PhD in Holocaust studies who's lived here your whole life, and who takes care of the only active Jewish cemetery in Warsaw. With Klara's knowledge of American Jewish culture and yours of Polish Jewish culture and history, you'd make a formidable pair and have a much stronger impact," he said, staring at Filip.

"I have to agree," Glenia said. "We could help you with who to reach out to on the Commission for the Preservation of America's Heritage Abroad. We've continued to have some contact with them over the years, but it would need to be both of you." She pointed from Filip to Klara. "We have some other American connections who could help you reach out to the American Jewish community, about where you should plan to visit and speak in the United States," she said, becoming more engaged.

By the time they finished their lunch, Filip said, "There's a lot to think about. Thank you both for coming today." He took in a deep breath as he stood up after their meal. "We'll be in touch. It was wonderful to catch up with you," he continued, shaking their hands goodbye.

Klara followed in kind. "It was so nice to meet you," she said, smiling and shaking Glenia's and Michal's hands. "We look forward to hearing from you."

"And we look forward to hearing from *you*," Michal said, gazing directly at Filip.

After leaving Glenia and Michal, Klara couldn't stop talking. "What a great idea, Filip! We could travel around the United States together, giving talks about the dire state of Jewish cemeteries here and the importance of preserving them. We could talk about the renewal of and appreciation for Jewish culture. What do you think? Maybe we could go for two weeks. Have you ever been to the US?" She was rambling on and on, oblivious to Filip's silence.

When she finally stopped for air, he spoke in a measured tone. "Klara, this really wasn't my plan," he said, turning and looking at her. "It's your plan. I want to support you, but I have my own work, and it's engaging. And my son's here."

Klara's brow furrowed, still caught up in her excitement. "But you heard Glenia and Michal. It wouldn't be the same if it were just me. Your background and expertise is vital—you have to come."

"I *have* to come?" Filip repeated, clearly irritated. "You know I have a life here—my son, my work."

"Of course, you do," Klara replied, backtracking. "But it wouldn't be the same if you didn't, and we have an opportunity to do something really meaningful that could have an important impact on the Jewish history of Poland. We'd be a great team. I'd *really* like you to come with me. Won't you at least think about it?" she asked, almost pleading. He sighed, which she took to mean he'd consider it. Klara didn't push it further, knowing he wasn't convinced she truly viewed them as a couple. Although she said she did, she hadn't really been making him a priority. Now she was asking so much of him. *Maybe I'm not being fair*, she conceded.

❖ ❖ ❖

Over the next few days, they didn't speak. Filip said he would be busy working, and Klara was occupied too, but also too proud to be the first to call.

"You should call him," Rachel said one evening when Klara had joined her for dinner at her home, noticing she was gazing at the phone.

"Why should I call him?" Klara asked, rubbing her forehead with her fingers.

"Because you want to. And from what you've told me, he's interested in you, but he doesn't know where you stand," her aunt said as she put the teapot on the stove. Klara knew her aunt was speaking the truth, but she held back.

In continuing to think about what Rachel had said the next day, Klara realized she was acting like a stubborn teenager who had drawn a line in the sand. She had to at least try—knowing the ball was in her court. Walking through Lazienki Park, she decided to invite Filip to listen to a classical music concert there on Sunday afternoon. They could have a picnic and just relax. Studying the breathtaking bronze monument of Frederic Chopin overlooking a pool of water surrounded by green grass, she knew that it would be a good place to start.

As she sat on a bench nearby, Klara watched the passersby until she was able to quiet her busy mind. She could hear her good friend's voice from another part of the world. "You must reach out to him, Klara," Rosario's voice told her. "You can do this. I am here with you." Klara took hold of her locket, rubbing it mindlessly while she sat thinking.

# CHAPTER 26

When she arrived at the Jewish Cemetery, it took Klara a while to find Filip, who was clipping branches in front of a section of the older tombstones.

"Don't you have someone who can do that for you?" she asked by way of greeting.

"Not really," he answered, continuing to clip. "Jan helps me out, but there's a lot to do. He's working over there," he said, pointing to a figure in the distance. He turned to face her with a scrunched brow, using his hand as a visor from the sun. "Did we have something planned for today?"

"No. I just thought I'd say hello. I hope that's okay," Klara replied, trying to smile. "We haven't spoken in a few days."

"I'm glad you stopped by," he said. "What have you been up to?"

She thought he sounded more casual than he should. Wasn't he wondering what she was up to every moment, just as she was with him? But she'd been too proud and confused to check in before now.

In truth, Hanna had pushed her to go see Filip. "What's wrong with you, Klara? Decide what you want. Filip won't be around forever," Hanna said. She then added, "If you don't want him, let him go, but don't scare him off." Klara didn't appreciate her cousin's tone, but she wondered what the difference was between letting someone go and scaring them off. She had too little experience in matters of the heart to fully grasp these nuances.

Klara realized she had drifted off into her own thoughts for a couple of beats too long. "I've been getting settled in my new apartment that Hanna helped me find," she said. "I think I mentioned I was going apartment-hunting with my cousin when I saw you the other day. Well, I found a cute, affordable apartment off Castle Square, not too far from the Old Town," she replied, trying to make small talk to keep the mood light. "It's a six-month lease. And I'm about to start my Polish language class at Warsaw University, so that will keep me busy."

"Great!" he said, maintaining a calm tone. Shielding his eyes from the sun, he peered at her. "So, you'll be with us for a while, at least through the fall," he commented casually.

Klara's mouth felt dry. She had expected—at least hoped—for a warmer reaction to the news that she'd be staying in Warsaw for longer, but she knew she had no right to ask for more than what she herself had been willing to give. "Yes," she said. Willing herself to speak, she licked her lips and asked, "Would you like to go to a Sunday Chopin concert at Lazienki Park with me? I thought we could have a picnic."

"I might just happen to be free on Sunday," Filip replied, amused, as he put down the metal clippers. "So yes, I'd love to. What are you bringing for lunch?" he continued, now with a twinkle in his eye.

"I haven't decided yet," Klara said, broadly beaming. *That's more like it.* "Maybe we can discuss it over dinner tonight?" she blurted out.

"I'm sorry, but I have plans with Jan tonight," he said regretfully, "and then I have practice with my band. But why don't you stick around, and you can meet Jan."

"You're a busy man," Klara replied, hoping she didn't sound too desperate or disappointed.

"Not too busy for you," he said, standing closer to her. "I can make time. I'll call you tomorrow, and I look forward to going to the concert with you on Sunday. I love Chopin in the park. What a nice idea." He put his hand on her shoulder. It felt good to her.

"I'm glad you think so," she said, the corners of her lips curling upward. His eyes crinkled as he smiled back at her.

A standoffish young man, wearing faded jeans and a white T-shirt, stood behind Klara, startling her with his voice. "I finished the shrubs on the eastern side," Jan said, apparently walking up on them as they were in conversation. He was a few inches taller than his father and about twenty-five years his junior, but clearly his spitting image—tall and handsome, with Slavic features and wavy light-brown hair.

"Jan." Filip smiled. "I have someone I'd like you to meet. This is Klara. I mentioned her to you the other day."

Jan nodded and said hello, examining her. She felt like an interloper. Holding up his clippers, he asked, "Where do you want me to work next?" essentially ignoring Klara.

"Um, over in the south area," Filip replied, taken aback by his son's curtness. "Have some water. Take a break. The work will still be there in ten minutes," he said, trying to add some lightness.

"I'm good." Jan walked away, making little eye contact.

"He seems nice," Klara said with a stiff expression, after their frosty interaction.

"He'll warm up. I've talked to him about you, and I think he's uneasy about it. He knows I like you but that we're still figuring things out. He and I have gotten closer these last few years, and I don't think he likes the idea of sharing me with anyone else, especially someone who hasn't made up her mind yet."

Klara knew that Filip was aware this last part was a dig, and it hurt. Her inability to commit and follow through was certainly her Achilles' heel, and Filip had even shared this with his son. It felt strange knowing she was the topic of conversation between them, like a frog being dissected underneath a microscope in her tenth-grade biology class. She felt her body shake almost imperceptibly, or so she thought, but Filip noticed.

"Are you all right?" he asked.

"Fine," she replied.

The sun was strong, and the nape of her neck felt wet. She blotted it with a kerchief Rachel had recently given her. "I'll see you on Sunday," she said to Filip, waving goodbye. "It was nice to meet your son," she added, lying through her teeth; it hadn't *not* been nice to meet him, exactly, just very uncomfortable. She realized she had never met any boyfriend's child before, young or adult. It made her see Filip's life as three-dimensional and more complicated. Jan was living proof that he'd had a life long before she'd met him. It was a stretch for Klara, who viewed life as a straight line rather than a highway with entrances, exits, and rotaries.

❖ ❖ ❖

Klara awoke on Sunday morning with a sensitive stomach. It felt as though a little gymnast had been doing cartwheels in her belly all night long. Her hands felt clammy, and she was tense all over. Why was she so nervous? It wasn't as if she were about to propose marriage to Filip; she was just going to spend the afternoon with him. She showered and carefully dressed, putting on her special blouse from the Yucatán. Although he'd seen it before, it immediately made her feel connected to Rosario and her strength and wisdom, something she badly needed right now. She chose a billowy white skirt that she had purchased at an open market a few days earlier and brushed her long, wavy hair, allowing it to dry naturally. She'd put it up later if it got too hot. Slipping on her strappy sandals, she looked at herself in the mirror. Seeing that the clasp on her locket chain had moved to the front of her neck, she turned it around to the back and checked that she had her father's amber stone in her purse for safekeeping and extra good luck. After making a few final touches—she put on some newly acquired makeup, naturally colored blush and lipstick—she was ready to go.

When she met Filip that afternoon outside Rachel's home, he took one look at her and was speechless. After realizing he was staring, he finally observed, "You look so nice, Klara. You took my breath away." Klara wasn't sure which of them was more embarrassed.

By the time they arrived at the concert, the park was packed with people. It was a bright, clear, seventy-five-degree day. The benches were all taken, and the grass was dotted with hundreds of blankets. They soon found a spot and spread out their blanket.

"I brought some sauvignon blanc," Filip said, holding up a cold bottle of white wine and rummaging in his backpack for a corkscrew. "I cooled it in the fridge last night."

"Nice." Klara handed him two glasses. She set out some *chleb pszenny*, or simple white bread, and a dish of *golabki*—cabbage rolls with minced beef, onion, and mushrooms. Then she added a separate container of pickled cucumbers, mushrooms, and cabbage as a side dish.

Filip poured two glasses of wine, handing her one while commenting with approval, "Your palate is becoming very Polish."

Klara beamed, pleased that he had noticed her efforts. "What should we drink to?" she asked. "How about to Polish cuisine?"

"To us?" Filip suggested tentatively, clinking his glass against hers.

"To us," she repeated, studying him with a little smile.

They ate and drank, making small talk and enjoying each other's company. Klara had promised herself that she would refrain from discussing her upcoming project, Polish history, or anything about desecrated Jewish cemeteries, which was not exactly date material. She also enjoyed hearing more about Filip's life and studies, and she warmed when he spoke about his son with obvious affection. When the music started, they relaxed on their picnic blanket and enjoyed Chopin for the next two hours, reluctantly standing up and stretching at the end. The pianist had played Klara's favorites: Nocturne in E Minor and Preludes in D-flat Major and in B Major.

"We could come again, if you'd like," Filip said while folding the blanket. "There are often Sunday concerts here, and it's also nice to just come and people-watch."

"I'd like that," Klara replied, smiling as she packed the leftover food into the picnic basket. "I honestly didn't know if you'd accept my invitation for today," she added without looking at him. "You've been a bit standoffish, and I didn't want to push too hard." At that, Filip stopped what he was doing and took Klara's hand, observing her and waiting until their eyes met.

"You didn't push too hard," he said, shaking his head. His voice sounded deep and clear. "Look, Klara, I'm a serious man, and I'm serious about you. I've been trying to follow your lead and figure out what it is that you want. But every time we move forward, you seem to back away. I need to know if you want 'us' to happen, or if we're just friends, as you said a few days ago. I've stepped back a bit the last few days to give you space, but now I need to know."

Filip's hand felt warm and strong in hers, and his piercing green eyes penetrated her. She knew she had been unfair to him, playing with his emotions. At the same time, she had the peculiar sensation that she was getting ready to make a giant leap.

Taking a deep breath, she replied, "Yes." She paused for a moment. "I want to give us a genuine chance. That's the real reason why I got an apartment of my own and enrolled in the Polish language class. I have come to love Poland and getting to know my new family, and I'm drawn to rebuilding desecrated Jewish cemeteries. But I have to admit that my real reason for wanting to stay is you, Filip," she said softly, feeling as though she were suspended in time.

Filip wrapped his arms around her, and she returned his embrace. He kissed her, and she kissed him back. She pulled back a little, looking directly into his eyes before speaking. Being honest and able to trust him was momentous for her. Even so, he had made it easier and had proven his worth ten times over. She decided in that moment that she would open up to him. It was time.

"There are some things I need to tell you about me, about my history, that have made it very hard for me to let anyone in—ugly things. I imagine you might not understand my feelings, but I'm more afraid that you might feel differently about me after you hear what I have to say."

"You can trust me," Filip said, holding Klara's hand firmly, and gazing into her eyes. "Whatever it is."

"That's a really big leap to take, without knowing what I'm about to say. But thank you," Klara said quietly, squeezing his hand in return.

They walked through the park, past patches of geraniums and poppies until they found a quiet, shaded spot under a towering oak tree. They took off their sandals and sat. As Klara spoke, Filip rubbed her feet.

"My mother never told me what actually happened to my father when I was a child, only that he left us. I always wondered, but I didn't find out that he died in a train crash until just before coming here a few months ago. All these years, she allowed me to think that he left me and hadn't cared about me. It hurt particularly because I loved him so much. It made me reluctant to get close to any man, as I couldn't trust that they wouldn't do the same—leave me like he did. I recently learned, through old letters he wrote to my aunt, like the ones you translated, that he'd always intended to come back for me."

Filip listened patiently as she spoke. When it was clear Klara had finished, he said, "Your father would have been so proud of the person you've become."

"Yes and no," she replied. "He would have been proud of my professional accomplishments but sad that I've been so alone." She hesitated for a moment. "I also think he would have wanted to hurt that monster—the monster who hurt me."

"Who? What monster?" Filip asked, shaking his head.

Klara inhaled deeply again. "That's the ugly part. It was a family friend, my mother and grandfather Sigmund's friend, Jacob Herschler." Klara began rubbing her upper arms and holding herself tightly. "They thought he could do no wrong, and practically worshipped him. He owned a men's shirt factory in New York City and was actually responsible for bringing my father and several other young Polish Jewish men to New York to work there during the war. He saved my father from the Holocaust and eventually introduced him to my mother, his best friend's daughter. His best friend was my grandfather," she said, looking pale and tired.

"I see," Filip said. He let go of her feet, sensing that she needed space.

"Jacob Herschler made my skin crawl. The very thought of him still does. When I was eleven, and he was in his late fifties, he started paying more attention to me. Before that, I was like furniture to him, but suddenly he started spending more and more time in our apartment. My mother couldn't do enough for him. When I'd complain that he was there too often, she'd yell at me and go on and on about what a great man he was. She was so proud that my grandfather had such an important friend," Klara continued. "But she didn't know what he did to me behind closed doors—or didn't want to know. He touched me inappropriately . . . in ways he never should have." She hid her face as a cry escaped her lips.

"My god!" Filip said with horror in his voice, reaching out to Klara, but she put up her hand.

"I need to finish," she whispered.

"My mother denied that such a 'wonderful' man could ever do such heinous things to a young girl. She said that I must be making things up or was simply 'crazy.'" Klara grew more and more angry as she spoke. "I learned then that I was all on my own, and I just needed to get out of there as soon as I could. I graduated from high school a year early and basically never went back, except for infrequent short visits and for my grandfather's funeral several years ago. Jacob Herschler died about three years before that. I learned two lessons from my childhood: that life wasn't fair, and that I couldn't trust anyone—not my father, who I thought had left me; not my mother or grandfather, who didn't protect me. And certainly not Jacob Herschler," Klara declared, stone-faced. "And because of that, it's been next to impossible for me to trust anyone."

"I am so sorry," Filip said as he gently held her hand. "I figured there must have been something that was holding you back, but I had no idea it was this. But I'm not any of those people. You can trust that I won't ever hurt you."

Klara fell into his arms and folded up like a small child. She decided that she had shared enough for now about her past, and that she could leave out the part about her mother wishing she were a boy. A few moments later, her face became more animated. "Finding out that my father meant to come back for me has meant everything," she said, tears rolling down her cheeks. "It means that I'm lovable, that he did want me after all."

"Yes, you most certainly are lovable," he said, hugging her. "And those 'ugly things,' as you call them, have nothing to do with you. They're about that disturbed man and his own deviancy, not about you." Filip's expression and cadence indicated that he would have killed Jacob Herschler if he were still alive.

"But I couldn't feel that way before now," Klara said, continuing to cry. "I just felt so ashamed. As if there were something wrong with me that made my family treat me like something less than human. But knowing my father loved me and how important I was to him changes everything about how I feel about myself, even what that pig Herschler did to me. Those ugly things don't define me in the same way as they did before."

"I'm so glad you found out the truth about your father. But however your father felt about you, you'd be lovable anyway. I'm just glad you can believe that now," he said, locking eyes with her.

"Thanks, Filip." Sniffling, she eked out a smile. "But it just hasn't felt that way." She closed her eyes and rested her head on his shoulder as he stroked her hair. The position of the sun had started to shift as the afternoon waned. They lay there under the hundred-year-old oak tree, Filip wrapping Klara in his arms. She couldn't remember ever feeling so peaceful, not since before her father had left, when she was a little girl. She recalled the amber stone and clasped it tightly in her hands as she snuggled with Filip.

# CHAPTER 27

From the day of the outdoor concert when Klara fully opened up to Filip, they were officially a couple—one with separate apartments and lives, but a couple nonetheless. Jan, Filip's son, stayed with him a few days a week, and preferred to have his father to himself. He wasn't happy having to share him with someone else just as they were finally bonding as father and son. They also spent some weekends away hiking and camping. Jan would be starting university in September, and he had been spending much more time with his father than in the past. Missing her own father after all these years, Klara could appreciate that. She did her best to understand, hoping Jan might eventually come around to accepting her. It was part of what allowed her and Filip's relationship to work as well as it did.

Meanwhile, she was delighted to finish furnishing her new place, using castoffs from Rachel and Hanna's apartment, which gave it a cozy aesthetic that felt like a warm embrace to Klara. One humid afternoon, while Hanna was helping her hang colorful floral curtains, she suddenly asked Klara, "Have you written to your mother at all since you got here?"

Klara was taken aback. "What made you think of her?" she asked with an expression that looked like she had just sucked on a lemon.

"I don't know." Hanna paused for a moment, shrugging her shoulders. "You're setting up a new apartment here in Warsaw and plan to stay for several months or so. I just wondered if you've told your mother."

Klara busied herself with a task. "I sent her a postcard when I first arrived, and I recently wrote to her telling her that I'll be staying for at least the next few months," she said more forcefully than she had intended. "I'd rather not think about her, especially now, knowing how much she kept from me about my father, that she let me believe—*no,* that she *made sure I believed*—that he never intended to come back for me. I now know from his letters to your mother many years ago that it was all a lie."

About six weeks had passed since she'd first arrived in Warsaw. After asking Holbrook College permission to take a sabbatical for the fall semester, Klara heard back from her department head. She would be allowed to take a leave, but in the future, she should give much more notice. At that point, Klara was already sure she would stay in Poland, regardless of the answer, leaving her faculty position if necessary—but for now, that could be avoided.

She was making a new life for herself here in Warsaw with her father's family and with Filip, people who cared about her more than her mother ever had. She wanted to keep it safely to herself for the time being and not give her mother the chance to burst her happy bubble. That she *deserved.* Once she told her mother about her plans to stay, she had no doubt that she would shoot them down. Klara didn't want to hear it.

❖ ❖ ❖

Klara's schedule was suddenly very busy; she had her Polish language classes in the morning and would then meet Filip at the Jewish Cemetery in the afternoons to review their weekend research excursions throughout Galicia. Despite her active schedule, she made sure to visit Rachel and Hanna a few evenings a week, which sometimes included Hebrew lessons with her aunt. She hadn't traveled halfway around the world in search of her family for nothing.

Filip came by when he could to spend time with Klara at her new place. They settled into a comfortable routine of spending at least four nights a week together. They also spent many weekends traveling to Jewish cemeteries across the Polish countryside. Before long, they were inseparable, fully intertwined in each other's lives. Filip had become more amenable to the idea of traveling to the United States together sometime in the future to try to raise funds to rebuild the Nazi-desecrated Jewish cemeteries. Even Jan was warming up a bit to Klara, agreeing to have her join them for a movie now and then.

By early December, Klara had given notice to Holbrook College, telling the Anthropology Department's chair and the college president that she would not be returning at all. She needed to stay in Poland for the time being and allow her life to take its course, whatever that might be. She wrote to her good friend and colleague Sheila.

> *Dear Sheila,*
> *I know you'll think I'm crazy, but I just gave notice to Holbrook that I won't be returning in January, or at all. Warsaw is where I belong for now, researching the lost Jewish cemeteries alongside Filip. I think I'm falling for him. Don't get too excited; time will tell. I'm hoping we might make a*

*trip to the US sometime in the next several months.
If so, I owe you a dinner—at least one, probably
several. Would you mind please holding onto my
things for a little longer?*

*Aren't you the one who's always encouraging
me to take chances?*

*I know you'll understand. Thanks a million!
XO Klara*

After making this big life decision, Klara was ready to
contact the Commission for the Preservation of America's
Heritage Abroad. *You can do this*, she told herself, once
again feeling like "Professor Lieberman," a coveted role she
thought she'd left behind in Maine. That January, Klara wrote
to the commission explaining her interest in their report
from twenty-five years earlier on the state of Polish Jewish
cemeteries, memorials, and synagogues at that time. She also
described her and Filip's academic and professional backgrounds. She proposed the idea of traveling to the United
States in the spring to raise further funds to reconstruct Polish
Jewish cemeteries to their pre–World War II state, in homage
to those who were already buried there and those who died
in the Holocaust and were never properly buried at all. She
wrote of their many visits over the last several months to
these now mostly ruined cemeteries, the findings of which
they would present to the American Jewish community at
Jewish Community Centers (JCCs) and synagogues.

One day, as she was waiting for a reply, Filip put an arm
around her shoulders and said, "If they'd like us to come,
I'll go with you." Klara could feel her shoulders drop and
her chest soften. She was not alone.

Finally, in early February, she received a response. The
commission welcomed them, stating that their funding for
further research had dried up years before. But if Klara and

Filip were interested in undertaking a trip to the United States, the commission would help them plan their itinerary and connect them with the Jewish community in a number of states. Klara was over the moon.

They agreed the trip would be two weeks long, as that was the amount of time Filip could take off from work, and that a minor portion of the money they raised could be used to cover their trip expenses. They hoped to travel the first two weeks of June, a trip that the American Commission could help them coordinate over the next few months. That also meant they would be back for the annual Krakow Jewish Cultural Festival the first week in July. By late March, all was settled—they were going to the States in mid-June. Although Klara had shared limited written communication with her mother over the past few months, letting her know she was fine, she couldn't decide whether or not to visit her when they were in New York. That was clearly a much bigger deal.

She had tried to explain her relationship with her mother to Filip. "You know, it's not your classic 'difficult relationship.'" After watching her continuously perseverate over whether she should visit her eighty-four-year-old mother on their upcoming trip, Filip encouraged her to talk to a psychotherapist, as the impasse had become all-consuming for Klara. The idea of speaking to a therapist was something Klara had always avoided, instead simply burying her emotions, despite learning the hard way that that rarely worked.

"Come on, Klara," he had urged. "A therapist could help you sort out your feelings about your mother and gain some clarity around what you want to do. This one comes highly recommended and understands that lots of people have difficult relationships."

Klara felt an out-of-body experience as she watched herself agreeing to disclose her most intimate feelings to a complete stranger. Old, familiar shame bubbled up in her, and she wanted to run, but she didn't. Against her primal instincts, she agreed to meet with Dr. Kowalski. At that moment, it occurred to her how deeply she felt for Filip, and how much she trusted him to stretch herself like this. As he hugged her, she felt herself return to her body.

After feeling like a spinning top, going round and round, Klara finally made an appointment with Dr. Kowalski. It was a perfect sunny April morning. The corn poppies were blooming, their vivid red petals in full sight. Until the last moment when she left her house, Klara wasn't sure whether she would follow through.

On her commute to the office, she grew pensive. It would soon be a year since she'd first arrived in Warsaw. So much had happened during that time, she thought: she had met and become close with her father's family; visited his gravesite after learning he was buried here, which she still regularly did; met Filip, who had become hugely important to her; begun learning Polish and Hebrew and Yiddish; and made weekend outings with Filip to forsaken Jewish cemeteries that had first been desecrated by the Nazis and then forgotten for seventy years. Thinking about all that she had accomplished these last several months took her breath away. She knew she was a changed person in many ways, but opening up about her personal life to a complete stranger, even a professional one, was a challenge she wasn't sure she was up to.

# CHAPTER 28

Dressed in a light peasant blouse and long flowing skirt, with her wavy brown hair loose, Klara arrived at Przyokopowa Street 28, near the former Jewish Ghetto. The discreet office plaque, which read *PSYCHOLOG* on the outside red brick wall, told her she was in the right place. As she sat down on Dr. Lena Kowalski's tan easy chair, her body sinking into its soft, worn cushions, she stared around the beige-painted room with matching decor and an array of potted green plants on the console by the windowsill. She wondered how she would explain all she'd gone through this past year, and more importantly, her current dilemma. How could this woman, perhaps fifteen years her senior, in her well-coordinated ecru pants suit, with a set of pearls and coiffed hair, begin to understand her messy, disjointed life?

Klara looked at Dr. Kowalski's warm eyes and gentle smile.

"So, what brings you here?" the psychologist asked her.

"It's a long story," Klara said, exhaling what felt like the weight of the world.

"I have time," Dr. Kowalski replied, as she continued to look into Klara's face with a patient stillness.

Deciding to take a chance, Klara showed her the letters she had received ten months earlier—the one from her mother, and another more formal one from the Polish government, with its official coat of arms emblem, showing a white eagle on a red background.

"I've kept these letters to remind myself that my mother actually sent them to me. I was teaching archaeology at an American college in Maine last summer when I received these letters," Klara said, after taking a deep breath. "It's in the northeastern United States." Dr. Kowalski nodded.

Klara proceeded to jump into the story of how she quickly made the decision to travel to Warsaw, and what she'd been busy doing since she arrived ten months ago.

"And now I'm returning to the US to present information on what's left of Jewish life here in Poland and the small Jewish renaissance that's begun, and I don't know whether or not I can bring myself to visit my mother. Filip, my partner, and I are going to the States in two months, and I'm furious with my mother for hiding the truth about how my father died, his plan to come back for me, and that my aunt, his sister, had tried to reach out to me several times but was turned away by her. I'm irate that she could never get over having a baby girl instead of a baby boy, that she ignored me as a child and didn't believe me. I'm livid about how self-involved and narcissistic she has always been. I don't know if I should visit her when we go to New York. I feel really torn about it."

Although Klara felt odd pouring out her heart, Dr. Kowalski listened and made supportive and validating remarks. "It's up to you what feels right, Klara. Clearly, you've been very hurt. There's certainly a lot more for us to discuss, but it's your choice to set the limits you need in your relationship with her. You get to decide that."

Just hearing those words, "You get to decide," felt like a thousand-pound weight had been lifted from Klara's chest. No one had ever told her that in regard to her family. These were such simple words, yet they carried such profound meaning. By the time she returned home after her first therapy appointment, Klara was both physically and emotionally drained. She couldn't help but go right to bed for a long afternoon nap.

Filip called later that evening. "How'd it go?"

"I can't remember the last time I felt this exhausted," Klara replied, "but it went surprisingly well. I actually opened up, and then I couldn't stop talking. Dr. Kowalski made me feel comfortable. I won't lie. My nerve endings are a bit more exposed, but I'm definitely going back next week. Thank you for encouraging me to go." And she meant it. She'd have never gone if Filip hadn't found a therapist for her and practically walked her to the office door.

During those two months of meeting with Dr. Kowalski prior to traveling to the US, Klara had a mixture of traditional forty-five-minute weekly talk therapy sessions, interspersed with hour-long Eye Movement Desensitization and Reprocessing (EMDR) sessions. She had never heard of EMDR. Dr. Kowalski mentioned it after a handful of sessions, explaining, "It's a technique used for people with various levels of trauma, from simple phobias to complex forms of post-traumatic stress disorder, or PTSD. It can also be used to treat complicated grief, which can be another form of trauma." Klara was open to hearing more. Dr. Kowalski continued, "It was initially used with war veterans and survivors of childhood sexual abuse, but now it's used more broadly. I think it could help you in discharging some of the trauma in your nervous system in relation to your mother, particularly how she hid the secret of your father's death from you."

Klara hadn't yet revealed her history of abuse by Jacob Herschler to her therapist. There would be time later. The main issue at hand was dealing with her mother. She hadn't realized just how much she had compartmentalized her overall broken relationship with her mother and her mother's shaming and damning responses to her about Jacob Herschler.

"EMDR can help an individual process trauma more quickly than traditional talk therapy, as it can aid in accessing traumatic memory more easily," Dr. Kowalski initially explained. "The person can then feel the emotional pain and release it. However, the more complicated and chronic the traumatic events, the more EMDR sessions are needed to access and release the memory and feelings. And we'll need to slow it down at times, so it doesn't become too much." She hesitated, waiting to see whether Klara had questions.

Klara nodded, feeling somewhere between being in the moment in Dr. Kowalski's office and being back in her mother's Queens apartment in the late 1970s, even without the EMDR. Although Jacob Herschler's face popped up, along with her mother's and her grandfather's, she still chose not to mention him at this time. Maybe she'd discuss it with Dr. Kowalski once she returned from her trip to the US. That whole horrid part of her life just felt too insurmountable to deal with now, even all these years later. It was enough that she had brought it up with Filip and Hanna. Jacob Herschler was dead, and she wouldn't have to face him if she decided to visit her mother. She buried the image of his face deep down inside. Realizing Dr. Kowalski was speaking again, halfway through her sentence, Klara snapped out of her looping thoughts.

"Excuse me," Klara said. "Could you repeat that last part again?" She shifted in her chair, aware that her mind had drifted off, something of a familiar occurrence these days.

"Sure. I was saying that it's helpful if we first work on who and what you'd like to use as your internal emotional resources, so that you can call on them in the work, and that way you won't feel so alone."

Klara was confused. "I don't understand," she said.

"We're going to help you identify a peaceful place, a nurturing figure, a protective figure, and a wise figure. They could be real or imagined—someone from your life, or a book or movie. If it's a person, they could be alive or no longer here. It can even be something like a spirit animal you connect with."

"That's not really my thing," Klara said. "I'm more of a scientific person." She straightened her back as she began involuntarily tapping her foot on the rug.

Once they came up with a list of resources, Dr. Kowalski took out a small handheld battery-charged device attached to a set of wires, which she gave to Klara. At the end of each wire was a small pod. "You put one in each hand. I'm going to turn it on, and you'll feel a slight buzz." As soon as the device was on, Klara felt a vibration, first in her right hand, then in her left. It kept alternating back and forth. "If you want, you can add the headset too. You'll hear a coordinated buzz in each ear." Klara was reminded of the elementary hearing tests in the school nurse's office, but soon agreed to use both headset and handset together.

"Tell me when the intensity and the speed feel right. You'll know," Dr. Kowalski told her. "Also, it works best for most people when they close their eyes."

Klara closed her eyes and allowed the vibrations to alternate between her hands. She did have a sense of what felt right. "That feels good," she said. The scientist in her needed to know the underlying thinking behind this technique if she was to put any stock in it. "Tell me again how this is supposed to help me," she said, feeling silly holding the pods.

Klara had thought about doing EMDR for a couple of weeks before agreeing to try it. "What do I have to lose?" she said to Dr. Kowalski one day.

"I think you can get a lot out of it, and we can go as slowly as you need. If it feels like too much at any point, we'll take a break or stop for the day. Okay?"

Klara nodded, feeling like she was about to dive off the deep end. Over the course of the last month before going away, she did four rounds of EMDR.

After Dr. Kowalski executed the protocol, she recalled moments of her childhood and adolescence she hadn't thought about in many years, and then the healing began to happen as she sat in that large, tan easy chair across from her therapist. Although the process included alternate hand sensations, the sounds from the earphones worked better for her. She settled in and listened to a little beat, softer than a click, more like the snap of a finger and thumb. She first heard a click in her right ear and then in her left; back and forth the clicks would go. EMDR put her into a semi-dream state. And suddenly there was a movie playing inside her head. Her last session before traveling to America was remarkable. She saw herself opening the shocking letter her mother had sent her only a year earlier that her father was dead and buried here in Warsaw. It was a lot, and she found herself unexpectedly crying puddles of tears. She wiped them away with a handful of tissues, and proclaimed loud and slowly, "Shame on you." Then she felt and heard herself say the words "Shame on you" aloud. It was directed at her mother. The divide between the movie in her mind and her physical self had blurred.

The next thing she remembered was Dr. Kowalski encouraging her, guiding her out of the session, inviting her to return to the room. She slowly opened her eyes, looking over at her. Dr. Kowalski wore a smile and said, "Welcome back," as she lifted the earphones off her head, placing them on the coffee table in front of her. She felt as if she had more of herself, like she was more grounded.

"Would you like to tell me what happened?" Dr. Kowalski said.

"Would I ever," was Klara's initial response. She took a deep breath and said, "I told her off, really told her off.

Shamed her. God, did that feel good!" Her hands rested quietly on her lap, not grasping like they were at the beginning of the session.

Klara knew she still had a lot more work to do, but it was time to travel to the United States for her and Filip's speaking tour about the small Polish Jewish renaissance and the sad state of the decimated Polish Jewish cemeteries that needed money and attention. It was odd; she had lived there for most of her life, but the past year in Poland made her question whether she was flying home or to just another destination to tour. The big question of whether she would visit her mother still loomed large. While Dr. Kowalski had helped Klara to understand her issues more clearly—in particular, her grief about her father and her anger toward her mother—she wasn't yet certain about her final decision. Would she visit her mother? She was still debating the pros and cons. The pro was being a "good" daughter by doing the right thing and checking on her elderly mother. The cons seemed to be much more convincing: not being able to forgive her mother for her lies, hating her mother for her regular dismissal of her and her constant withholding of love. Clearly, the cons won. Why, then, did she still have a nagging feeling that she would regret not visiting her mother?

Dr. Kowalski was talking to her. "Klara, you've done a lot of good work these last few months. I think once you get there, you'll know what you do or don't want to do. Let me know when you return. I believe in you and your ability to decide what's best for yourself," Dr. Kowalski said, as a final send-off.

*Will I? Will I know what's best for myself when I get there? I'm still not sure*, she thought as she made her way to the bus stop.

# CHAPTER 29

---

## *June 11, 2015*

Arriving at JFK airport in New York City after a nine-hour flight, Klara found her stomach was well beyond butterflies flapping; it was doing flip-flops. It wasn't just the turbulence of the airplane but the reality of being back in the United States, and New York City in particular. The implications of the possibility of seeing her mother in the near future had triggered Klara's stress response, alerting her to the likelihood of an impending hurricane or, better yet, a five-alarm fire.

*I still have two weeks to decide whether to visit my mother*, Klara reminded herself.

As she was so preoccupied with her worries, she was unable to take in the wonder of the New York skyline, despite the fact that it was a beautifully clear, sunny day. While Filip looked out his seat window, pointing, oohing, and aahing at Manhattan Island, trying to catch Klara's attention, she remained stuck in her head.

"This is amazing," he said, observing how one small island, just under twenty-three square miles, could hold so many skyscrapers and people. He wondered aloud, "It's incredible that almost nine million people really coexist here together—having emigrated from all over the world!" He shook his head, as though it were some sort of miracle.

Once they landed, the first thing Klara noticed were crowds everywhere; the line to get through customs took two hours alone. The second thing she observed was that the majority of people were speaking English, with Spanish and then a myriad of other languages mixed in.

"Is it this busy with people everywhere?" Filip asked, a bit overwhelmed, as they were packed in line like sardines.

"Not like this, except for some parts of New York City, like Times Square and the Long Island Expressway. And also the Ventura Freeway in LA and other busy airports like JFK. You'll see."

Following a long wait to get through customs, they grabbed a quick meal before boarding their next plane. They would fly to California that afternoon and then make their way back East to New York over the next two weeks. Eating lunch at an airport restaurant before flying six hours to Los Angeles, Klara and Filip reviewed their itinerary.

"Welcome to the Big Apple," Klara said, holding her arms out, trying to distract herself. She was more than a little aware of a lump in her throat when discussing New York as their final destination, knowing it was emotionally entangled with the big question of whether to see her mother when they returned to the city at the end of their trip. She tried to push down her panic, focusing instead on the many cities they would be visiting.

"New York, Boston, Philadelphia, Baltimore, Washington, DC, Boca Raton, Cleveland, Chicago, St. Louis, Houston, Phoenix, San Francisco, Los Angeles. More than twelve cities in two weeks," Filip said.

"Excuse me?" Klara said, hearing his voice, but in a fog of her own making.

"The cities we'll be traveling to during our stay here. Which ones have you been to?" he asked, expectantly awaiting her answer.

"Sorry to disappoint, but maybe about half of them, mostly the ones on the East Coast. I've never been a big traveler in my own country. I guess that sounds a little lame." She crossed her legs, put a napkin on her lap, and opened the airport restaurant menu.

"No, I get it. It's a big country," Filip said, clearly trying to comfort her. He had visited just about every country in Europe, as well as Southeast Asia, Australia, and a couple in Africa during his bachelor years. "I know we won't have much extra time, but I'd love to listen to some blues music in Chicago and New York. Do you think we could fit that into our tight itinerary?" he asked with a grin.

Klara smiled. She wasn't at all surprised that this was Filip's one request. Over the past year, he'd played many a worn B.B. King and Muddy Waters album for her on his old stereo turntable as they kicked back, closing their eyes and drinking Grolsch beers. He liked to listen to his music old-school style. She liked that.

"Flight 2407 will be boarding shortly," the loudspeaker shouted.

"That's our flight," Klara said, looking at her watch. "We should hurry." They were taking American flight 2407 to LAX at two o'clock that afternoon. Klara and Filip sat next to each other in row 23 E and F. He was kind enough to take the middle seat as she opened the blind and stared out the window.

"You're sure you don't mind?" she asked demurely, pointing to the middle seat.

He shook his head and smiled.

"We'll switch next time," she said, knowing this would be their longest flight, except for their trip back to Poland.

As the airplane began to taxi from the tarmac onto the

runway, Klara placed a stick of gum in her mouth, offering one to Filip. Once the plane took off, she peered down at the Atlantic Ocean below them. Now she was ready to take in her surroundings. She had grown up going to Jones Beach with her mother and grandfather at least twice a summer back in her youth and loved the ocean. Her mother packed lunches and beverages for all of them, towels, a large cotton beach blanket, and suntan lotion she'd slather all over Klara. Although almost everyone wanted to get a golden tan back in the day, sun protection against ultraviolet rays was not yet a thing, and she would easily burn. While her mother took care of most of the necessary items, her grandfather was responsible for the beach umbrella and chairs.

"Did you remember to pack the umbrella and beach chairs?" her mother asked Klara's grandfather each time. It was always in German, their private language; Klara was about ten years old when she began to decipher it.

"Yes, he did," Klara responded, also in German, much to her mother's surprise. "He already packed them."

Her mother stared at her and made a sucking sound with her teeth as she shook her head, disapproving of Klara's know-it-all bravado.

They'd pile into their mid-seventies, pale-yellow Oldsmobile, leaving early Sunday morning, taking the Cross Island Parkway to the Northern State to the Meadowbrook, and getting a prime spot near the shore by nine in the morning. Klara loved riding on the highway with her back window rolled down, feeling the wind blow through her hair, staving off the heat. It seemed like the car's air conditioner was broken at least half the time. Her mother would tighten her brightly colored paisley headscarf around her neck, yelling, "Roll it up! I just had my hair done," and then proceeded to madly fan herself with a folded *Good Housekeeping* magazine once the window was closed.

When they finally arrived, the beach would be lightly sprinkled with brightly colored sun umbrellas spaciously placed several feet apart. By the end of the day, it was impossible not to step on others' beach blankets or accidentally hit someone with sand while shaking out their towels. Klara always enjoyed wading in the water, and as she got older, jumping over or swimming through the waves. She loved building sandcastles and digging moats that would fill up with ocean water, and she always took great pleasure in eating the peanut butter and jelly sandwiches her mother would pack; they never failed to taste even better at the beach. These few days were a welcome respite from the rest of her daily life.

As the airplane climbed into the sky, Klara could see the deep shadows of the ocean water fill the panoramic view below, as once-large motorboats left haphazard trails of foam behind. The bright blue sky was marked with lines of white stratus clouds. Soon the ocean and sky met, with little delineation between the two. Finally, the water disappeared altogether, and all she could see was sky for miles with white cotton patches of clouds. Eventually, the whole sky below became one big patch of white, with the bright blue heavens shining above. Klara was never religious, but traveling up in the sky high above the earth, particularly starting out on their pilgrimage, she felt something close to spiritual. It was as though an unfamiliar calm came over her like a warm gray flannel blanket. Leaning her head on Filip's shoulder, she soon fell asleep.

❀ ❀ ❀

As the pilot announced they'd be landing in Los Angeles in the next twenty minutes, Klara felt Filip's hand on her shoulder. She didn't recall dreaming or even sleeping for the last several hours.

"We're almost there," he said. "You missed lunch, but I saved you a snack," he added, holding up a bag of pretzels.

Rubbing sleep from her eyes, Klara looked at him. "Thank you," she replied, trying to get her bearings. It was five o'clock Pacific time when their plane landed.

They'd be presenting at eight o'clock that night and knew they were cutting it close. Luckily, they had booked a hotel near the airport, and the Westside Jewish Community Center was only a mile away.

❀ ❀ ❀

The talk with accompanying slides went better than they could have imagined, and there was a lot of interest.

"That went well," Filip commented when they were done the first evening.

"It sure did," Klara agreed with a smile.

The next several days went similarly well. They'd fly to a new city in the morning, followed by a meal, a quick rest, and a tourist destination if they had time. In Chicago, they visited the famous Bean sculpture and admired the city's well-thought-out architecture from a two-hour boat tour on Lake Michigan, followed by a stop at Buddy Guy's Legends to listen to some classic blues. In Boca, they waded in the ocean for the afternoon. In DC, they met with members of the Commission for the Preservation of America's Heritage Abroad and toured the Holocaust Museum and the Smithsonian. In Philadelphia, they visited the Liberty Bell and the Museum of Art. In Boston, Klara was thrilled to meet up with Sheila, Diane, and Barbara at downtown Faneuil Hall, where she introduced them to Filip.

"He's a keeper," the three friends whispered loudly when Filip stepped away to get a cup of coffee. Klara said little. "Really," they said, prodding Klara's shoulder.

After saying goodbye to her Cambridge friends Diane and Barbara, Klara and Sheila strolled Market Street window-shopping while Filip walked around Quincy Market. "I just wanted to thank you again for packing up my house and mailing me my things," Klara said to Sheila. "I know this isn't nearly enough, but until I can be your personal tour guide in Poland, I wanted to give you this." Klara handed her friend a small gift bag.

Sheila's face brightened. "Thank you." She reached into the gift bag, pulling out three small neatly wrapped boxes. Opening each, she found herself staring at a matching set of beautiful orange amber jewelry set in silver—a large brooch, along with earrings and a bracelet.

"Amber is Poland's stone," Klara explained. "I wanted to get you something special to show my deep gratitude for packing up the house. I couldn't have done it without you," Klara said, putting one hand over her heart. "Think about when you, Jack, and the kids might be able to come visit Warsaw. I'll take the week off to be your private tour guide."

"I'll hold you to that," Sheila said, hugging her as they were saying their farewells. "And seriously, Klara, Filip seems great. I really hope things between the two of you work out."

"Me too," Klara found herself saying, before she realized that perhaps she was being a bit too unfiltered. But then she smiled, and Sheila smiled back.

❖ ❖ ❖

Later that afternoon, before picking up a car rental and driving to the JCC in Newton, Klara and Filip took Boston's MBTA Red Line to Harvard Square, which was much more built up than it had been when she was a student there in the 1980s and '90s, with many two-story buildings. But then she quickly recalled it had already become ritzier when she was still teaching there just eight years ago. Of course, she had to take Filip to Harvard's notorious quad. *How many years did I spend there?* she nostalgically mused, barely able to believe the passage of time. So much had changed in her life since she was last there. Cambridge would always have a special place in her heart. After all, this had been her home for twenty-five years. It was where she got to create her own life and live it the way she chose, no longer under the thumb of her mother and grandfather.

The audience at Newton's JCC was welcoming and receptive, just as the others had been, promising to visit Poland and to send checks to rebuild Jewish cemeteries and refurbish old synagogues. That night, they stayed at the Newton Marriott, only a ten-minute drive from the Mass Pike. Early the next morning, they'd drive to New York City. Klara had visions of her mother's face and imagined hearing her voice asking, *Aren't you going to visit me?*

"My heart won't stop racing," Klara told Filip that night in their hotel room, as she held her chest. "If I didn't know better, I'd think I was having a heart attack, but I know from experience it's just a panic attack."

Filip put his arm around her. "You did great tonight, and you'll do a great job tomorrow night."

"No. It's not about tonight. It's about New York. It's about seeing my mother. I still don't know what I'm going to do." She had felt the same when she had to defend first her thesis and then her doctorate in front of the entire Archaeology Department. All those questions had made her want to cringe and run away, but she hadn't. She had stood her ground, just like she would now.

Filip hugged her for a long time, and she welcomed it.

# CHAPTER 30

The following day, Klara found herself driving across the Throgs Neck Bridge from the Bronx to Queens in a white Chevy rental sedan to an airport hotel, where they'd spend the next two nights. It was the thirteenth and the next-to-last day of their two-week whirlwind tour. She and Filip had spoken about the early stages of a Jewish cultural revitalization in Poland, along with the need to rebuild Nazi-desecrated Jewish cemeteries and synagogues there. They had traveled to more than twelve cities, meeting with the Jewish Community Centers (JCC's), some synagogues, and Jewish Federation leaders in each one. Tonight, the final night of their tour, they would be presenting at the 92nd Street Y in Manhattan and then flying back to Poland the following afternoon. Despite feeling physically and mentally drained, they were also invigorated by the positive response they had received from their audiences. People talked about taking Jewish heritage tours to Poland and seeking out the cemeteries where their ancestors were buried, as well as donating money for the renovation and upkeep of old, forgotten Jewish cemeteries.

Now that they were at the hotel, it was time to rest before their final talk.

"I'll set the alarm for four," Filip said. "That way we'll have enough time to shower, change, and eat dinner before heading into Manhattan by subway at six thirty this evening."

Klara nodded, trying to keep a neutral face, but she couldn't stop worrying about seeing her mother. She was glad Filip did not seem to notice, or at least had not remarked that he had. She tried to think about other things. It had been quite a trip. Looking forward to returning to Poland for at least the next several months and likely longer, Klara knew in her gut that she would not be back here any time in the foreseeable future. She had resigned from Holbrook College's Anthropology Department months before, and her dear friend and colleague Sheila had sent her belongings, understanding Klara had found her true home in Poland.

Before closing her eyes, Klara pushed herself to call her mother. They spoke briefly, and it was done. She would see her mother the following day.

The alarm blared at exactly four o'clock, and Klara hadn't slept a wink.

She was about to tell Filip of her decision when he offhandedly asked, "By the way, have you called your mother yet?"

Klara was pacing around the room, about to get ready, and filled with nervous energy. "I was just about to tell you—I called her while you were napping. She's expecting us in the morning. Of course, she's annoyed that I waited until now to get in touch with her."

"Have you thought about what you hope to get out of the visit?" he asked thoughtfully, knowing how strained the relationship between Klara and her mother was and wanting to make sure she was prepared.

"I can't say for certain, but I just feel I need to see her and to confront her about the things I learned about my father that she kept from me for so long. I need to hear her tell me face-to-face why she deceived me these past forty-some years. I think that might give me some kind of closure on my relationship with her, so I can move on."

Klara had thought it through, replaying her many conversations with Dr. Kowalski over the past two weeks, and in the end, she realized she needed to take this opportunity to see her eighty-four-year-old mother now, as she didn't know when she would next see her. She remembered that she was a very different person than the one who had gone to Poland over a year ago, a much more embodied one. Rubbing her gold pendant, she reminded herself she could handle it now; then she rubbed her father's piece of amber that she kept in the black velvet pouch in her pocketbook.

"It will be okay. I'll be right there beside you," Filip said, hugging her.

"I know you will." She smiled.

❖ ❖ ❖

That night at the 92nd Street Y talk, the audience applauded loudly when Klara and Filip had finished their presentation, peppering them with many questions and compliments. When the two finally walked out of the building, Klara turned to Filip.

"We did it," she said, smiling. "Our final talk."

"Yes, we sure did. I think we make a pretty good team," Filip said, grabbing her hand.

"This calls for a celebration, and I have the perfect place in mind. How about some blues?"

"Perfect," Filip said.

She hailed a yellow cab on Lexington Avenue.

"We're going to the West Village, to Arthur's Tavern on Grove Street," Klara told the driver. "I think you'll like it a lot," she said, turning to Filip.

Once there, they drank to their success and to the band's rendition of Robert Johnson's "Crossroads," clinking glasses. Neither of them would forget this moment.

The song, and its name, seemed quite apropos, as Klara literally felt she was at a major life junction, needing to choose which direction she would next take. In the short term, the emotionally easier one was to spend the next morning sleeping in and then fly back to Poland later that afternoon. But Klara knew she had come too far in her personal growth to cop out now. She heard Dr. Kowalski's, Rachel's, Hanna's, and Rosario's voices telling her she was strong enough to visit her mother, particularly with Filip's help.

"You are not alone," they said. "We are all here with you."

Pondering this, Klara stood taller, took a deep breath, and could feel her resolve. No, she would take the harder road, the one she wished she could avoid, knowing in the long run that it was the one that would give her permission to move forward with her life without regrets. She kept this to herself, wanting to take full ownership of her choice.

Although she knew it was the right decision for her, that night she slept in fits and starts, intermittently recalling flashes of nightmares. Her mother was yelling at her. Jacob Herschler was taunting her. Her father was waving goodbye forever; she would never see him again. She abruptly awoke more than once with a light layer of perspiration covering her skin. Splashing cool water over her face, she looked in the bathroom mirror, telling herself, *You can do this*, although she wasn't convinced she fully believed her words. Lying down next to a sleeping Filip, she hugged an extra pillow closely and tried to will herself asleep.

When she awoke, rays of bright sunshine were streaming through the sheer curtains. Filip was half-dressed in a T-shirt and boxers, making coffee and reading their complimentary *New York Times*.

Klara bolted upright. "What time is it?" she asked.

"It's still early. Don't worry. Only eight thirty," he said. She lay back down, relieved.

"Good morning," he added with a knowing look and a reassuring smile.

She wasn't so sure.

❖ ❖ ❖

In the taxi on the way to her mother's apartment in Forest Hills, Klara thought about all she had been through these past several months. Ever since she arrived in Warsaw and met her aunt Rachel, her life had been transformed. *She* had been transformed. Here she was, at the end of her journey and professional tour of the States with Filip, soon to confront her mother about a life-changing lie her mother had perpetuated for years. Yes, she was with the man she hoped would be her life partner, getting ready to fly back to another country she now considered her home. But she was still shaken. Despite her nerves, she was able to proudly think about her newfound professional purpose: studying and preserving the artifacts of her own ancestors, not only others'. She thought about Rosario's question to her almost two years earlier, "Why are you always searching for other peoples' artifacts? What about your own family?"

That simple question had ignited a dormant flame in Klara that even she hadn't known existed—a desire to find out who she was and where she came from—and even more pressing, a burning need to belong to and be a part of something greater than herself. Her mother's letter to her over a year before about an inheritance had forced her hand, pushing her to travel to Poland. Meeting and developing meaningful relationships with Aunt Rachel and her cousin Hanna built on her wish to connect with others and challenged her ability to trust in them. Ultimately, through her trust in them and information she learned about her father, she was able to take a huge leap of faith in taking a chance with Filip. Amazingly, she had been able to sustain her relationship with him these past months and looked forward to their future together. Rosario, Rachel, and Hanna had been her lifeline and would always remain so. Filip was her partner.

While going up in the elevator of her mother's building with Filip, Klara touched her locket, while Filip kept track of their suitcases. As the doors opened to the third floor of her childhood apartment building, Klara channeled the three most pivotal women in her life: Rosario, Rachel, and Hanna.

*You can do this*, she heard them say. *We're here with you.* She felt Filip squeeze her hand. He was most definitely there with her, in every sense. The hallway floor was covered with the same brick-red tile that had been there for the past half century. The surname on apartment door 3A read GREENBAUM, her mother's new husband's last name. They rang the bell, and an eighty-something-year-old woman with poorly dyed brown hair and wearing a beige skirt, a dark-green cardigan, and light-blue house slippers opened the door. Her mother ushered them in, sizing up Filip in one glance, with neither a smile nor a greeting.

"Don't forget to take your shoes off and leave your suitcases by the door," her mother ordered.

"Mom, this is my friend Filip Jablonski," Klara said, putting her arm around his waist.

Bessie looked him over. "Jablonski, that's Polish, isn't it?" she sneered. Then, without missing a beat, she declared, "It's about time you had a man in your life, Klara." Fuming inside, but choosing to ignore her mother, Klara handed her a chocolate babka that she had bought at a local bakery on their way over.

"Where'd you get that?" her mother asked.

"From Zeigler's down the street."

"He's no good anymore," her mother said, shaking her head and scrunching her nose like she smelled something unsavory. "His cakes and pastries aren't as fresh as they used to be." Her mother took the babka and threw it in the trash before taking out her own dessert from the fridge.

"I got this pie at Seymour's Bakery two blocks away. His are better than Zeigler's. As I told you on the phone, if you'd given me more notice, I would have baked something myself."

"I know, Mom. I'm sorry. We just didn't know our plans until yesterday," Klara replied, hoping that this might serve as an explanation for not calling her mother earlier. Not that she was too concerned—this visit was already going as poorly as she had expected.

While her mother busied herself with the dessert, her husband, Morris, slowly shuffled into the room. Klara barely knew him, as he and her mother had only gotten married a couple of years ago. He wore suit pants and a white shirt. Klara tried to be polite, but the fact that he was Jacob Herschler's former son-in-law sickened her. She knew that it wasn't Morris's fault. He hadn't done anything to her, and he seemed decent enough, but any connection to that monster from her childhood elicited a negative reaction in her. When they all walked into the dining room, her mother exploded without warning.

"How dare you!" she screamed at Klara, gesticulating with her hands.

"Excuse me?" Klara replied, confused.

"How dare you go to Poland and stop communicating with me? How dare you cut me out of the inheritance? How dare you leave me out of your life? Who do you think you are? You have no right whatsoever. You left me all alone here!" Her mother's face was beet red.

Klara took a deep breath, and Rosario's face came to mind. Next, she thought of Aunt Rachel and Hanna. She felt as though she were channeling each one's strength and courage, as Filip stood behind her, his presence comforting and supportive. She was about to lash back and stand her ground, but then she saw something she hadn't expected: tears in her mother's eyes. Her mother tried to hide them, turning around momentarily, but Klara had seen them clearly. She had come here with so much built-up rage, never expecting to feel sorry for her mother, but now that was exactly how she did feel.

As Klara felt her mother's pain, years of squelched anger toward her morphed into something far more complex. Without thinking, she slowly walked toward her mother, putting a hand on her shoulder. Bessie's body jerked away from Klara just before she let out a wail and leaned forward, rocking back and forth to calm herself. For a moment, Klara felt like everything was unreal. Then she saw Morris usher her mother to a seat and heard her own voice say, "I'm so sorry, Mom. I really didn't think you cared. You have Morris, and I did send you postcards and notes letting you know I was safe and with Dad's family. As for the money, I did have the Polish government send you your portion. Technically, it should have all gone to me, as you had already separated from my father when he was killed in the train crash, but I decided to split it with you. So, no, you were not entitled to all of it."

Bessie stepped even farther away from Klara, fixing her hair and dabbing her eyes with a tissue. Her outburst had passed, and she was now back to business. "Yes, I did get a share," she said brusquely. "You're right, I'm fine. I have Morris. I can see you have your own life now," she continued, glaring at Filip with the chill of an icicle. "I just thought you'd show your own mother a little more civility."

Klara could feel the chill emanating from Bessie. "Civility?" she began. "You want to talk about showing civility?" But she stopped herself, knowing her mother was trying to reclaim her pride. In that brief moment, she had revealed her vulnerability, that she missed her daughter, maybe even cared about her more than she liked to admit. Klara didn't want to upset her mother any more than necessary but was resolved to take care of what she had come to address—the need to confront her mother.

"I came to see you before returning to Poland." Klara tried to strike the right balance of sounding warm but firm. "Poland is my home, at least for now. But I came here to ask you about something, and I want an honest answer for once." Klara took a deep breath before continuing, determined to see this through. "I've learned a lot these past several months about what really happened to Dad and how much you kept from me, making me believe he left us—left me. I know now he had always planned to return for me, and you knew that," she said, pointing at her mother. "How could you let me believe otherwise for all those years? How could you allow me to think he might still be alive—that he might be out there somewhere, but wanted nothing to do with me—when you knew perfectly well he wasn't?" Klara glared at her mother, her heart beating furiously.

Bessie listened to her daughter, showing little expression. "I have nothing to be sorry for." Now she was the one pointing. "I protected you. I gave you a good life and did what I thought was best. Your father was a weak man . . . and then you cut me out of your life. You left me alone. You're the one who should apologize." She crossed her arms in front of her chest.

Klara realized that, while she had needed to see her mother for what could well be the last time, this visit was not going to give her the closure she so yearned for. She'd have to work on that on her own and in her therapy with Dr. Kowalski. She would stop now and not bring up the fact that her mother wished she had been a boy, or her mother's denial that Jacob Herschler had abused her. There was no way Bessie would ever admit she had done anything wrong; it just wasn't in her DNA. She had always cast Klara as an "ungrateful child" and herself as a victim, and she certainly wasn't going to change her stripes now.

But much to Klara's surprise, this lack of closure she thought she so badly needed didn't devastate her. Rather, her mother's reaction reinforced what Klara had known all along—that her real connection was to her father's family and now to Filip as well. She and her mother would never forgive each other for the other's perceived sins, and that was just the way it would be. Klara was finally happy in her life. She was not going to allow a relationship that was beyond repair to undo that, although she knew she would need to grieve it.

"You're not alone, Mom," Klara responded calmly. "You have Morris now, and I have Filip and Dad's family—Aunt Rachel and my cousin Hanna. You have Aunt Rachel's address and phone number and my email address if you or Morris need to get in touch with me, as my current address is temporary. I'll write and keep in touch, and I hope you can do the same. I wish you well, but I can't stay here any longer. If and when you're ready to be honest with me, you know how to reach me. As for my portion of the money from my grandparents' land, it's going toward the upkeep of Dad's gravesite, and so many others as well. You have your portion. Goodbye, Mom."

Before Bessie could say anything further, Klara walked out the door with Filip behind her, grabbing their suitcases.

In the elevator, Filip put his arm around Klara's shoulder. "Are you all right? That was a lot. I'm so proud of you for how you handled it all."

"Thank you so much for being by my side," Klara said, letting her head rest on his shoulder.

"Do you want to talk about it?"

"What I want to do right now is to go home," she said.

"Home?"

"Back to Warsaw."

"Yes, home would be nice. We'll be there by morning. We have a plane to catch," Filip said, smiling. "Back to Poland."

"Back home," she said, smiling at him and squeezing his hand.

# SOURCES

While in Poland, I bought the following books, which I've referenced:

*Rediscovering Traces of Memory: The Jewish Heritage of Polish Galicia* by Jonathan Webber

*The Fall of the Wall and the Rebirth of Jewish Life in Poland: 1989–2009*, Published by the Taube Foundation for Jewish Life and Culture

*FKZ* program from July 2013's Jewish Cultural Festival

I'd like to acknowledge Barrett Briske's efforts in attempting to track down a book I refer to on page 175: *It Is the Stones That Tell the Story.* I saw it in the Galicia Museum's gift shop in Krakow in July 2013. It was a book of photos that reflected the museum's exhibition at that time. Barrett searched online for this book and also emailed the Galicia Museum. Unfortunately, in the end, we were unable to track it down and confirm publication details. I would like to thank the creators of this book for its impact on me. I wish I had bought it—both for its powerful photos and so I could share its details here.

# ACKNOWLEDGMENTS

*Klara's Truth* is the result of over ten years of research, writing, editing, taking a Novel Writing Master Class at Sarah Lawrence Writing Institute, participating in writing groups and workshops, and a taking a Jewish heritage trip to Poland in 2013.

I am so grateful to Brooke Warner, Crystal Patriarche, and Shannon Green at She Writes Press for believing in my manuscript and helping to usher it into the world. Thank you also to the She Writes editorial staff for their keen eyes and feedback in copyediting and proofreading, and to She Writes Press for connecting me with Krissa Lagos and Barrett Briske, who completed important tasks that would have taken me days to accomplish. Thank you, Julie Metz, for the book cover design that so beautifully captures the essence of this story. I am grateful to publicity guru Crystal Patriarche and her wonderful team, Tabitha Bailey and Grace Fell, for helping me spread the word about *Klara's Truth* as a novice author and newbie regular social media user, and to Maggie Ruf for her fabulous website design skills.

I especially want to acknowledge Leslie Wells, a very talented and seasoned editor whom I was fortunate enough to work with, and whose developmental editorial assistance and feedback supported me in further developing this story, giving it greater depth and a real potential life as a novel.

I would also like to thank Debra Hand for her eagle-eyed copyedit and overall input as she wisely encouraged me to check my work, and for cheering me on to keep going, and Brian Hand for his astute legal assistance.

Thank you so much to my fellow writer Lynda Peckel, whom I originally met at the New York Pitch Conference in December 2015, who taught me what it meant to write a novel through our exchange of material and critical feedback. Her lifelong writing expertise was vital in supporting me to add more complexity to particular characters as well as to more completely fill in the narrative. I also appreciate sharing a writer's group with Fran Hawthorne and Vicky Oliver from New York Pitch in the early days of this novel's beginnings.

I am indebted to Stephanie Newman, whom I originally met in the fall of 2018 at Sarah Lawrence Writing Institute's Novel Writing Class, and who encouraged me along the way in sending out multiple query letters, and eventually strongly nudged me to query She Writes Press. This book might not have found a home if not for that nudge.

To Pat Dunn and Jimin Han, my teachers at the Writing Institute at Sarah Lawrence College, as well as Julia Sonenshein for her additional time reviewing my work.

I would like to express my deep gratitude to my first reader of an early edition of my manuscript, Karen Stamatis, who motivated me to keep writing and gave me invaluable input.

My heartfelt appreciation to my friends who read pages, chapters, and offered editing advice—Rachel Ades, Barbara Buxbaum, Nancy Cagan, Andrea Eisenberg, Dara Epstein, Martha Glantz, Kristina Hals, Linda Stewart Henley, Cindy Pisani Katz, Marlo Klein, Denise Lewis, Tone Lindgren, Rhonda Regan, and Laurie Hirsch Schulz. Thank you to Donna Jenson for sharing her EMDR experience with me. I am grateful to the She Writes spring 2024 cohort of writers for their informative meetings and publishing advice. I'd like to convey a special thank-you to a new acquaintance, Jenna Blum, a wonderful writer and CEO and cofounder of A Mighty Blaze, a digital platform for authors. I so appreciate her wealth of knowledge and advice about publishing and social media specific to writers.

And finally, thank you to my family: my husband Alan for his tireless support in reading and rereading my chapters and manuscripts, and for his wise advice and unwavering belief in me, as well as his excellent culinary abilities; my daughter Olivia for her time, support, and belief that everything I wrote was fabulous (even if it wasn't always so); and my daughter Bella for her social media know-how, and for putting up with my how-to questions.

# ABOUT THE AUTHOR

Susan Weissbach (Friedman), LCSW, is a psychotherapist with a specialty in women's issues, family therapy, and trauma-focused therapy. A graduate of Hamilton College, Boston University's MSW/MPH program, and the Ackerman Institute for the Family, she is also EMDRIA certified and a Somatic Experiencing Practitioner (SEP). She has been in practice for more than twenty-five years. She is not currently accepting new clients. Originally from Long Island, she now lives in Westchester County, New York, where she enjoys practicing yoga and mindfulness, going for walks in nature, listening to music, and spending time near the ocean. Susan has been married to her husband for thirty years and has two daughters in their twenties. *Klara's Truth* is her first novel.

*Author photo © Janna Giacoppo*

## Looking for your next great read?

We can help!

Visit www.shewritespress.com/next-read
or scan the QR code below for a list
of our recommended titles.

She Writes Press is an award-winning
independent publishing company founded to
serve women writers everywhere.